Life's Manifesto

~ Nate Tung

Life's Manifesto

Nathan Truong

Copyright © 2010 by Nathan Truong.

Library of Congress Control Number: 2010906663
ISBN: Hardcover 978-1-4500-7785-9
Softcover 978-1-4500-7784-2
Ebook 978-1-4500-7786-6

All rights reserved. No part of this book may be reproduced or transmitted in any form or by any means, electronic or mechanical, including photocopying, recording, or by any information storage and retrieval system, without permission in writing from the copyright owner.

This is a work of fiction. Names, characters, places and incidents either are the product of the author's imagination or are used fictitiously, and any resemblance to any actual persons, living or dead, events, or locales is entirely coincidental.

This book was printed in the United States of America.

To order additional copies of this book, contact:
Xlibris Corporation
1-888-795-4274
www.Xlibris.com
Orders@Xlibris.com
80331

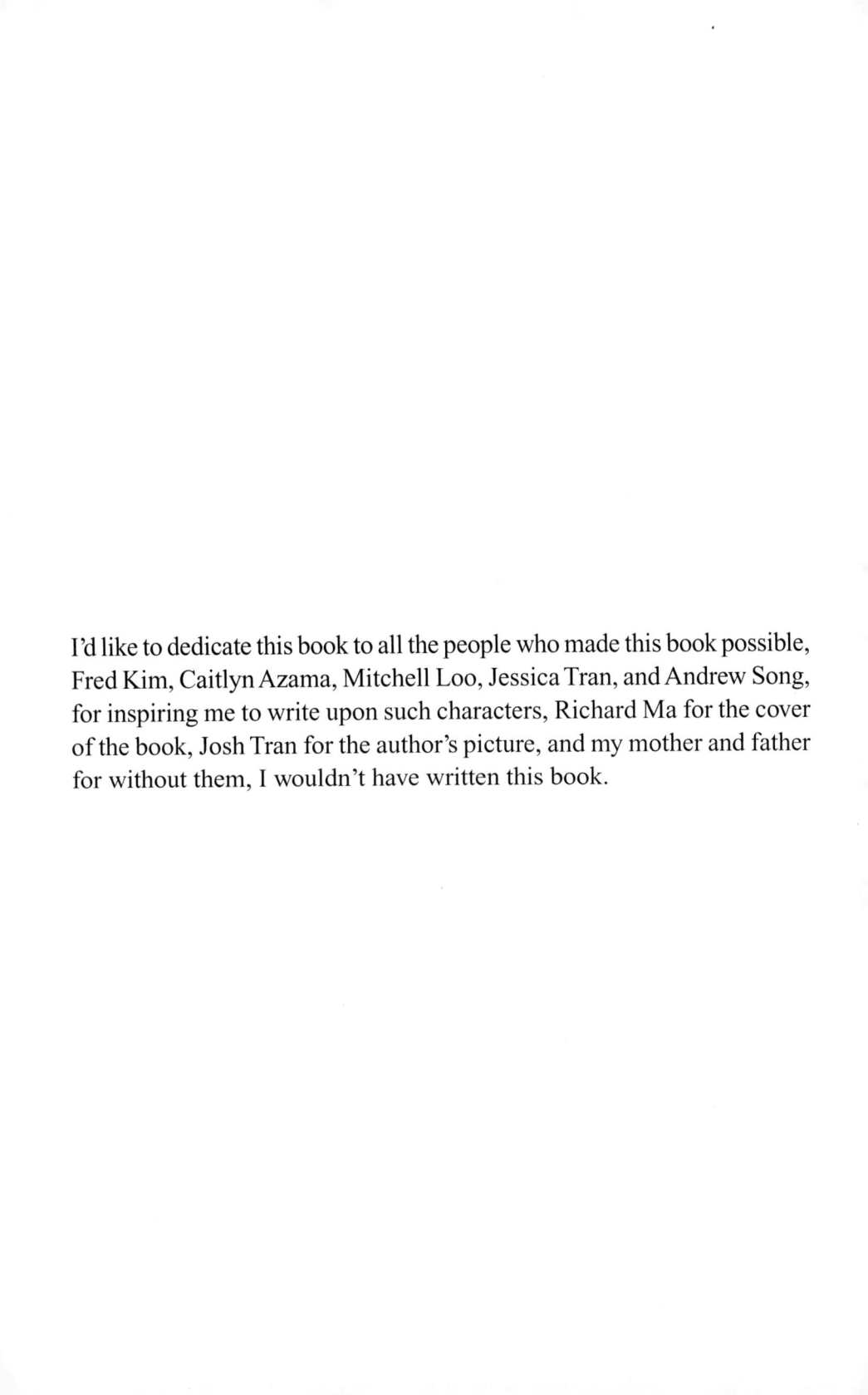

I'd like to dedicate this book to all the people who made this book possible, Fred Kim, Caitlyn Azama, Mitchell Loo, Jessica Tran, and Andrew Song, for inspiring me to write upon such characters, Richard Ma for the cover of the book, Josh Tran for the author's picture, and my mother and father for without them, I wouldn't have written this book.

Nathen~

I was waiting patiently for the receptionist to call me in for my what? My fiftieth interview? After fifty interviews, I felt the need to celebrate my failure since it wouldn't get me anywhere else. I sat in an uncomfortable wooden chair half drenched in my coffee. I had spilled coffee on me when I abruptly stopped at the sight of a red light . . . except it wasn't the correct red light I was supposed to be watching out for. Hopefully, the air-conditioning would dry it off as I waited.

I was the only one waiting in the room, excluding the receptionist. The receptionist was an old woman, probably around her sixties who wore those glasses with a chain attached to them. Her hair was fairly white with small streaks of yellow like a dog continually urinating around a vast field of snow. She popped large bubblegum bubbles as she listened to her iPod through her tangled earphones. I wish I had an iPod, but I keep forgetting to purchase one, and what's absurd is I always seem to remember when I'm stuck in traffic.

Waiting here, I felt like I had all the time in the world, and what can *you* accomplish in this long wait? What can I accomplish in this long *wait*? I had brought nothing with me except irksome documents that I could pretend to read to make myself seem busy and intellectual, or pens I could fiddle around with to make myself look childish.

What had happened to enjoying life? All the days I have lived through, my social life had revolved around boringness before high school hit me, and after a few years, high school left me. My best friends from high school are still around today, hidden under their busy and well-paid jobs and families of their own. Did I have a busy and well-paying job to drown in? No. A family of my own? No. I do have a lot of money in the bank, just nothing special to spend it on. I live my life very cheaply. Having cheap noodles for all three meals a day is a simple way of saving money that I enjoy. I live in an apartment in Los Angeles which is slightly fancy, yet warm and homey. I have another apartment over in Hawaii my father had bought for me as an apology, but that's another story.

An ambulance arrived at the front door, and medics ran out of their vehicle with their supplies and headed inside toward the interviewer's door.

"What's going on up in here?" the receptionist asked yanking out her earphones from her wrinkled ears.

I would have asked the same question, just not in such an improper womanly tone. I stood up from my chair, attempting to have a peek at what was happening inside the interviewer's room, but the numerous medics were blocking my view. The medics pulled the interviewer out on a stretcher and into the ambulance.

"He had a heart attack," a man informed the receptionist and me as he came from the interviewer's room.
"Oh dear lord!" the receptionist cried out, cupping her hand over her mouth.
"Does that mean I'm not getting that interview?" I semi-joked to the receptionist with a crooked smile smeared across my face.
"That man just had a heart attack, and all you care about is your damn interview?" She rose.

I immediately left the building. For the rest of the day, I drove around the city enough times for street performers to recognize my car. Then I stopped by a hot dog stand owned by an elderly Chinese man to buy some orange chicken. He was the only Chinese man that owned a hot dog stand and sold orange chicken, but the only problem was he didn't sell any hot dogs, just Chinese food. After that, I stopped by a park and sat on a bench to relax. I took in the fresh air, the cool breeze, and the cries of children wailing and enjoying their lives on the paint-chipped playground. Women dragging strollers along eyed me with caution, fearing that I was some form of kid abductor or child molester or anything else that involved malice toward their precious children.

I got home at 10:00 p.m., tossed the car keys on the counter, and dropped myself on the couch for a few minutes. I got up lazily and dragged myself over to the grand piano and played Chopin's "Fantasie Impromptu." I found it funny how music just makes you forget about your troubles . . . like a drug you can buy off the dealers lurking in the alleys at midnight. They reside behind my apartment, and I like to classify them as my neighbors that take the graveyard shift and make more money than me.

Jessica~

I left work early and drove straight home to finish up my Korean drama. I sat on the couch with my laptop in my lap, a tub of reduced-fat chocolate ice cream to my right, and my cell phone and box of soft tissues—just in case I tear up—on the left. From time to time during the drama, I would answer received texts and search for pictures of the cute Korean guys in the drama which would be saved as my desktop background on my laptop. I stuck my index finger in the tub of ice cream and licked it cleanly. Who needs spoons when you have fingers? That's why I prefer fingering rather than spooning. Ha-ha! Okay, bad, dirty joke.

When I finished the drama, I moved onto a different one, hoping it wouldn't be as predictable as the last. Seriously, what is with all these writers? I could definitely write something better than all of them. Probably, the most surprising drama I ever watched was when this one dude and this one chick got married, and they had had a pretty happy marriage for like five years, and they had never had sex. Can you believe that? No sex for five freakin' years. That's like an adolescent boy who tries to keep his urges from masturbating for a month. Do you know how crazy that sounds? Then my first thought was that the man must be a gay. But in the end, he turned out to be a woman and I was like, "OH MY GOD!" A woman married a woman . . . who was really flat, had a manly voice, and very manly facial and body features.

My phone rang, and I picked it up quickly pausing the drama. It was Freddy.

"Hi, Freddy," I answered.
"Hey, we're out tonight?"
"Yeah, unless you want me to watch Korean dramas all night. Ha-ha."
"Okay, pick you up at 7-ish?"
"Sounds fine with me."
"Okay, see you later."
"Okay, I love you."
"I love you too, Jessi."

Freddy and I have been going out for about ten months? Eleven months? Something like that. This has probably got to be my longest relationship yet. I've had more in the past . . . high-school ones. High school . . . ah . . . good times . . . good times . . .

It was 6:50 p.m., and I was all dressed and ready. I sat myself on top of the dinner table, fiddling with the tablecloth. The doorbell rang, and I ran toward the door.

"You ready?" Freddy asked.
"Yep. Let's hit it."

Mitch~

Wow, that was a drag. I couldn't watch anymore *SpongeBob*. My boy, four years old, was sitting in front of the TV laughing his ass off to a talking sea sponge and a talking starfish making really corny jokes. I yawned a few times during the show, and when it was over, I had to go tuck him in bed, tell my daughter to go to bed—which I knew she wouldn't—and then finish off the night with a romantic comedy with my wife. Boy, am I psyched up for all of this . . . As soon as the episode finished, I scooped him up and ran him upstairs to his bedroom laughing as hard as he did when viewing talking seafood. I opened my daughter's bedroom door to inform her that lights should be out in half an hour which I'm sure she ignored as she talked away on her cell phone. I slowly pulled myself to my bedroom where my wife sat on the bed with a bowl of popcorn in her lap. The movie had just started, and I lay down beside her. I took a kernel and popped it into my mouth.

Half hour into the movie and I had to say it's all right even though chick flicks aren't my forte. I got up to check up on that daughter of mine. As I walked down the hall, I heard a faint noise of footsteps and the sound of leaping into a bed. I opened the door to find her covered under sheets. I didn't say anything and smiled, closing the door quietly. Teenagers, what are you going to do with them? Ha-ha. I'll let her stay up late, like I did when I was a hardcore rebel.

"Hurry up and sit down, honey. This is the best part!" my wife called.

I sat beside her and looked at her face. She was smiling, and with that, she made me smile. She laughed, and then she gave me a double take, turning away from the movie.

"What are you smiling at or for?" She chuckled, placing her hand on mine.

I continued to smile at her, not saying a word until we had a staring contest. The contest went on for minutes, until I gave in.

"Ha-ha! I win!" she yelled out excitedly, raising her hands in the air. "So what's my reward?"
"The ending of this movie," I joked.
"Ha-ha! Fine!" she exclaimed, slapping my arm.
"I love you."
"I love you too, Mitch," she replied, giving me a kiss.

Andy~

Ah, nothing better than spending a night playing tennis with my son. The downside to this cool night—he was winning. We were prepping up for his tryouts in a few weeks. My wife and my daughter were sitting on the bench playing around with some "flowers." My wife tried to convince my four-year-old daughter that they were weeds, not flowers, but she denied the fact. She used the "flowers" as pom-poms cheering for her older brother to win. I thought it was kind of cute.

When we were done prepping, we hit a pizza place for a bite to eat. My daughter fell asleep before the pizza arrived, and we tried to wake her up so that she could have something in her stomach, but she wouldn't budge. After that, we got ourselves ice cream cones and walked down the pier under the moonlit sky—a few stars here and there.

Finally, we arrived home around 11:00 p.m. We were all exhausted, so it was a cold shower and off to bed except for my son. He stayed up a little later with his laptop in front of him in his bed.

"Night, honey," I said, kissing my wife good night.
"Night," she mumbled. "Andy?"
"Yeah?" I asked, about ready to close my eyes.
"The kids know you're a great dad, right?"
"I hope so." I chuckled.
"They told me after you went off to work."

I didn't say anything. I closed my eyes and smiled.

Nathen~

I found that I had fallen asleep on the piano. I got up, my eyes half opened, to get myself a cup of coffee, and in the process of doing so, I tripped over a chair and fell to the floor. I got up, cursed at the chair angrily, and kicked it, making sure it knew who's boss. Yeah, I'm boss. A few minutes after burning my tongue with the coffee, I jumped back on the piano with blank sheet music in front of me. I felt the need to write music because I had nothing better to do. Update my resume? Why bother. Look for more jobs? I failed fifty times . . . Should I set a new record with a fifty-first failure? Could be an option. After scribbling a few notes onto the blank paper, I glanced over at the clock on the wall which looked like it was going to fall off. It was 3:34 p.m.

As I was about to head toward my bathroom, my phone rang. I picked it up and answered, "This is the residence of Nathen. How may this call concern me?"

"Okay, Nathen, honestly, there are better ways of answering phone calls," Jessica said.
"Oh, hello, Jessica."
"Hey! How did that interview go yesterday?" she asked in her excited tone she always used.
"The interviewer had a heart attack; I asked about my interview and kicked myself out."
"Ooh . . . ouch. We should celebrate . . ."
"Yes, celebrate my failure . . ., but yes, I was thinking the same thing."
"Come over to my place around 5-ish. I have champagne and Korean dramas!"
"No excitement can top watching Korean people cry and talk about their problems with a bottle of an expensive beverage," I said sarcastically.
"Gosh, why do you have to be so depressing?"
"Blame everything that makes my life miserable."
"Ha-ha, okay! I'll see you at five!"
"Hmm." I mumbled and hung up the phone.

I proceeded to the bathroom to relieve myself. I felt the need to bring something over to Jessica's apartment as a gift. I left the house in the same suit I spilled coffee on, went to an interview with, and slept in. I climbed downstairs which counted as my daily workout and drove off to the Chinese hot dog stand to purchase some orange chicken. I'm sure Jessica would appreciate orange chicken as a gift.

13

I arrived at her door at 5:00 p.m. exactly. I knocked on her door a few times in no rhythmic pattern but more in a metronome monotone.

"Hey, Nathen!" she exclaimed happily.
"Hello," I replied to her greeting.
"Come on in!"

As I came in, I noticed Freddy sitting on the couch watching a Korean drama in a lazy, slumped position.

"What's up, Nathen?" he greeted.
"Hi, Freddy," I greeted, giving him a weak wave.
"I'll go get the champagne!" Jessica exclaimed, running into the kitchen with her arms flailing in the air as I watched her go.
"Have you checked her out before?" Freddy asked me abruptly, as I took a seat next to him on the couch.
"No . . ."
"Aw, come on, don't lie." He winked.
"No, I haven't."
"She's so cute! How can you not?"
"Um . . . orange chicken?" I offered, showing him my box of Asian chicken.
"Sure." He accepted, quickly opening the box shoving orange chicken into his mouth.
"Okay!" I shouted abruptly, "I admit, I have checked her out before, but that was because I didn't know her name, and I was searching for her name tag all around her body."
"HA-HA-HA!" He laughed out loud, almost choking on a piece of chicken.

Jessica exited the kitchen with three glasses of champagne. We all grabbed a glass from her, holding the glasses in the air.

"A toast," she said as she gave a dramatic pause, " . . . to Nathen's failure."

"To Nathen's failure!" we shouted in unison. The glasses clinked, and we gulped the delicious liquid down our throats.

"Failure never felt and tasted so divine," I said.

"You brought orange chicken over?" Jessica asked, sticking her fingers into the box to retrieve a piece, popping it into her mouth.

"Go ahead and indulge yourself in it," I said.

I watched them as they gobbled the entire box down, and from that sight, I knew that they were meant for each other.

"Hey, Nathen," she started with her mouth full, "do you wanna go out to dinner with us?"

"Um, no, thanks, I'll pass," I said, standing up, about to show myself to the door.

"You're leaving already?" Jessica asked.

"Is there a problem with that?" I asked.

"Well, no, but it would be nice if you stayed a little longer. You've only been here for about three minutes. Watch a few Korean dramas with us," she suggested.

"No, I should go. I have . . . something to do," I lied.

"Okay, fine," she said taking a bottle of champagne with her, as she walked me to the door. "Take this," she instructed me, holding up the bottle.

"No, I shouldn't."

"No, it's all right. Take it."

"No, save it for you and Freddy when something special comes up." I smiled and left.

Andy~

"Come on, wake up, Austin! We're leaving in ten!" I shouted at my son as I opened his bedroom door.

"Where are we going?" he grumbled, his face in the pillow.

"To Mitch's house. Get up!"

He immediately jumped out of bed and got dressed as I left. What is with him whenever we go over to Mitch's house? I quickly forgot about the question when I headed down to the garage to get my soccer ball—the one I've had since the beginning of freshmen year back in high school. Wow . . . high school . . . I could never forget those four years . . . ever . . .

I started the car and watched as everyone jumped inside.

"Everybody ready?" I asked.
"Yeah, let's hit it," Austin called out.
"Hip ip," my daughter Sarah imitated.

We drove toward Mitch's house for a little barbeque we'd planned. I was telling my wife about my boss's obsession with Yoda and how she could do a great impersonation of the little green guy. She even had a green light saber hanging right beside her plaque on her wall. When I was telling her this, I noticed this strong odor coming from Austin.

"Austin?" I asked.
"Yeah, Dad?" he said, pulling out his earphones from his ears.

Kids and their iPods these days! It's like they can't leave the house without one, but I guess you can't live without music. At least I don't have to play his songs on the radio anymore . . . or my wife's songs. I bought her one too. So now I keep the radio to myself, and they can listen to whatever they put on those fancy music players. But back to that smell.

"Austin, are you wearing . . . cologne?" I asked him, my eyes darting from the street to the mirror.
"Um, n-no," he stuttered.
"Dude, who's the special someone?" I teased him.
"I'm not wearing cologne, okay?" he shouted, placing his earphones back into his ears.

My wife coughed up a laugh.

Mitch~

The doorbell rang, and I called my wife to get it as I flipped over the boneless beef, pork, and chickens on the grill.

"Hi! Come on in!" I heard my wife say.
"Is Monica home?" Austin asked.
"Yeah, she's upstairs in her room."

I met Andy, his wife, and his daughter outside.

"Hey, Mitch!" Andy greeted me with a hard pat on the back. "Smells good!"
"Hey, Andy. How does it go?"
"It goes great. Life is good," he said, setting himself in a chair with his hands resting under his head.
"That's cool."

Andrew's son, Austin, raced upstairs to see Monica, my daughter. Both of them were in the same grade and went to the same school together . . . the same school Andrew and I went to. Austin knocked on Monica's door.

"Come in," she said.

Austin slowly opened the door and poked his head inside. Monica didn't even turn around, her eyes glued to the computer's screen. Austin stepped into the room shyly and scooted himself toward her.

"Hi, Monica," Austin said. His throat felt like it was being heavily gripped by a sweaty hand.
"Hey, Austin," she said monotonously.

"Whatchya doin'?" he asked, shoving his hands in his pockets, slightly leaning toward her chair.

"Talkin' to friends . . ." Monica took a whiff of a heavy yet delightful smell in the room. "Austin, are you wearing cologne?"

"Um, yeah. You like?" he asked excitedly.

"Aha. Cute."

Austin blushed and slowly backed away from her.

"Hey," Andy started, making sure neither Austin nor Monica was around to hear him, "do you think there's something goin' on between Austin and Monica?"

"Aha-ha! Why would you think that?" I asked, placing out the food on paper plates.

"Austin was wearing cologne today, and he never wears cologne unless he sees Monica."

"Ha-ha. Maybe. We'll just see."

Over by the plastic chairs, the wives were talking over glasses of iced tea, and the younger kids were playing on the grass. The weather was great; it was warm with occasional passing breezes.

Later on, Andy brought out our soccer ball, and we played until we were covered in sweat. It was an intense game as the wives and kids cheered us on. In the end, I won . . . I always win. Ha-ha. It was a good game.

Jessica~

Freddy told me to meet him at this Italian restaurant where he reserved seats for us. When I got there, there was no sign of him. I stood outside for a few minutes on the lookout for his car. I was disappointed and cold, so I walked inside, and the waiter directed me to my table. I took a seat, the waiter left me with no menu but a note. It was folded up, and so I unfolded it. It read:

Break Open the Bread.

I dragged the breadbasket in front of me and broke a rather short baguette, and I admit it took some time and some muscle—two of the things I lack. When I broke it in half, crumbs falling all over my dress, a diamond ring and a small note fell out. I unrolled the note.

Jessica, Will You Marry Me?

I jumped up and screamed, and when I was about to make a fool of myself by screaming and jumping around in a circle, Freddy grabbed me from behind and hugged me.

"YES! YES! YES!" I screamed. "This man that's grabbing me inappropriately right now just proposed to me! AND I KNOW HIM!"

I turned around and kissed Freddy, not minding the other customers sitting around me. When the kiss was finished, everyone clapped and cheered.

"Oh my god! Freddy! I love you!" I cried, tears running down my face.

We left the restaurant and went back to my place. I opened that bottle of champagne we used to celebrate Nathen's failure, and I was glad he refused my generous offer. But . . . he acted as if he knew that Freddy was going to propose to me. As I filled the two glasses, I asked, "Freddy, did you tell Nathen that you were going to propose to me today?"

"No, why?" he asked curiously.

"I don't know. It was as if he knew you were going to do so today," I explained handing him a glass.

For the rest of the night, well, I don't want to get into great detail, but it was absolutely . . . breathtaking . . . literally.

Nathen~

I was up early in the morning and decided to go through high-school yearbooks. I looked through all the pictures and even the ones I wanted to dodge—the pictures of me. I laughed at myself . . . how pathetic! I read through all the comments classmates had written and laughed until I cried, which is rare. The last time I ever laughed and cried at the same time was when I caught my calculus teacher dancing in a bright rainbow spandex in a dance class not far from the high school I attended. I was just passing by the dance studio when I was with my mother desiring the need to purchase new clothes. The phone rang.

"This is the residence of Nathen. How may this call concern me?" I answered.
"Okay, seriously, Nathen. STOP SAYING THAT! Or else, I'm going to hang up and start this phone call all over again," she scolded.
"You called," I reminded her.
"Oh, guess what?"
"What?"
"Guess!"
"You . . . got engaged?"
"Yes . . . how did you know?"
"Wow. Engaged . . . that's . . . that's . . . something," I said, ignoring her question.
"Nathen, how did you know?"
"I . . . I promised not to tell."
"Nathen, please?"

I hung up the phone. I needed to inhale fresh air. I left my apartment and rushed to the Chinese man and ordered some orange chicken. I withheld my temptations as my mouth watered. I promised that I wouldn't touch the orange chicken until I reached the park. I made it through, and I ran to the same bench I had sat on with the great view of the playground and the little, happy children. I turned off my cell phone so that I wouldn't hear from Jessica and happily munched away at the orange chicken with a pair of wooden, disposable chopsticks. I watched as the children ran around, being free and young . . . something I had missed.

When I was half way finished with my chicken, I noticed a man jogging around the playground listening to his iPod. He reminded me to go buy one, but as soon as I left the park, I'd probably forget. When I looked up at him again, he seemed vaguely familiar. I stood up and walked toward him, but couldn't catch up with him, so I ended up jogging with him. I finally reached him and gently tapped his shoulder. He didn't seem to notice, so then as I was about to pick up speed, I tripped over a crack in the sidewalk and ended up pounding his back with my fist as I fell to the ground. He turned around.

"Hey, you okay?" he asked me, giving me a hand.
"I'm fine," I answered, examining his face.
"Okay," he said, helping me up and turning around to continue his afternoon jog.
"Excuse me," I said quickly.

He turned back to me.

"Yeah?" he asked.
"I think I'm familiar to you," I said.

He gave me a long stare like I was some insane being, but then his eyes lit up.

"Nathen?" he said my name.
"Yes, this is he. But strangely, I don't remember your face," I sadly admitted.
"It's me, Mitch," he told me.

"Oh . . . Mitch . . . MITCH! Oh, fancy meeting you here! What has it been? Ten years now?" I was completely shocked.
"Yeah, something like that. Wow . . ."

The sound of a little boy sobbing grabbed Mitch's attention.

"Aw, what's wrong, Howard?" he asked.
"I fall!" he cried.
"Where does it hurt?"
"Om my reg."

He gave his leg a sweet and petite kiss, and in return, he gave him a hug and a kiss, and ran off to a swing to sit on.

"Quite adorable." I smiled.
"Yeah, he is," he agreed, placing his hands on his hips as I was actually referring to the event that just happened.
"Well, I'm sorry to ruin this confrontation, but I must be going now," I said, walking away slowly.
"Okay, well, I'll see you around sometime later."

I nodded my head and went my way.

"Hold on! Wait! Nathen!" Mitch yelled.
"Hm?" I turned around.

He came jogging to me with a small sheet of paper in his hand.

"Here. Call up sometime," he said, jogging away as I thanked him.

Jessica~

Okay, Nathen, what are you hiding from me? I drove toward Nathen's apartment. As I drove, I listened to my tires making a swishing sound as the streets were covered in water from the aggressive sprinklers. I found a parking spot and came out of my door in high heels because I love the sound of high heels clicking against the streets. I slammed the door; an echo followed. I looked around the neighborhood and thought of one word: decent, not too shabby at all. I climbed up the stairs which was very difficult in high heels, so I took them off and walked barefoot toward his door. I stepped on a few pebbles and broken glass that made me whine "ouch" a lot, but no blood, which was good. When I reached his door, I slipped on my high heels. In the process, I heard the sweet sound of beautiful piano music coming from his room. I knocked a few times, tidying myself up.

The door opened, and he whispered, "No! For the thousandth time, I would not like any of your drugs."

"Nathen?"

"Oh, Jessica, it's just you. I thought it was those damn girl scouts again. Please, do come in." He offered, opening the door all the way as I was slightly confused about the topic of girl scouts selling drugs. I glanced around, wary of any suspicious little thug girls in uniforms.

He closed the door and locked it as I made myself at home, jumping on his couch as if it were a trampoline.

"Jessica, please. You have high heels on," he said.

"My baaad," I apologized, jumping off.

"Would you like a cold or hot or warm beverage?" he asked, poking his head out of the kitchen.

"No, I wouldn't. But you know what I would like to know? I would like to know how you knew that I was proposed to before I even told you." I yelled.

"You asked me to guess, and I guessed," he yelled back.

"No, no, no. You know something. Something's goin' on . . . and I wanna know!"

"Jessica, I promised not to tell. I really did promise."

"TELL ME!" I yelled at the top of my lungs.

"Freddy is going to kick my ass for saying this. I just know it," he admitted.

"Don't worry. I'll make sure he won't. Your ass is in good hands." I smiled.

". . . Wonderful. Okay, you know that ring you're wearing on your index finger? By the way, you're supposed to wear it on your ring finger," he started.

"I am not married yet."

"Okay, that ring, that diamond ring. I bought it."

"Come again?"

"I bought that ring. That ring, with my own money."

I looked at my ring; the diamonds sparkled under the lamplights in the room. I took it off and turned it over a few times in my hands. Nathen? This ring? He bought it? His own money? I laughed out loud, and he responded with a weird look on his face.

"Wow, Nathen. I knew you should've become a comedian. Remember? I told you that back in high school." I coughed up as I was still laughing.

"Um, I wasn't trying to be funny," he said seriously.

My laugh quieted down a little until I was completely serious and took a look at the ring again. He came up to me with a little piece of paper. I took it and found it was a receipt. Freddy . . . why?

"Did Freddy ask you to buy the ring for him?" I asked curiously.

"He has financial problems, Jessica. He was really desperate for a ring, and so he asked me to help him. I was hesitant at first, but he . . . he loves you," Nathen explained.

I felt like knocking Nathen out, but I couldn't be mad at him. I should be mad at Freddy. The ring slipped from my fingers and landed with a thud on the wood-surfaced floor. I crumpled the receipt in my hands as tears formed in my eyes.

"God! Stupid Freddy!" I cried, falling to my knees which hurt a little.

"Would you like a beverage now?" he asked me.
"It would comfort me," I sniffled.

He brought a glass of wine and a box of tissues for me, pulling me up from the floor and to the couch I had used as a trampoline. He didn't say anything. I didn't say anything. I turned off my cell phone just in case Freddy gave me a late night "I love you." I didn't feel like talking to him right now. I took small sips just in case Nathen decided he wouldn't give me anymore, but later on, he gave me the entire bottle. It was quiet until he sat down at the piano and played Chopin's "Fantasie Impromptu." It was like the only song I heard him play back in high school, and it was his favorite song he enjoyed playing. But I like it too. My small sips grew longer as he played beautifully. I dabbed my eyes dry from time to time. But what was strange was that as he played, I started to cry more. I didn't know why. The way he played, the emotions he put into it, were all so beautiful. It was probably the only time he got emotional.

Nathen offered me to stay overnight, and I happily accepted. He handed me a soft blanket and a fluffy pillow, just the way I like my sleep.

Andy~

Mitch and I were going to meet up at the park to kick a ball around. I brought Austin along, and he asked me if Monica was coming too. I told him yes. Ha-ha. Another clue? Something was going on between Austin and Monica. I gotta tell Mitch this. You know what would be funny? If—I'm just saying "if"—those two get married, Mitch and I would be related. Ha-ha.

I met Mitch on the fields while Austin went his separate way onto the tennis court.

"Ready to get your ass kicked again, Andy?" Mitch asked me.

"Ha-ha. Yeah, right." I replied, kicking the soccer ball I had brought along in his direction.

He quickly stopped it with his foot and bounced it upward, catching it on top of his head. After three seconds of head balancing, he dropped the ball and kicked it toward me. I really didn't know how to do anything fancy, so I just kicked it upward a couple of times. Then, after some warm-up kicking, it was game time.

"What's up, Monica?" Austin waved to her. "Ready to play?"
"I serve?" she asked, pulling out her racket and tennis ball.
"Sure."

Austin took a minute to stare and gawk at her legs.

"Hey! Austin! Eyes on the ball!" she yelled at him as she served.

Unfocussed, he couldn't take his eyes off her, and the ball landed on his side of the court and rolled off, out of play.

"Hey! Buddy! Focus! Tryouts are in a few days!" she yelled at him.

After an hour of a game baking in the sun, we took a seat on the bleachers. We took out our Gatorades and gulped them down like alcoholics at a bar that serves drinks for free.

"Hey, Andy, you will not guess who I ran into the other day," Mitch started.
"Who?" I asked, out of breath.
"Nathen."
"Nathen?"
"Yeah, back in high school? Remember?"
"Oh, how is he?" I asked, memories of high school flooding back into my head.
"I didn't ask. He called, and I told him to meet me up for lunch tomorrow."

"Nice."

Next week was my anniversary, and my wife and I were thinking about leaving town for about two to three days—leaving Thursday night and coming back in the afternoon on Saturday—to Vegas. But what about the kids? I didn't want to haul the kids on our special days. I wonder if Mitch could watch over Austin and Sarah for me.

"Hey, Mitch, could you watch my kids for like three days next week?" I asked him.
"Oh, sorry, bro, I can't. I got a project to do next week. I need to work late. So does Leslie," he explained.

Leslie and Mitch. Ha-ha. Goes way back to high school.

"Why don't you ask Nathen?" Mitch suggested.
"Nah, are you crazy? I can't just ask him to watch my kids after what? Ten or fifteen years without meeting him again? It's just not right. I'd have to buy him a drink before I'd ask him that," I said.

Although, it is a good idea.

Austin and Monica sat on a bench to rest. Austin was breathing heavily, sweating crazily. Monica didn't look like she broke a sweat, busily sending text messages. Austin grabbed a Gatorade from his tennis bag and handed it to Monica without saying a word.

"Thanks," she said without looking up at him, continuing with her texts.

It was silent after that. Austin took a while to catch his breath.

"Wow," he huffed, "you're pretty good."
"Thanks, and you . . . you need some work. Give me ten laps around the court."
"What?" Austin asked in disbelief.

"Ten laps! Go!" Monica yelled, and her eyes still focused on her cell phone. "You can gawk at me while you run." She smiled.

Austin immediately jumped up and started his run. Monica fell off the bench laughing. Austin couldn't help but laugh at her fall as he took his run slowly absorbing her beauty with his eyes.

Jessica~

I woke up to the smell of noodles Nathen had made me for breakfast. I got up from the couch and sat in front of the bowl of noodles, picked up the pair of chopsticks beside the warm bowl and happily dug in. Nathen joined me with his own bowl, smaller than mine, and then, I felt fat.

"You finished my bottle of wine last night," he said, starting his breakfast.
"I'm sorry," I apologized with my mouth full.
"It's okay. I was meaning to finish it. So I should thank you."
"Anytime, Nathen." I smiled.
"There's more noodles on the stove if you wish to have more. Please help yourself."
"Thanks."

He left the kitchen to make my "bed," putting away the pillow and the blanket. I wanted to ask him if I could keep the pillow. It was like a marshmallow. I just absolutely loved it! But I felt like I was asking for too much. He gave me a comfy place to sleep for the night, complimentary music, and an Asian yet yummy breakfast.

"Oh, I met someone at the park the other day," Nathen said.
"Who?" I asked, helping myself out to seconds. "Gasp! Did you get her phone number?"
"Um, it was not a she."

"Oh, well, Nathen, I respect you and your decisions. I'm . . . happy for your . . . gayness. Yes. Go, gay!" I cheered, my fist shaking in the air.
"No . . . it was an old friend," he corrected me.
"Oh, whoops. My bad!"
"Apology accepted."
"Who was it?"
"It was Mitch."
"Oh my god! Aha! That jackass back in high school? Wow."
"People change you know."
"Yeah, whatever. I find it amazing yet cute who he married. Anyways, what was he doing at the park?"
"Jogging while his son was amusing himself on the playground."
"Aha. Nice."
"I'm meeting him for lunch tomorrow."
"Have fun with that," I said, washing out my bowl, placing it in the sink.

Mitch got on my nerves. Ugh! He was a HUGE irritation in my life back then. I, honestly, made a voodoo doll of him—which was made out of college-ruled lined paper and I stabbed pens in him. Then I would cut up his body with a pair of scissors and throw him away, and if the first killing of the doll didn't satisfy me, I made another one; sometimes with extra features like boobs, just depending on my mood. But like Nathen told me, people change. I wonder how much he changed . . . 5 percent? Maybe.

"Okay, Nathen. I think I'm gonna leave now. I need to go home and brush these dirty teeth." I pointed to my teeth. I picked something out between my teeth and tried to flick the plaque into the trash can, but I'm sure I missed.
"Okay, I'll walk you out," Nathen said, pushing me out the door kindly.

He walked me out to my car without saying a word. He waved good-bye to me, and in return, I imitated him. I drove out of the lot and went on my way toward home. I turned on my cell phone and inserted my Bluetooth into my ear and found that I had five missed calls; all from the same guy, the same guy that made Nathen buy him a ring for me. He could've proposed to me with an onion ring, and I still would've said yes . . . maybe . . . But he didn't have to go to Nathen for a ring, a beautiful diamond ring. It was just not right. I didn't know whether to be mad at him or . . . gosh . . . I turned off my cell phone. Where was the ring? I left it back at Nathen's apartment. I felt it was the right thing to do. I hid it inside the fluffy pillow, so I think it would probably take him a while to find out.

Mitch~

I met Nathen for lunch at a Chinese restaurant for some dim sum. I couldn't remember the last time I had dim sum. He got there before me. Usually I was the faster one. Well, back then, I was faster. While we were finished with our orders, we waited for our drinks to arrive.

"So what do you do for living, Nathen?" I asked.
"At the moment, nothing," he revealed.
"Oh, I'm sorry to hear that."
"No, it's okay. I have enough money to support me."
"That's good."

The conversation grew dead after that. Aha. It reminded me of the times when we had many dead and awkward conversations. Well, that was because Nathen was such a dead and awkward person to talk to. But it's nice to see him once again after all these years.

"So Mitch, how are you and Leslie?" he asked.
"We're good. Everything's goin' smoothly," I said.
"That's nice . . . and the children you own?"
"I have a son, Howard, seven years old, the one that fell down in the park. And Monica, she's fifteen. She goes to the same school we used to

go to. Same with Andy's kid. Oh, by the way, can you do Andy a favor and watch his kids this Thursday to Saturday?" I asked for Andy. Andy owes me one . . . if Nathen says yes.

"Um . . . sure. I'd be quite honored," Nathen agreed.

"Okay, I'll give Andy a call. If you'll excuse me," I said as I got up from the table.

I walked outside and made my call. As I was waiting for Andy to pick up his cell, I looked over to Nathen through the window. Our drinks had arrived. Dead and awkward . . . he wasn't like that before . . . before the accident happened to his . . .

"What's up, Mitch?" Andrew answered.

"Um, Nathen said yes. He'll watch them for you," I told him.

"All right, thanks, man. I owe you one."

"Hell, yeah, you do," I joked.

"Okay, see ya later."

"Bye."

I hung up and walked back to the table. I took a sip from my iced coffee I had ordered.

"So Nathen, how 'bout you and your wife and kids?" I asked him, taking another sip.

"Um, I don't control a wife or own any kids," he said rather embarrassed.

"Oh, um . . ."

I didn't know what to say after that. I kind of . . . kind of felt bad for him. Actually, to be honest, I felt bad for him all these years, even back in high school.

"I didn't choose to be a loner. Loner status just . . . chose me. Absurd as it sounds, between you and me, I think I was meant to *be* a loner," Nathen whispered to me.

Sometimes, I couldn't tell if he was joking or not. Like right now. That was what made him so funny. I couldn't help but laugh, and I tried to hide it with a fake cough and a napkin to cover my mouth and hide my smile. We talked a little more with more awkward and dead words just like the old days. We finished our meal, and the bill came. I looked at the amount we owed and counted the bills in my wallet, but before I could pull them out, Nathen had covered it.

"I'll take care of it, Mitch," Nathen told me, getting up to take the bill back up to the counter.
"Nah, it's okay. I'll handle it," I said, trying to stop him.
"No, don't bother. I can handle it."

Then we literally got into a fight over a bill. He won in the end; probably, the first thing he's ever won between us. As I was waiting for him to finish up the bill, I looked up at the sky—a few clouds here and there, but mostly clear. I thought about the upcoming project for work and how many hours I'd have to put into it. Just as long as it puts food on the table.

"Thank you for this, Mitch," he said.
"No, thank you. It was nice seein' you, Nathen," I said, walking away slowly.
"Wait, before I forget."

He handed me the business card of the Chinese restaurant.

"Um, I don't think I'll be needing this, but thanks anyways," I told him, handing him back the card.
"The location of my address is on the back of the card written in pen. It's for Andy," he corrected me.
"Oh, okay. I'll give this to him," I said, turning over the card. "Bye. Have a good one."
"The same unto you."

Jessica~

When I entered the parking lot, I saw Freddy at my door on his cell phone probably trying to call me. He noticed my car and ran down to see me. I took a deep breath and opened the car door.

"Jessica! I was so worried about you last night. Why didn't you pick up your phone?" he asked me, grabbing my hand as he caught up to me.

I pulled his arm away and tried to run as fast as I could to my door, but I was in high heels, so that was pretty much impossible. When I reached my door, I dug through my purse for my keys.

"Jessica," he called my name again.

I dropped my keys. God! I was so clumsy. As I was about to reach down for them, he picked them up for me. I aggressively pulled the keys away from him and opened the door. I didn't want to see him. I didn't want to talk to him. I just wanted him to get away from me . . . temporarily.

"Jessica, what's wrong?" he asked, grabbing my hand once again.
"Freddy! Just . . ." I stopped.

I took a seat at the kitchen table and covered my face with my hands, hiding tears. I tried to sniffle as softly as I could, but I failed. Freddy took a seat beside me, placing his hand on my back and his head rested on mine. After a minute or two of silent sobbing and peaceful silence, I lifted my head up too quickly, and our heads bumped into each other. I reacted to the pain with a wimpy "ow" and rested my head on the table again. After a few minutes of that, I lifted my head up slowly, making sure I wouldn't bump my head into anything again. I turned to his face to find him wearing a "worry" mask. He pulled a strand of hair away from my face and smiled. I didn't feel like smiling.

"Freddy," I started, taking a deep breath, "why did you ask Nathen for a ring?"

He changed his "worry" mask to a "shocked" mask.

"Did . . . Nathen tell you that?" he asked me.
"Yeppers . . ."
"Well, he's lying, Jess," he stressed from his mouth.
"Freddy, *you* don't have to lie about it. Nathen has the receipt."

He got up from his chair and slammed his hands down on my sink. Hopefully, it didn't break.

"I'm sorry, Jessica. I'm . . . sorry. I just . . . don't have any money left," he admitted to me in person.
"Freddy, why didn't you tell me?"
"I don't know . . . I just thought . . . damn. I messed up big time. I don't even have enough money for gas. I've been asking people for money."
"Including me," I sadly added.
"Yeah. Last week. I asked for ten dollars from you, so I could buy some toothpaste and a new toothbrush."
"Is that why you asked me to pick a color?"
"Ha-ha. Yeah."
"Well, I hope you're enjoying your hot pink toothbrush."
"Ha-ha."

I walked over to him to give him a hug. I asked him if he would promise not to ask for money anymore unless he really needed to. He promised with a handshake, a hug, a kiss, and an "I promise."

He ended up getting a second job working as a waiter at a Chinese restaurant. Sometimes, he would get free dumplings from the kitchen and was kind enough to share them with me. I would happily accept his generous and mouthwatering offers unless I felt fat. If that happened, I would watch him pig out.

Andy~

I was beat. I sat at my computer typing up some stuff with my eyes half open. I went into the kitchen to get some coffee to wake me up. I stayed up all night training Austin for his tryouts because they were tomorrow. While I had to leave for work at five in the morning, he got to sleep in until noon passed. I wished I was Austin's age again. I wanted to sleep in. I found I slept on my coffee which was overflowing and spilled all over the floor. I quickly got some paper towels and cleaned the mess up.

"Greetings, young padawan." My boss greeted me in her Yoda voice.
"Oh, hey, Janet." I yawned.
"Spilled some coffee I see."
"Yeah. Just cleaned it up."
"Farewell, my Jedi apprentice," she said, leaving the kitchen.

To be honest, Janet is a freak, but she can do one hell of a good impression of Yoda. I've been trying to get as close as I can to her so that I would have a higher chance of getting a raise when I ask her for one. For the past two Christmases, I've bought her life-size mannequins of Yoda for her ranging from two hundred to five hundred dollars. I feel that I'm getting close to asking. I'll probably do it next week . . . or month.

Then I wondered if I should pay Nathen for watching my kids. I thought I'd pay him. I thought it was right. But I thought he'd decline the money because that's how all Asians are especially when we go out to dinner. We fight over who pays the bill and the only way to end the war is to surrender and let them pay for it. Asian customs.

Nathen~

My doorbell rang. I answered it to find Andy and his two children.

"Hello, Andy," I greeted.

"Hey, Nathen. Nice place you've got here," Andy complimented, glancing around the room.

"Thank you."

"Well, okay. I'll be back here on Saturday to pick them up. You guys, be good, all right?" Andy instructed them, scratching the top of their heads like the way you would do to a dog.

"All right, bye, Dad," his children said in unison.

I closed the door behind him. Austin and Sarah stood beside the door, their bags to their sides waiting for further instructions.

"Um, you can make yourselves at home," I told them. Sarah dragged her bag over to my lamp beside the piano and set up her little sanctuary of stuffed animals and small pillows and blankets. Austin sat down on my couch with his iPod. I'm guessing that's all a teenager needs. I sat in a chair with my iced coffee and watched them. Wow, such quiet beings!

As I was about to use my bathroom, I heard someone playing the piano. I turned around and saw Austin playing. All of sudden, the need to pee disappeared. I sat down on the couch and listened to him play. It was quite beautiful and relaxing. When the piece was finished, Sarah and I stood up and clapped enthusiastically—a two-person standing ovation.

"Nice piano," he complimented.

"Oh, thank you. That song "River Flows in You" by Yiruma?" I questioned.

"Um, yeah. You know it?"

"I, um, haven't found the sheet music for it yet. Would you mind playing it again?" I asked shyly.

"Sure," he said, sitting back down.

Ah, it was played as beautifully as the first time, and at that moment, an idea struck me. When he was finished, I asked him, "Have you ever played for money?"

"Uh, no."

"Well, first time for everything. Let's go."

We left my apartment, and before I went downstairs, I left Sarah with my neighbor, Mrs. Bracken.

"Hello, Mrs. Bracken. Would you mind watching Sarah for me?" I asked her kindly.
"Will I get paid?" she asked in her motherly voice.
"Of course."

I dropped Sarah off, and Austin and I took a walk down to the lobby.

"Mrs. Bracken has a strong fetish for cooking, so don't worry if Sarah is malnourished," I whispered to Austin.

I asked the lobbyist if we could borrow the piano for a half hour, and he agreed. I pulled the piano and its bench out onto the street as Austin just watched me. I induced a fair amount of struggle which involved a lovely few gallons of sweat from my body. Why thank you for your assistance Austin. I pulled a felt-tip hat from the bench and placed it beside the leg of the piano. It was a good thing I lived on a busy street with busy people.

"Just set yourself up and play," I instructed him.

He did so. Soon, people were distracted and stopped for a minute or two to listen to him. Everyone who stopped to listen had one thing in common—they needed to press the pause button on their busy lives and breathe in peaceful music. Then the money-making happened. People placed bills into the hat as I stood as close as possible to local bystanders fiddling with their pockets, purses, and man purses.

After a half hour, he stopped playing, and I brought the piano and the bench back inside as Austin brought the money-filled hat. I agreed with myself that my workout for the day was over. We climbed back up and retrieved the tummy-filled Sarah.

"Awesome! We made twenty bucks!" Austin exclaimed.
"That is where you are wrong, dear Austin. We just made more money than your father will ever make in thirty minutes," I corrected him.
"What?"

I emptied my pockets and revealed thick rolls of bills.

"Holy crap!" he stated, astounded as I unrolled the bills and started counting.
"Yes, crap is sometimes holy. Three hundred and ten . . . twenty . . ."

In the end, I counted four hundred and fifty-one dollars and forty-nine cents plus the money Austin had made on his own. That totaled up to four hundred and seventy-one dollars and forty-nine cents.

"Shit man, you are good," he said, his mouth dropped.
"Bah werd," Sarah said rather cutely.
"Austin, watch the language, and I'll give you half." I offered.
"Damn good deal. All right."
"Just promise me you won't mention this to your father."
"Sure."

I did so, and he literally bathed himself with many bills and few coins. I know it's wrong to pickpocket the pockets of many innocent people, but it's how I make money since there's no other way of doing it because I don't have a job. I don't tell people this because I know that most of them will not understand. But if I did leak this information, which I did with Austin, the community of hard-working men and women and the community of homeless people would all hate me for what I do in order to make money.

Jessica~

I stopped by Nathen's apartment to tell him about my life and what not. I had brought along some home-baked cookies in a woven basket for him which, I have to admit, I have maybe taken one or two . . . or five on my way here. I knocked on the door.

"Oh, hello there, Jessica. Do enter. Please make yourself at home as I command myself to the commode." He answered the door, running off to the bathroom. As I entered the living room, I found a teenage male and a female toddler next to the piano. I dropped my basket on the tile with my mouth gaped open wide enough for small swallows to nest in. Nathen has kids? Since when did Nathen have kids? He never told me about this! Is this what he's been hiding from me? Kids? Oh dear lord! I wonder where his wife is hiding! In the closet? Sleeping under his bed? Singing in his shower? OH MY GOD!

"NATHEN! WHO DID YOU HAVE SEX WITH AND HOW COME YOU NEVER TOLD ME?" I screamed out loud, probably loud enough for the other apartment dwellers to hear me.

He replied to my loud question with a toilet flush and came out and asked, "Hm?"

"Where have you been hiding these kids, Nathen?" I yelled at him, turning to the two children. "Gasp! They are so adorable!"

I ran over to the youngest one and squeezed her cheeks. I tickled her little tummy, and she giggled which melted my heart. Then I came up to the older one and scratched his head. He was cute! Cute as in like "Freddy" cute.

"Don't worry, I'll tickle your tummy too!" I told him, giving him a little tickle on his stomach.

He laughed due to excessive tickling by ME!

"Ha-ha. Um, those children don't belong to me. They're Andy's." Nathen told me, as he folded his hands across his chest, taking a lean against his wall.

"Oh my god! Gasp! Andy from way back then? Like 'high school' way back then?" I asked, shocked.

"Yep, same one." Nathen smiled.

"Wow, his kids are cuties; I'm jealous."

"Thank you." Austin and Sarah said in unison.

"How cute! Their names?" I asked.

"Austin and Sarah."

"Gosh, I'm really jealous," I admitted, my arms folded across my chest, "Even if Andy was a jackass just like Mitch. No offense, Austin and Sarah."

"It's okay," Austin said.

"Bah werd," Sarah said.

"Come, little ones! Have some cookies!" I told them, picking up the basket I dropped.

They happily munched away on them, and I was happy—happy that they liked my baking.

"So how are you and Freddy?" Nathen whispered the question to me.

"Oh, we're good now. We're all good. He, um, got a second job at some Chinese restaurant and brings home free dumplings from time to time, so it's all good." I smiled.

I love Korean people. That's why I'm with Freddy. Ha-ha. Before I left, I wanted to take a picture of Andy's kids with my camera and probably save it as a desktop background for my computer at home.

"Okay, picture time, kids! Just look cute, and that will be just fine," I told them.

The camera flashed, and I left, taking my woven basket with me. The basket wasn't mine; it was my grandma's. The woman wove it herself as she went through a Native American phase, appreciating their culture and what not. I wish I were as talented as she. I wish I could weave things. She did offer me weaving lessons at her weaving classes at the community center, but I was too lazy to go.

"Okay, bye, kiddos!" I waved good-bye to them and left his apartment.

I drove back to work and was envious of how lucky Andy was. How lucky he was to have two very cute kids and probably a beautiful wife. Maybe if I stuck with Andy a little longer back in high school, I would've been lucky and ended up like Mitch. Well, you can never change the past; you can only tamper with it.

Andy~

We booked a room for just the two of us at The Venetian. It was really nice, yet really pricy, but yet, all things in Vegas are pricy.

"Ah, this room is amazing, Andy!" my wife exclaimed as I dragged our bags inside.

She took some time to stare outside on the balcony. I took a stand next to her, my arm around her shoulder.

"It's amazing." She breathed.
"Amazing does cost you a fortune," I joked.

She left the balcony to take a look at the bathroom which was also nice. I stood outside the balcony for a while to think to myself. No matter where you go off to for a relaxing break from life, there is always something to worry about. I wondered if the kids were all right with Nathen. I'm not saying Nathen is a bad "babysitter." It's just putting my children in the hands of a friend I haven't seen in ten years is somewhat of a mistake. Isn't it? For all I know, he could've changed from a genius to a drunken drug addict. But most drunken drug addicts don't live in such nice apartments. Then there's work. I'll have to be working overtime when I get back home.

"Andy, do you think the kids are going to be all right?" my wife asked as she stepped out on the balcony with me.

"Honey, don't worry about them. This is our time together, and we need to leave our worries back home. All right?" I told her, my hands wrapped around her.

We left to take a long walk along the Vegas Strip. We stopped at shops to rest and buy stuff. My wife took a while leaving the shops as I waited outside. Then we spent the night gambling until our pockets were filled with plenty of coins. We exchanged them for bills at the counter and went off to a sushi bar. I'll tell you, Las Vegas has ways of swallowing your money really fast.

We got back to our room at one in the morning, and we were completely beat. But while we were asleep, Vegas was still awake with its bright lights and its slot machines making a huge racket especially when jackpots were being hit.

Mitch~

I was in bed looking through a few documents from work before I got some sleep. Leslie jumped in with me and kissed me on the cheek. She covered herself with piles of blankets and turned the other way.

"Night, honey," she murmured.
"Oh, I almost forgot to tell you this," I started, putting away my documents. "I met Nathen for lunch a few days ago."
"Nathen? From high school?" she asked, turning around, pulling the sheets away from her.
"Yeah."
"Is he holding up okay?"
"I guess so. He didn't seem troubled or depressed at all, but he's still socially awkward."
"Same Nathen." She sighed, staring at the ceiling.

I stared with her and wondered how he could be holding up if he didn't have a job. How he could be holding up all alone after the accident with his family? His family died in an unexpected massacre from a neighbor. The neighbor suffered from disassociate identity disorder or, as we all know it as, split personality disorder. The woman lived alone and had medications for her disorder. She refused to go through therapy because she absolutely despised doctors. She had three different personalities: herself, a kind, warm-hearted grandmother, and a mentally disturbed middle-aged man. People have rumored that her personality of the middle-aged man came from her grandfather who had abused her mentally and physically.

So what happened was that Nathen stayed home to study for a huge calculus final, which I remembered studying for, while his mom, dad, older sister, and two younger brothers went off to the park. But the neighbor stopped them for some small talk inside her house, and that's when her personality switched from herself to the mentally disturbed man, and she butchered the five of them. No one heard any screams or saw anything suspicious.

Later on, she placed the chopped up bodies on the grill, and that's when people started calling the authorities because of a suspicious smell—the smell of burning flesh. Finally, she hung herself with an electrical cord in her living room. The neighborhood was a fairly good one without any troubles or complaints and was usually very quiet. It was all over the papers and the TV. Nathen tried to stay away from the press as much as possible which was good for him. But god, I don't know how anyone can live through that. Before his family was killed, he was such a lively person, but after the massacre, he just excluded himself from the rest of the world. He sat by himself at lunch tables, didn't raise his hand during class to answer a question, and didn't work in groups at all when completing group assignments. But he was still a genius, he worked hard, and he ended up going to UCLA when Yale and Harvard wanted him. But he said he wanted to stay somewhere near home, so he could visit his family's graves, and that his dad wanted him to go to UCLA.

I do remember once, after his family was gone, he asked me if I could be his partner for a project. I was going to partner up with Andy, so I told him no, and I regretted not accepting him as a partner. God, I felt like such an asshole. Andy and I got a B for that project and, of course, Nathen passed with an A. Later on, I started sitting next to him during lunch—because you know I was a nice guy and not a complete asshole—and started talking to him no matter how awkward it was. Then Andy. But Jessica beat us to it. She was there before Andy and I came. Jessica . . . ha-ha . . . wow . . .

The idea of a massacre sounds so far-fetched to me but it really did happen. How could something so unexpected happen like that out of the middle of nowhere?

Nathen~

"So who was the chick yesterday? Your girlfriend?" Austin asked me as I was preparing breakfast for him.
"No. Just a friend. Her name's Jessica," I told him.
"That's cool."
"Speaking of Jessica, believe it or not, but, she used to be your dad's girlfriend back in high school," I revealed.
"Whoa . . ."
"Yeah, I know. But Jessica dumped him because she just lost interest in him I believe."
"Well, her loss."

I smiled, dumping noodles into his bowl and Sarah's bowl.

"Nathen, you're pretty cool," Austin told me.
"Aha. Are you just saying that because I gave you half of the money I made?"
"No, you're actually pretty cool. I thought you were some boring loner at first, but, no."

"Thanks, I highly appreciate that. You're probably the first to ever call me cool."

"Really? Wow."

I didn't know if I heard or understood this clearly and correctly, but did Austin just classify me as being cool. Cool as in a positive epithet/interjection that is a part and parcel of the English slang. Amazing . . . I am cool. Cool. Ha-ha. My fancies were being tickled at the moment. I needed some time to digest Austin's kind words that slightly appealed to me emotionally.

"Austin, are you ready to make some more money?" I asked him.
"Sure. Let's do it."

Then it happened. We made about the same amount as the previous day and evenly split the money. For the rest of the morning, Austin played through some of the music that I had written. I didn't expect him to play it well, since it was somewhat hard. But it was nice to hear another person play my music. I highly appreciated that.

"Okay, Austin, what is it that you desire in life right now?" I asked him, taking a seat on my couch.

"Uh, an iPhone," he answered rather quickly.

"Then let's not deny that desire," I said, getting up, picking up Sarah from underneath the piano. "Oh, and by the way, you're using your own money."

"That's fine with me!" he exclaimed, getting up from the piano.

We left the apartment building and jumped into my Smart Car. Since a Smart Car is a two-seater car, Sarah had to sit on Austin's lap. Hopefully, the authorities wouldn't catch us riding with an infant illegally. I drove to the nearest Best Buy, and after a few minutes of much excitement for Austin, we left the store with Austin being satisfied.

"Thanks, Nathen," Austin said, ripping open his boxed goods, ignoring the disappearance of the receipt that flew out of the open car's window beside him.

"Why thank me? You're the one who made the money," I told him, and my eyes glued to the road. "You have to understand that, without you as a distraction to the chaste strangers, it would have been a bit more difficult to pick pockets. So basically, I used you."

"Well, being used never felt so good," he said, turning on his new iPhone.

"Aha-ha. Anything else that you covet?"

"No. Not really," he answered quite casually.

"Well, by the looks of you, I think you have everything you want: a great father, a loving mother, an adorable sister, a warm home, a girlfriend, and all the small necessities that enhance your adolescent lifestyle."

"Ha-ha. Um, no girlfriend."

"No?"

"I guess we have one thing in common; we are still 'girlfriend virgins.'"

"Ha-ha. You are absolutely correct," I admitted.

No, I have never had a girlfriend. I just . . . there's a story behind this simple . . . something that I promised myself that I simply forgot about. It's . . .

"No girlfriend? In your entire life?" Austin asked me.

"Sadly, no."

"That sucks, man. To live all your life and not have someone to share love with."

"Share love? As in physically?"

"Um, sure, but I meant feelings."

"Oh yes, of course," I coughed. "And you? You have not shared feelings of love with anyone?"

I was wondering if this conversation was at all awkward for him because it was a wee bit awkward for me.

"Uh, no. Not yet. But there is . . ." he stopped.

"Someone?" I finished the sentence for him.

I found this conversation quite intriguing. What is it with adolescent love stories that engross you into wanting to know all, including the smallest details? Because I was quite interested.

"Okay, I like Monica," he admitted to me as his cheeks turned red.
"Who is this Monica specimen?" I asked.
"She's, um . . . Mitch's daughter."
"Mitch? Wow . . . quite interesting."
"You know Mitch?"
"Yeah, he's is a good friend of mine."
"Oh, that's cool."
"So . . . have you talked to this female being of Mitch's?"
"Yeah, but I don't think she likes me very much," he revealed quite sadly.
"I see."
"I like her a lot, but . . . I don't think she sees that. Why doesn't she like me? What's wrong with me?"
"That's a rhetorical question, right? Well, to me, you seem like a spiffy young chap," I admitted.
"Ah, thanks."

He said nothing more. It was a quiet ride home.

"Hey, do you know how to play tennis? I need to practice for a tournament," Austin asked me as we marched up the stairs, a sleeping Sarah in my hands.
"Um, no, but, Jessica does," I told him.
"Cool. Can I play her today?"
"I'll have to call."

In a few minutes, we met Jessica at the park. She was performing a few squat thrusts on the tennis court with her arms outreached.

"You ready to play, Austin boy?" she asked him.
"You're on."

Then the game began. Austin was to serve, and the ball flew at Jessica's face which she quickly dodged by running away toward her water bottle. Austin bent over, laughing at her.

"Austin! Don't do that! That ball almost hit my face, and I work hard for my face! Why do you have to hit it so hard?" she screamed at him.
"That's what she said!" he laughed even harder.
"Okay, that's it. Your ass is mine!" she yelled, chasing after him with her racket.

Sarah and I watched as Jessica badly swung her racket at Austin, missing every time as they ran around the court. Sarah was giggling loudly, clapping her hands on the bench beside me.

"Damn cute Korean teens and their ability to run fast!" Jessica yelled.

Jessica stopped running and slowly walked over to her bottle of water which she finished in seconds. Austin walked back to our bench still laughing. Sarah got up and handed him a water bottle.

"Thanks, Sarah," he said tiredly.
"You wercome," she laughed, clapping as she got back up on the bench.

Jessica walked toward our bench and warned Austin, "I'm going to tickle you again the next time you hit a ball like that."
"Fine, but only after you tell me how my dad's lips were," Austin shot back.
"WHAT? NATHEN? YOU TOLD HIM I KISSED ANDY?" she screamed at me.
"Um, sorry?" I apologized.
"Nathen, I'm gonna tell Freddy to beat you up, and if that doesn't work, WE'LL BOTH BEAT YOU TO DEATH!" she threatened me.
"I'm sorry!"

"And maybe I'll include what you stole from Diana at her party back in high school and tell little Austin here! Free of charge!" she added.
"No! Don't tell him! I'm sorry!"
"What did you steal, Nathen?" Austin asked me curiously.
"I'll tell you, Austin!" Jessica shouted, "He stole . . ."
"Say no more!" I shot at her.
"NATHEN STOLE DIANA'S PANTIES!" Jessica screamed jumping up and down.

Austin laughed so hard he fell off the bench.

"I threw them out!" I admitted.
"HA-HA-HA! Wow, Nathen, you? Steal panties?" he laughed. "I think I'm gonna piss my pants."
"Wa pannies?" Sarah asked.

I was very embarrassed which was obvious by my blushing.

Andy~

My wife and I were driving around looking for another hotel to stay at, since we got kicked out of The Venetian. My wife suggested something cheaper, but no, I decided we would stay at the Bellagio, and I had to admit that it was way more beautiful than The Venetian . . . and possibly my wife. Nah, just playing. *Nothing* is more beautiful than my wife.

"Honey, this is beautiful and all, but I think we're spending way too much," she admitted.
"Ah, it doesn't matter. Let's just enjoy ourselves," I told her.

I stepped out onto the balcony to take some pictures with the professional camera I just bought. The pictures turned out really clear and beautiful. My wife jumped on top of the bed, landing on her stomach. She laughed and flopped herself upright to have a look at the ceiling. I stepped out and asked, "What are you laughing at?"

"I can't believe what you did to get us kicked out of The Venetian."

"Well, you told me to!" I said, jumping on the bed beside her.

At night, we went out to the pool area for a swim when the pool was closed. I took a look at the pool, and it seemed decent enough to swim in, and when I was about to turn around to take a look at the Jacuzzi, my wife pushed me in the pool, and I fell with a mighty splash. It was extremely cold. As soon as I got to the surface, I splashed some of the water on her as she laughed and screamed. She hopped into the Jacuzzi, and I stepped out of the pool shivering with my teeth chattering like crazy. I met my wife in the Jacuzzi, and warm water never felt so relieving.

"How was the pool?" she laughed at me.

"Colder than your cruel black hole of a heart," I retorted.

"That's mean!" she scoffed, splashing water in my face.

I guess I deserved water in my face.

"I dare you to take off your swimming trunks!" my wife laughed.

At this point, I didn't know what I was thinking. I did tell myself that the idea was stupid in the first place. Maybe it was one too many drinks I took a few hours before. I got up from the pool and started untying the string to my trunks and quickly pulled them down, and to be honest, I was feeling a little . . . horny. Ha-ha. I jumped back in the pool, hot water splashing everywhere and dragged her down under the water and kissed her. It was my first time ever kissing someone underwater, naked, and the experience being a little different. We popped our head back to the surface after a few seconds.

"Oh my god! Put your trunks back on before somebody sees you!" my wife whispered loudly.

I got up and right then and there; the manager saw me, and I quickly pulled up the trunks and tied it together.

"YOU TWO! OUT OF THE POOL AREA! NOW!" the manager yelled at us as we snickered and left the area.

"Hey, look man, I'm sorry," I apologized casually.
"Get your stuff and leave my hotel," he ordered.

So we did just that. Now we're here at the Bellagio. I lay down beside her on the bed, staring at the ceiling with her. I don't know if I was hallucinating or something, but I could make out an "I love you" on the ceiling. I heard my wife's stomach growl and laughed.

"You hungry?" I asked.
"Yeah," she said, turning to me, kissing my cheek.
"McDonald's?"
"Two golden arches are fine with me." She smiled.

We went off, got our order, and sat on a bench to eat a few blocks away. As we ate, we watched many tourists walk by as street performers did what they loved doing for a few coins and dollar bills. This one guy was rolling this crystal ball-like object across his arms and fingers giving it an appearance that it was floating. It was pretty tight which I later found out was called contact juggling. We dropped a five-dollar bill in his hat when we finished dinner and walked back to the hotel, hand in hand. She was slightly leaning on my shoulder which ached a little, but I didn't mind.

Jessica~

I hadn't seen or heard from Freddy for a while. He hadn't called me or sent text messages to me like he used to when he was less busy. Freddy and I were supposed to meet today for some wedding stuff. I thought I should get that ring back from Nathen. I thought I'd stop by later today. I liked stopping by Nathen's apartment . . . well, now I do . . . because of Austin and Sarah. God! Why does Andy have to have such cute kids? Their cuteness is absolutely irresistible. Oh! If I go on a scavenger hunt through my room, I could probably find that note that Andy wrote to me way back then. He was the one that asked me out. He came to me. Yeah, I attract them, boys. Ha-ha.

Hmm, a scavenger hunt sounded like something I wanted to do tonight. Maybe a little accompanied music during the search would help, and why not a *small* tub of Haagen-Dazs? Or, even better, why not a *big* tub of Haagen-Dazs? If Freddy was still busy on Friday, why not two big tubs of Haagen-Dazs and a nice, little Korean drama? Yep, nothing is better than spending my time wisely.

I was at work and not doing what I was supposed to be doing . . . whatever that was. I brought my laptop along and watched Korean dramas underneath my desk. I would quickly close down my laptop and hide it underneath my skirt when coworkers would pass by which happened quite often. So I'd usually get to finish at least one episode at work. Sometimes, Tiffany, a friend of mine, would watch with me. Tiffany and I met at the underground gym beneath our work building. I was doing a couple of laps in the pool. Then she came along and started doing a few laps, showing off her oh-so-slim body. My game-side told me to race her, and I did . . . she beat me.

"It's okay, Jessica. Maybe next time," she smiled, handing me a Gatorade.

I grabbed the energy drink from her hands and gulped it down. I used to hate Tiffany because she was so much better than me at everything:

turning in documents before me, knowing how to get around a bunch of work, having a better lunch than me, and, of course, swimming. She was so nice but evil in a way. AH! I hated her. She was like a Nazi Mormon.

But that was the past. Tiffany and I are friends now because I beat her in a race four months after my loss.

As soon as I got off from work, I rushed down to Nathen's apartment. I felt like coming home to my family; Nathen being my husband, Austin and Sarah being my kids. Aha. I barged into his apartment and opened up his closet.

"Um, do come in," Nathen said.

I had disturbed his duet with Austin. He got up from the piano to see what I was up to. I told him, "I need to borrow this pillow."

"What significance does it hold to you other than the fact that it is quite fluffy?" he asked.

"My ring is in it, and I need something to rest my head on when I'm watching Korean dramas tomorrow night if Freddy doesn't show up," I answered sadly.

"Oh, I see."

By the time I got home, I'd feel so lonely. Sure I have a cell phone with people to text and call and Internet so that I can chat with people on Facebook, but I won't be able to speak with them *in person*. All I have to do tonight is watch Korean dramas, most of them with the same old plots and situations. Oh, wait! I also have a scavenger hunt tonight that I hope will keep me busy all night, and Haagen-Dazs. I love my Haagen-Dazs. Hey, why not ask Austin if he can keep me company?

"Hey, Nathen, do you think maybe I can borrow Austin?" I asked quickly.

"Austin, would you like to join Jessica for an evening, preferably today's evening?" Nathen asked him.

"Um, sure. Why not?" he agreed.

"Yay!" I clapped, "Come on! We'll have so much fun together!"

I waited for Austin to gather up his things for the night.

"Behave yourselves, you two," Nathen informed us.
"Okay, Daddy!" I joked.

I took Austin's hand and ran toward my car, forcing him to run with me. We both jumped into the car and headed back to my place.

"So Austin, how's life treatin' ya?" I asked him.
"Life is treating me sweetly," he answered casually, placing an earphone into his right ear.
"You have a girlfriend?"
"No, not yet."
"Aw, sad face," I said, moving my lower lip down.
"Ha-ha. How 'bout you? You have a boyfriend?"
"I'm engaged," I smiled.
"Congrats."
"Thank you!"

It was quiet for a minute, until I brought up, "Nathen told me that you had a crush on Monica."
"Then why did you ask me if I had a girlfriend?" he shot back.
"I don't know. So Monica. Mitch's daughter. Ha-ha. I remember when Mitch used to be such an asshole. He would always tease me and your dad when we were together." I laughed. "So does his 'asshole-ness' passed down?"
"No, Monica isn't an asshole. She's sweet, funny, hot, and maybe a little bossy at times, but in a funny way," he leaked.
"Aw, how cute! Little Austin has a little crush on Mitch's daughter."
"Yeah, yeah, yeah. Go ahead and tease me all you want. You're not gonna tell my dad this, are you?" he asked quickly.
"Pfft! Why would I?" I scoffed.

As soon as I got home, I ran to the fridge to pop open two tubs of Haagen-Dazs, Austin behind me. I threw him a tub and a spoon.

"Thanks," he thanked.
"Oh, by the way, you can leave your stuff by the door in case I sleep in and run late for work; that way you can pick it up as we run out the door and to the car."
"Um, okay."
"So you know what you're going to do tonight?" I asked him.
"No, probably watch a Korean drama with you? Nathen said you like to watch those a lot."
"Ha-ha! Yes! That and something else."
"What?"
"A scavenger hunt!"
"Yay," he said with the least bit of enthusiasm.
"You don't seem enthusiastic?" I said.
"Yay!" he said again, sarcastically.

This boy . . . he cracks me up. We walked over to my room and faced my closet.

"Okay, hunting time," I started, turning on my computer and played "Dancing Queen" by Abba, "and PS, if you come by a bra or thong, please don't steal it."
"Don't worry, I won't. I'm not like Nathen."
"Okay! Spoons ready? And Haagen-Dazs!" I exclaimed, as we stuck our spoons in the tub and began eating. "And search!"

I opened the closet door, and I shoveled through a whole bunch of junk. When I came by loose change, I quickly stuffed it down my pockets, continuing my search.

"You are the dancing queen, young and sweet, only seventeen. Dancing queen, feel the beat of the tambourine, oh, yeah. You can dance, you can jive, having the time of your life. Oh, see that girl, watch that scene, dig in the dancing queen!" I sang, using my silver spoon as a microphone. "Come on! Sing with me!" I commanded him, but he shook his head.

"What exactly are we looking for?" Austin asked, changing the subject.

"Oh, a note that your dad wrote me that made me go out with him."

"Is it this?" he asked, pulling out a small piece of notebook paper from underneath an old notebook.

"I don't know." I stopped, my heart beating faster for no apparent reason. "Read it to me."

"Three words, eight letters, just say it, and I'm yours," he read.

I laughed and lay down on the floor beside Austin. Those words . . . I remember he gave me that note when he came into biology and passed by my desk. I was half asleep because I was up all night "studying." Then, I remembered that my heart was beating really fast during the entire class, and I waited until everybody left, when the classroom was finally empty except for the teacher, to hug him and whisper those three words, those eight letters, into his ear. *I love you.* The teacher's presence made it a little awkward for us.

"Your dad was an asshole too, but that was only when he was with Mitch. But when he was by himself, without a Mitch, he was really sweet."

"So why did you break up with him?" Austin asked me, taking a spoonful of his ice cream.

"I just stopped liking him because I don't know. I just didn't like him anymore even though he was sweet. Your dad was a good man, and I hope he still is," I said, staring at the ceiling, not at least once having eye contact with the boy.

"Thanks, I guess."

"You can go back to Nathen's if you want. I'll drive you back right now." I offered.

"You're gonna be okay all alone?" he asked, thinking of me.

"I guess so. Tonight's hunt for a piece of paper finished earlier than I expected."

"Well, if you want me to stay, I'll stay."

"Well, I kinda do want you to stay . . . 'cause I need to know if I snore or not," I smiled.

"All right. I'll stay," he said, getting up to dispose of his ice cream.

Mine was still full and was slowly melting. I didn't feel like eating anymore. I just suddenly lost my appetite.

"Hey," I caught his attention before he left my room.

He stopped and turned toward me.

"To be honest, if I was your age, I would go out with you if Monica breaks your heart."

"Ha-ha. Um, thanks," he thanked shyly, hiding his blush as he walked away.

Why did I just say that? God, I was so stupid. Look at me! It was like I had some kind of crush on this kid! What was wrong with me? Okay, I needed a drink, but before that, I needed to drop this kid back to Nathen's, or he was going to ruin my head with feelings and thoughts. Ugh! When I looked at Austin, I saw Andy, and all these high school memories were making me like Andy again. I needed Freddy. Where was my Freddy? He was busy at a Chinese restaurant that gave him free dumplings. Look at what was happening as Freddy was slowly disappearing from me, I was keeping myself busy with thoughts about replacing him with a married man who I saw in his son who was in my apartment! Okay, this boy really needed to leave my apartment.

"Um, Austin?" I sputtered. "I think it's best if you go back to Nathen."

"Why?" he asked.

"Um, I'm fine all by myself," I lied.

"Um, okay."

"Wait by the door," I told him, grabbing my car keys.

I took the tub of ice cream and placed it back in the freezer, and met Andy, I mean Austin, by the car. Crap! I was getting them mixed up . . . okay, he was definitely ruining my head.

"Why the sudden change of plans?" he asked me as I zoomed past cars.
"I just need some thinking time alone . . . alone in my apartment. That's all," I semi-lied.
"Oh, okay."

I knocked on Nathen's door.

"Jessica? Back so soon?" he answered the door.
"You can have him back," I told him.
"Why? Were you two misbehaving?"
"No, nothing out of the ordinary," I told him.

Austin walked back inside to find his sister sleeping under the piano with stuffed animals. I left without a good-bye. I didn't know why . . . my mind was just being ugh . . . I was going to go home and have a drink. During the ride home, I thought about the story Tiffany told me. A rich gal had married this hobo because she thought he looked cute and fuzzy. Then a week after they were married in Reno, the hobo stabbed her to death with a rock in her backyard where she was sunbathing. He finished her off by dumping her in her own pool where the chlorine-filled water turned red. He spent a few hours stealing her jewelry and other sweet necessities and left in her car with a lot of cash in his pockets. As much as I didn't want to believe it, I was a sucker for amazing stories, even if they are sad like Nathen's.

I went to bed finishing an entire bottle of wine and that tub of unfinished ice cream. No matter how much I drank or ate, Austin or Andy just wouldn't leave my mind.

Nathen~

I cleaned up the dishes sitting in the sink while Austin and Sarah were getting ready to go to bed. Austin carried her to bed, and as soon as she was under the sheets, she woke up full of unsuspected energy. As soon as I finished the dishes, I turned my way to their room.

"Sarah, bed time for you. Austin, stay up as late as you want, just try to keep the noise level down, and the use of my lights should be at a minimum," I told him.
"Yes, sir," he saluted.

I closed the door for them. I sat down at my piano and scribbled a few notes on a music sheet hoping in the end, when I finished it, I could call it a song.

"Sarah, it's time for bed," Austin told her.
"Okay, brodder," she said, jumping under her sheets.

Austin tucked her in nice and warmly.

"Ausin?" Sarah called out his name as he turned off the lights.
"Hm?"
"Do you rike Uncle Nayten?"

Austin took a few minutes of thought as he pulled out his laptop.

"Sarah, he's not our uncle," he corrected her.
"Aw, I wiss. I rike Nayten," she said, hiding under her sheets.
"I like Nathen too," he said, looking at the iPhone he bought the other day. "It would be pretty cool."

I ended up falling asleep on my piano like most of the time even though it was quite uncomfortable, but one can get used to uncomfortable when sleeping on a piano, the only downside being an ached neck and back.

Andy~

It was our last day of our mini-vacation from the world. The last day was spent her way: shopping. We ran from store to store buying heavy stuff. I carried all the bags for her. We stopped at a place to get a few stuffed animals for Sarah, and another place to get Austin an iPhone because he'd been begging for one. After we finished brunch, we went back to the hotel to drop off all her heavy stuff.

"Andy, I feel lucky today. Let's hit the slots," she told me.
"Sure. Let's lose all our money," I told her.

I spent my hours at tables with cards and poker chips while she pulled down knobs of slot machines. I wasn't feeling lucky at all and was losing my money by the minute. After a few hours of no luck, I ran around the casino in search of my wife. I found her at a slot machine in a far corner yelling at it. I would do the same thing at the tables except there were people around me.

"Hey, honey, time to go home." I tapped her on the shoulder.
"Fine," she said disappointedly. "Did you win anything?"
"A few chips. Nothing special."
"All right, let's go home."

We walked over to the counter to exchange my chips, and in the process, the lad behind the counter laughed at me. My wife turned around and spotted a slot machine. She looked down at the coin in her hands.

"Honey, I'm gonna try one more slot machine," she told me, walking slowly toward her destined machine.

She slipped the coin in the slot and pulled down the knob. One by one, she pulled down the knob carefully and the last knob . . . The machine had given her a jackpot. She jumped up and screamed and ran to me forcing me into this long and back-cracking hug. I didn't know she was that strong.

"I WON! I WON! ANDY, I WON!" she screamed in my face.
"I know! I'm right in front of you!" I told her, trying to calm her down.

We exchanged the millions of nickels into dollar bills and ran back to the hotel. As soon as we got inside our room, she tossed the bills in the air, most of them landing on the bed as she was screaming with joy. Instead of packing up, she dragged me on to the bill-covered bed, and we did it there, rolling around in the filthy bills. Later on, during the car ride back home, she described it with three words: dirty, sexy, and money.

Nathen~

I had slept in through serving the children their most important meal of the day, breakfast. I quickly got up and ran into the kitchen, wiping the drool off my face. When I was about to grab a box of noodles, I had found two unclean bowls in the sink and one bowl of noodles ready for me. I walked around, looking for Sarah and Austin. I walked into the room I allowed them to stay in where I found Sarah having a little tea party with her stuffed animals. That would be a great Kodak moment.

"Where's your brother?" I asked her kindly.

She responded with a point with the use of her index finger, pointing toward my room. Now what would he be doing in there? I slowly walked over to my door, attempting to sneak up from behind and scare him with my thundering adult voice and actions. I slowly opened the door and peeked through to see him looking at my wall. *The* wall. I stood next to him, staring at the wall with him.

The wall was covered with pictures of Asian couples I had taken over the years. It was a small hobby of mine until it turned into a rather larger obsession than I expected it to be. To stop this obsession, I threw my camera out the window which I'm sure broke, or, if it survived, a hobo might have added something special in his shopping cart that day. Not only was it an obsession or a hobby, it was to show me, personally, how lonely I was in the world. It was a marvelous, colossal degradation for me especially when the Asian people in the photos were smiling together with their—what seemed fake—pearly, white teeth. They got to live their happy lives, where I lived a life where happiness had either left me or had been dead since what happened during in high school . . . the massacre. Something about degrading myself just made me feel good about myself. It pleased me.

"Why did you take so many pictures of so many Asians?" Austin asked me.

"It was a hobby of mine, and this hobby of mine showed me how lonely I was in the world," I admitted.

"If it does that, why don't you just take it down?" he fired back.

"Because I also like being happy for other people, even if they're strangers," I told him.

"Wow, you're one complex dude."

"Thank you, I believe. So it's the last day, what shall we do today?" I asked him, changing the subject.

"Whatever you wanna do for a change."

"I was actually looking forward to whatever you wished to do."

"I don't wanna ask too much from you, so I'm good," he said, leaving the room.

I sensed a microscopic form of animosity between us. What did I do? What hateful crime did I commit? I guessed I had nothing to do today.

After four hours had passed, Austin and Sarah were ready to leave; I had done nothing. All I had accomplished for the day was a staring contest with my wall of Asian people. I hadn't been in my room for approximately two months I believed. I'd been either sleeping on my piano or the couch, so I had missed my room a wee bit.

The doorbell rang, and I went to retrieve the door. As I expected, it was Andy here to retrieve his children.

"Greetings, Andy," I answered the door.
"Hey, Nathen," he greeted, giving me a pat on the back.
"Daddy!" Sarah squealed, running into his arms.
"Hey, honey! Did you have fun?"
"Yesh," she hugged him, as he picked her up.
"Hey, Dad," Austin greeted casually, grabbing his bag.
"Hey, kiddo. Ready to leave?"
"Yep."
"Go meet your mom in the car while I talk to Nathen for a sec," he ordered them as they went away with the mother. "Hey, Nathen, um, thanks for watching the kids for me and Lily. I owe you."
"No problem, and there's really no need to owe me. You're kids are wonderful and, well, kept me company, so I guess you can consider us even," I told him.
"No, I really do owe you one," he said, pulling out his wallet.
"No, please, put those American bills away. There's really no need."
"No, it's okay, I just won the jackpot, well, Lily won the jackpot."
"Well, that is really quite outstanding, but please, save it for future electric and water bills. Those are quite a monster these days especially having two children."
"Okay, fine. I surrender. Well, it was nice seeing you again."
"Yes, you too," I said, closing the door as he waved good-bye.

Andy~

I jumped in the car where everyone was waiting for me. I opened up the glove compartment and took out the iPhone I had bought and threw it to Austin which he caught.

"Oh, thanks Dad," he said uneasily.
"What's wrong, son?" I asked him.

"Oh, nothin'," I sensed him lying.

I ignored it for a minute to hand a bag of stuffed animals to Sarah.

"There you go, sweetie," I told her, opening up the bag and driving at the same time.

Lily helped me out and pulled some stuffed animals out for her to play with in her car seat. I looked at them through the mirror above me and smiled. Today was probably one of the best days of my life, other than my wedding day and my honeymoon. My wife won the jackpot. Dirty. Sexy. Money. And it was great to see the kids again.

"How was Nathen's?" I asked them.
"FUN!" Sarah exclaimed, clapping.
"It was all right. Nathen's cooler than I expected," Austin admitted.
"Ha-ha. Well, did he tell you about what happened to him?" I brought up, a little uncomfortable about bringing it up in the first place.
"No?" he said unsurely.
"His family was massacred."
"Andy, not in front of Sarah," Lily whispered to me.
"What the hell? How? Why?"
"I don't want to go into details. Too gory, but yeah. He was really a depressing and miserable person back then. So is he still like that when you spent three days with him?"
"No, not at all. He just seemed lonely," Austin told me.

I didn't say anything. I didn't want to say anything more. It was a quiet ride home. I didn't think I'd have to work overtime because of this jackpot, so I wouldn't have to stay late for work to hear from Yoda, Janet.

Jessica~

Oh my god! I had been lying down on the floor all day, beside my closet, staring up at the ceiling and doing absolutely nothing. I'd been trying to call Freddy and sending him text messages, but he wouldn't reply. I tried to call again, but all I got was his stupid voicemail, "Hey, this is Freddy. Uh, I'm not here right now, but I'll try to get back to you as soon as possible. Ciaooo." Then where the hell are you, Freddy? I sent him another text message and dropped my phone beside me. He proposed to me with a ring that Nathen bought for him, and now nothing was happening. Was there supposed to be a wedding coming up? Between me and Freddy? Or not? In my other hand, I had the note Andy had given me back in high school. I was slowly falling for Austin's dad. I blamed Freddy! I needed him, or should I blame myself? My stupid self. I thought I needed another drink. Look at me! I was drowning myself in alcohol to get rid of my problems, . . . but it was not working at all.

If I did stick with Andy all the way through, that would be like a miracle—a miracle which Mitch had gone through. He married Leslie. Leslie went to school with us for a while, until she transferred because she moved. They had a relationship back then, even after she moved. It was sort of hard for them, but they made it through when they met each other again when they attended UCSD. Leslie was such a nice, sweet person. Mitch was an asshole. They were meant for each other! Catch my irony/sarcasm? How could a nice girl like her go for a poo-head like Mitch? But anyways, they stuck with each other. Perhaps, sticking with each other till the end. I wanted to stick with someone till the end. Freddy? Andy? Austin? Austin? Why did I just internally suggest Austin for myself? God, I'm such an idiot . . . and a soon-to-be predator aiming my love life toward little teenage souls. Okay, I seriously needed to get another drink.

Mitch~

I am so overworked right now. I literally don't have anytime to even have dinner with the family. All personal phone calls and e-mails are temporarily being unanswered. I don't even have time to complain about work and life right now. I'm working from home, so I could take small breaks without having my boss see me sleeping on the job. I'm only half way done with this pain-in-the-ass presentation. But after all this is done, which will be done by Monday very nice and neatly, I will be looking forward to a bonus. It's not a jackpot, but it's as close as I can get to one without having to hit a casino in Vegas like Andy. Okay, I admit, maybe I have slipped in a few personal calls from Andy, but that's because he's my best friend. We're like brothers, "brothas from 'notha mothas" if you wanna put it in Ebonics.

My wife's been worried about me. I haven't been coming to bed with her until morning comes up, around midnight and 1-ish. During breaks, I do have time to complain about life and work. I kind of feel like a student again. I feel like my daughter. Not in any female way though; no, not at all. I want to go back to those days, those golden days.

Nathen~

I'd been staring at my wall of degradation for a while now. I felt that I was all alone in the world. Austin, Sarah, and Jessica didn't count because they just came and went, and I needed someone to stay here with me—stay here in my apartment to keep me company, but not in any sexual pleasures like the Russian prostitute that lived with a neighbor of mine three floors down. His name was Roger, and he had decided to keep a Russian prostitute as a toy I believe because of his problems with women in the past. Roger didn't speak a lot of English, but Portuguese was his thing. He only knew "please," "thank-you," and "I like your dandy tie." I taught him the last one which took about a week for him to learn, coming by his house every day. He switched to shackles for her instead of duct-taping her to a chair. He switched to shackles so that she could use the restroom, but far enough so that it was impossible for her to reach a phone so that she could call for help. Before he left for work—his work including standing in front of buildings looking for work from random strangers—he gave her a plate of bread, peanut butter, and a bottle of water for her breakfast and lunch. He would feed her dinner when he came home. I needed a wife, but I thought having a wife did include sexual pleasures. Maybe a maid would do. Yes, a maid. As she would tidy up for me, I would talk to her and maybe pay her extra for listening to me drone on about my miserable life. Actually, I didn't need to have her clean my home because I could do that myself, so maybe I'd just pay her to listen to me. Yes, that sounded a bit right.

No, I thought I needed to escape. I needed to escape from this terrible way of living. I needed to escape from reality and go on a long vacation. Yes, that sounded excellent. I noticed a misplaced photo underneath my dresser and picked it up. I quickly grabbed a tissue to dust off the dust that the photo had collected. It was a picture of Katie. It must have fallen off the wall of degradation. I slipped a piece of double-sided tape on the back of the photo and posted it on the wall. Katie was a female that I admired dearly back in high school. She was a cousin of Mitch, and I made a really quite absurd promise to myself that I would go to Hawaii and find her. Why Hawaii? She had left Los Angeles, California, to attend UH Manoa. A promise like that could take years to accomplish because of the numerous people and many islands.

Hawaii? Vacation? Maybe a search? I believed my thoughts had a dash of puerile in them at the moment.

Jessica~

I met Freddy today at a café after many busy nights he had. He looked overworked and tired. I took a long sip from my iced coffee and gave him a long stare. He was falling asleep on me and his cappuccino. I tapped him on the shoulder, but he didn't move.

"Freddy, it's nice to see and hear from you again," I started, but he was still asleep on me, "but I don't think this relationship is going to work out. You're away a lot. I know, I understand that you're really busy because of that second job, but I really don't think this is going to work. You can keep your ring and propose to another young lady perhaps someone like me so that when you marry her or something, I won't have awkward conversations with her when I meet her. I'd know what she would like, and she would know what I like, and it'll be easy talk. Or you could just sell it or exchange it for store credit depending on where you bought it. Oh, wait, excuse me, where Nathen bought it."

I felt like I was talking to myself. He didn't move one bit when I was talking. I tapped on his shoulder again, and this time he jumped up, yelling, "W-What? Are you ready to order now?" He scared the crap out of me. I slowly covered his cold hand with mine. Even though it was cold, I felt warm inside.

"Did you say something, Jessica?" he asked me with weary eyes.

I shook my head no and continued to finish up the iced coffee.

"Oh, by the way," he started, "I'm gonna be off for a few months for a business trip, so I'm taking a small leave of absence from being a waiter and free dumplings."
"Sounds good," I told him with no enthusiasm at all.
"We'll keep in touch?" he asked me, squeezing my hand.

I pulled my hand away from his. I wanted to be with him. Now I didn't want to be with him. What was the matter with me? God, I was so fickle. Well, I'd give a good reason: I'm a girl, and girls are fickle most of the time I think, and if not, then I was born the wrong gender or something.

"What's wrong?" he asked me.

"Are you blind? Do I need to draw you an illustration at a preschool level?" I yelled at him.

Everyone in the café—coffee-loving-customers and lousy workers—stared at me. I was causing a major attraction of drama.

"I don't understand?" Freddy whispered, wanting to lower my voice.

"I know that you're busy, Freddy. I know, but you haven't been around for the what? Past two weeks? My life is boring and empty without you!" I loudly whispered.

"I'm sorry, Jessica. I don't know what to say," he apologized.

"I don't think this is going to work out, Freddy," I told him, this time he was awake.

"But we were going to get married," he said sadly.

Oh god, he has his puppy-dog face on. I felt like a terrible person right now. He deserved to dump iced coffee on me, and today was a good day since I didn't do my hair. Then, Freddy started to cry, and now I felt really bad. I made a boy cry for the first time I thought—first time without any physical contact. I kicked Mitch in the groin, and he cried. Now I felt like Mitch, an asshole. He ran out of the café covering his eyes. I raced out the door with him, but then came back and yelled, "Somebody watch my iced coffee for me." He ran to his car fumbling with his keys.

"I'm so sorry, Freddy!" I apologized.

"No! I'm sorry, Jessica," he sobbed madly, literally jumping on top of me to cry on my delicate shoulder, "I'm sorry! I feel really, really bad about all of this!"

"No, it's my fault. I . . . I shouldn't have yelled," I apologized, tears quickly forming in my eyes.

Big girls aren't supposed to cry!

"I don't want to end up all alone! I need you, Jessica! You! I don't want to end up like Nathen," he screamed out loud in the parking lot, falling down to grab hold of my legs.

"I don't want to end up like Nathen either!" I cried with him in a mockingly manner, falling over. To me, his superb acting was a bit over the top for me, especially, when he included Nathen into this.

There we cried with each other in the parking lot, a show of water works while the ice in my iced coffee slowly melted into the coffee giving it a bland taste. We ended up talking for a long time and cried a few more times. He ditched his day of work at the restaurant to go out to a movie with me. It was good to have him back. It was good to have him place his arm around my lonely shoulders again.

Andy~

Today was the day I'd ask Janet for a raise, but I was too chicken to do so. My heart was beating like crazy, and I was sweating like a fat guy eating chicken noodle soup during the summer in Australia. Okay. I should ask her during our lunch break. Nobody saw her when she was eating her lunch because everyone in the building, including me, thought she was a freak. You know, sometimes when we're working hard and seriously, she would come out of her office with her green lightsaber and start jumping on our desks, swaying that thing as if she really was Yoda. We didn't know what to do but stare at this crazy boss of ours.

When it was her lunch break, I quickly darted across the hall to see her in her office. She was eating a salad and looking up something on her computer.

"Um, Janet?"
"Yes, young padawan?" she greeted me.
"Can I speak to you about a raise?"

"Why not, I don't see? Have one, you will," she told me in Yoda's awkward phrasing of words.

"Thanks, Janet."

She responded with a munch of her salad. I left her door, mouthing a loud "YES!" as I coolly walked back to my desk. A moment to celebrate. But why did I need a raise? I had plenty of money. My wife just won the jackpot and a few more dollars from gambling before. I didn't need a raise. Kids weren't asking for too much, and the wife had everything she ever wanted with a huge shopping spree back in Vegas. I didn't need a raise. I couldn't go back and tell Janet that. Would you call this greed? I? Being greedy? I felt pretty much the same except the part of realization that I didn't need this raise, and now I was feeling bad about asking. Did I deserve a raise? No, I was just sucking up to Yoda-woman in order to get one. I cheated my way through. I didn't work as hard as George, a coworker working beside me. George's wife died of cancer while his daughter was ran over by a car when she crossed the street to retrieve her blue bouncy ball she'd dropped. He lived in a small home three hours from here. What a sad guy! George was always working, well, it seemed that way. Every morning I come in, he was sitting there. Every time I leave in the afternoon for home like everybody else, he was still there. I didn't deserve this; he deserved this.

Nathen~

I had been sitting here in front of this wall. I had accomplished nothing in the past few days. I hadn't written any new music or gone out on the streets pick-pocketing unwary strangers. I had found my professional camera in a closet and was craving the need to take more pictures of Asian couples.

I needed to escape. I ordered plane tickets to Hawaii online and called up Jessica, Mitch, and Andy. I couldn't go all by myself. I needed some people to keep me company on a long and dreary plane ride—over exaggeration—and some people to enjoy life with. But they all gave me the same response, not exactly the same, but just the response that danced around this one: "Nathen, we can't just drop everything we have and go to Hawaii with you. I'm sorry, maybe during the winter or spring break." I understood that they had jobs unlike me. I had mailed them the tickets anyways, since I had bought them before I called them.

I thought to myself: if I didn't want to travel alone, I should hire a personal assistant. So I did. I hired the best in the world who was rated five out of five stars in over thirty-six countries. Part of his job was for me to personally give him a name. I thought it was quite absurd at the time, but I liked the idea. Fast food restaurant mangers should do this more often when hiring new people.

"What should you name me, sir?" he asked me, with pencil and paper in hand, in case, he would forget the identity I gave him.
"Jordan, your name will be Jordan," I told him. "Do I need to include a last name?"
"If it's fine with you, sir," Jordan replied.
"Does it cost extra?"
"I'm afraid not, sir."
"Then I grant you the name, Jordan Wong."
"Thank you, sir."
"No problem, Jordan Wong."

He was a very pricy person. I had to pay him five hundred dollars for every day I spent with him excluding the day I hired him; it was his complimentary gift or free trial of his lovely assistance.

"What is it that I shall do for you, sir?" Jordan Wong asked me.
"Um, I need to pack right now, and if you haven't packed already, please do so," I told him.
"I have finished. Now what, sir?" he asked quickly.
"If you know how to play the piano, dust off my keys with your fingers."
"Yes, sir."

He played Chopin's "Waltz in C Sharp Minor (Opus 64 No. 2)." It wasn't a favorite, but it will do. As soon as he finished the piece, he asked, "Should I help you pack, sir?"

"No, it's rather safe that you don't touch my undergarments. We don't want diseases being spread, and would you please not address me as 'sir' anymore? I find it best that you refer to me as 'Nathen.' Will that work out for you, Jordan Wong?"

"I will try, sir . . . Nathen, and may I state that I do try my best to keep my hands very clean?"

"Also, if you would, please send a basket of assorted breads to Jessica, Mitch, and Andy. Thank you, Jordan Wong," I said, ignoring his comment about clean hands. Hands will never be clean or *very* clean no matter what. Germs will always return to your sanitized hands.

"Yes, Nathen," he agreed as he rushed out the door in search for assorted breads.

This feeling of being "bossy" was quite eccentric to me since it was usually vice versa. I was usually the one who was bossed around. I didn't like it, but I accepted it. "I added small containers of butter in the baskets if that was okay, Nathen," he told me when he returned. It was indeed okay. I called a taxi, we got our suitcases ready, and we were off to the airport. I didn't want the ride to be too quiet, so I asked Jordan Wong to entertain me with his words.

"Um, well," he started, "I mistook a prostitute for a police officer. I could explain! She was wearing a policeman, I mean, woman's outfit until I took a quick glance at her badges. They were covering her bosoms. The badges can spin like little windmill flowers. It was actually pretty neat."

The taxi driver choked on his doughnut because of laughing. I couldn't help but laugh as well.

"The woman almost kissed me! Who knows how many other men she laid a kiss on with those crimson red lips?" he started yelling.

"It is okay, Jordan Wong," I laughed, "It has happened to me as well."

"Me too," the taxi driver added.

This conversation reminded me of the time back in college when Jessica sent a legal prostitute over to my dorm so that I would lose my virginity. How she found a legal one, I did not know, but she did tell me she had "connections," and that she "knew some people." I was the only one in campus who hadn't lost theirs excluding Prof. Palmer and his trouble with women and men. I felt his pain but only in the interest of women. Hey, if that was the way he flowed, that was the way he flowed. I found out that the prostitute's name, the one Jessica sent over, was Meryl Streep because she was her inspiration. "I absolutely love her! Meryl Streep is such a great actress!" she exclaimed over and over again as if I hadn't heard her the first time. I asked Meryl if she liked to have fun, and she replied with a very provocative yes with the licking of the lips, and so I pulled out my chess set and taught her how to play chess. She had checkmated my king a few times, and we had bundles of joy and laughter. I asked her if she wanted to do anything else besides having intercourse with strangers, and she said she wanted to be a film maker. "I'm actually writing a script right now. Without giving anything away, it's basically a surreal Lebanese Lesbian porno featured on the grasslands of galloping porcupines and prickly horses." As mystical and absurd as her movie idea was—without doubts that she wrote her script when she was high—I gave her credit for pursuing in something that wasn't so degrading such as her job as a prostitute. And as she wanted to make a foreign pornographic film, I wanted to have "Hitler and Friends on Ice" or "The Return of Rasputin on Ice" or have a John Waters film on ice such as *Pink Flamingos*, and have a drag queen eat canine poo off ice. I gave her an iced coffee and paid her as she went on her way in search for more men to have fun with.

Jordan Wong and I had different seats on the plane to Hawaii, and I told him to keep himself busy by taking as many pictures of youthful Asian couples as he possibly could on the plane. I told him doubles were fine as long as they were from good and different angles. I handed him my professional camera. Before the flight started, he had already captured fifty. He was finished with his objective, so then I told him to keep himself busy by acquainting with the people sitting beside him. That should keep him busy for a while. I needed some sleep, and I did so quite comfortably because this seat was no piano. Would I really find Katie? I mean, I didn't think I would ever find her again. Ninety percent told me I should go back home and continue to spend lonely nights with a piano while the other ten percent was telling me to enjoy life. To be honest, I'd take any side of these sides of mine. I didn't mind either one of them. Maybe I should let Jordan Wong decide for me, but it seemed he was too busy with the people beside him when I took a quick glance at him.

Mitch~

I took a break from the project even though I knew I shouldn't. I was almost finished! Yes! I took a look at the mail and found that I received a basket full of bread and a small container of butter with a ticket to Hawaii. I told Nathen no on the phone yesterday. Nathen sure knew how to send gifts to people.

"Hey, Leslie," I called my wife in the kitchen. "Look at what Nathen sent us."

I held up the basket and placed it on the counter. She took the clear plastic wrapping off the basket and broke a baguette in half next to her ear. It made a very nice crisp sound.

"Good bread, but ewww carbs," she said.
"He also sent me a ticket to Hawaii," I added, handing it to her for a look.
"Wow, why is Nathen being so generous?"
"I don't know."

I picked up the phone and called up Andy.

"Hey, Andy," I called, guessing he was at work from the sounds of keyboards and telephone rings in the background.
"What's up?"
"Did you get a breadbasket and a ticket to Hawaii from Nathen?"
"Yeah, even when I told him no. I can't just drop everything and head off to Hawaii with the guy right now. Same with you?"
"Same with me."
"Well, hey, I'm busy right now. I'll call you later," he said, hanging up.

I got back to work, placing the ticket beside my laptop. I typed up a few more things hoping that I would be done by the time I tuck Howard into bed. Monica had school in a few days and hopefully we'd work out a carpool schedule with Lily. I glanced at the ticket. A trip to Hawaii would be nice right now. How did Nathen have the time and money to go on a vacation like that? I mean, he didn't have a job, and surely he couldn't have a wad of money in his pockets. It was almost impossible—to not have a job and have a lot of money.

I couldn't stand the house next to us. It was being demolished by teenage assholes. Car windows were smashed, lawns looked terrible, roofs were covered in toilet paper, and garage doors were being vandalized with red spray paint. What was it with kids these days? Whatever happened to discipline? Their house was not only making my house look bad, but the entire neighborhood. What did this house have against stupid kids? Or, what did stupid kids have against this house? And even worse, what if it happened to my house?

Jessica~

Freddy left for his business trip without a personal good-bye kiss. He just sent a text saying that he would be back in three to four months.

I let out a heavy sigh as I sat in front of my computer not wanting to do nothing at all at work. I fiddled with my mouse, making it click violently.

"Cheese for your mouse?" Tiffany asked me, placing a stick of cheese beside my mouse pad.
"Yay," I whispered unenthusiastically.
"Gosh, why are you so down, Jessica?"
"Freddy. He's gone. Three to four months. Hip-hip-hooray."
"Oh! You know what that means?"
"Korean dramas and ice cream?"
"No, save that for when Freddy doesn't come back."
"Don't say that, you're gonna jinx me," I said with the least of worries.
"Let's go clubbing!" Tiffany exclaimed, shaking my shoulders.
"Clubbing as in streaming colorful dance lights and expensive shots? Or clubbing as in taking your nieces for mini-golf and shaved ice?" I asked her.

I was so excited that one night she said we were going clubbing. I was totally pumped up! Until I hopped into the passenger seat of her car and spotted two little children in the back seat.

"Um, I don't think they're old enough to get into the night club, Tiffany."
"Yeah, they are. It's ages four and up," she explained, yet I was still confused.
"What kind of night club allows children at the age of four to go dance with older men and have drinks?"
"Oh, night club? No, we're going mini-golfing!" she exclaimed.

But it wasn't bad though; it was actually kind of nice even though the kids were better than me. I was so hungry that night; I shoved myself with tons of pizza. I felt like such a pig, so I bought an extra pizza for Tiffany and the kids.

"Yes, that kind of clubbing. You in?" she asked me.
"Sure. I'm up to it."

Hopefully, Freddy would know that I would not go after other men at clubs even though he was gone, but I was a bad girl, so I couldn't make any promises until I saw if there were any cute guys.

Andy~

As I was finishing up some documents before I left for lunch, George came by my cubicle. George and I had never talked to each other in person at all, just through e-mails. He knocked on the cardboard-like panels of my cubicle and said, "Howdy there, partner."
"Oh, hey, George," I said, finishing up a small piece and turned to him.
"So how are . . . how are you and . . ." he was hesitant. He scratched the back of his head and did some weird hand stretches.
"Lily?" I said, finishing his sentence.
"No, Janet, who's Lily?"
"Lily's my wife."
"Oh, a two-timer I spy with this little eye," he said pointing to his left eye with his left pinky a couple of times. "Scandinavian Scandalous. You know Janet's Scandinavian, right?"
"What are you talking about?" I asked, unsure of where this conversation was going.
"Isn't there a little somethin' between you and Janet? Hm? A little office love story behind your wife's back?"

What the hell was this guy talking about? I had no interest in women that sounded like Yoda at all.

"No, there's nothing going on between us," I said.

"Yeah, there is; that's why she gave you a raise! That's why she asked you out to lunch! There is somethin' goin' on, buster!" he started whispering loudly.

"I asked for that raise, and I wasn't the only one who got asked out to lunch with her; she invited all of us, but you decided not to come," I whispered loudly back, slowly getting up from my chair.

"No, No!" he yelled out loud, kicking down my cubicle wall.

He started to kick at the air really violently. He removed his shoes and chucked it at the plexi-glass windows. He removed his tie and started to whip the plants with it, chopping a few leaves off. He stripped himself to nothing but his black socks and ran around the floor screaming incoherently. Then he ran back to me, and I knew this wasn't going to end well at all.

"I'VE WORKED MY ASS OFF FOR TOO LONG! TOO LONG! I'VE TRIED TO WORK HARD ENOUGH FOR A RAISE! JUST A SMALL RAISE SO THAT I COULD FEED MY CAT! AND YOU! YOU! YOU STOLE THE LOVE OF MY LIFE AWAY FROM ME! MY JANET! MY BELOVED JANET! THAT WAS SUPPOSED TO BE MY FUCKIN' RAISE! MY FUCKIN' JANET! ARGHHHH!" he yelled, his face as red as the blood that was flowing through his visible veins.

Just as he was about to attack me, the security guards grabbed a hold of him and sent him out the door. Janet had asked him for a leave of absence from our department. I asked Janet if I could have the rest of the day off, and she agreed. I drove home thinking about George. What a sad little man! Now, I could profile him as a lunatic after that weird incident back at the office.

Jessica~

Before I left with Tiffany to the club, I watched a little bit of my Korean dramas and maybe stuffed myself with a little bit of my beloved Haagen-Dazs. Before I was stuffing myself with ice cream, I made some egg rolls for Tiffany. I thought maybe she would like some. She picked me up, and I was somewhat pumped for this "exciting" night.

"You wanna egg roll?" I offered, holding up the plastic container of such edible delights.
"No, why did you bring egg rolls for?" she asked.
"I made them for you."

She took my container of egg rolls, rolled down her window, and threw it out the window. How dare she!

"Hey! What did you do that for? That container was expensive," I yelled at her.

I had spent little time on the egg rolls, but that container was expensive. It was a really nice container. I loved it dearly. I used it to pack my lunch with. Well, I guessed I was going to have to buy a new one.

"Come on! Your spirits need to be uplifted, honey," she told me.
"But I'm gonna miss Freddy."
"Oh, stop worrying about the guy."
"Whatever Tiff-Tiff," I sighed, staring out the window.
"What is that? My stripper name?"
"I think you'd make a good stripper," I told her.
"Oh my god! Speaking of strippers, you know Michelle?"
"She works with HR?" I turned to her.
"Yeah. Oh my god! You know what she was doing outside the building? She was pole-dancing for some guy in a nice car, and it was so funny! Did you see it?"
"That's a sight for sore eyes."

We were almost there. I honestly didn't feel like grooving to loud blaring music, and I didn't feel like getting drunk with small shots. Tiffany seemed she was up to it. When we got to the club, she pulled my arm, and we jumped inside.

"Come on! Let's groove!" Tiffany shouted in my face, a little spittle of hers on my cheek.

While she did that, I walked over to the bar and sat down.

"What will it be, miss?" the bartender asked me.
"Do you have any Haagen-Dazs?" I asked him.
"No."
"Water will be fine then."
"Coming right up."

He pushed the glass toward me, and I drank up. He stood there like he was expecting a tip. Unlike Tiffany, who would give him a "nip-tip," I handed him a five-dollar bill. When Tiffany was really drunk and asked for more drinks, she would always give the "nip-tip." For those of you who didn't indulge in inappropriate activities, a "nip-tip" was when you tipped someone with the exposure of your nipple. It really didn't matter which one you revealed. I'd never done it myself because I was a good girl.

"Hey, can I buy you a drink?" a stranger asked me.
"Um, a water would be nice," I told him, resting my head down on the table.
"Good, then I don't have to pay. A water for this fine young woman here," he shouted to the bartender.
"Oh and before anything gets too intense between us, I'm in a relationship," I told him.
"Bartender, forget the drink," he yelled, leaving to the dance floor to try to pick up some more women with his cheesy dancing. That guy couldn't dance. He danced like a crippled Shakira.

I looked over to Tiffany who seemed like she was enjoying herself, and here I am enjoying myself.

Nathen~

We landed in Waikiki and took a taxi to the Waikiki Hotel.

"Please tell me you two aren't married," the taxi driver stated. "Or else, I'm gonna kick you out."
"Um, this man is my personal assistant," I told the driver.
"Okay. Good."

There was an awkward silence until I brought up, "Jordan Wong, do you own a wife?"
"Um, the last person I assisted told me I was too good to be married, Nathen," he replied.
"Interesting, have you ever owned a girlfriend?"
"No, Nathen."
"Well, then it looks like we're on the same page. You can consider us as 'single buddies' if you wish."
"Thank you, Nathen."
"No problem at all, Jordan Wong."

Well, I was here in Hawaii, and now the search should begin; the search for my long-lost love, Katie. I doubted I would find her, but it was worth a shot, right? I meant, what did I have to lose? As soon as we got into the room, we unpacked quite quickly. We had our separate beds, but we had to share the same bathroom, sink, and microwave. Why not start the search today? I sent Jordan Wong on a mission to search for all the department stores and ask the managers/workers if they had ever seen Katie. I had stolen a recent picture of Katie from Austin's laptop. I'm sure he didn't mind. And me? What should I do for the rest of the evening? I went along the busy crowds and took pictures of Asian couples and made a large sum of money from pick-pocketing. It was quite a fantastic evening. Jordan Wong and I met at a Todai for dinner and went our way back to the hotel with a walk beside busy and fancy stores. I took interest in taking more photos of Asian couples. I thought I took so many photographs that they were pictures of the same couples.

When the lights were off, and we were in bed, I found it quite awkward and eerie that a man was sleeping in the same room as I was. I should have given him his own room. I thought he would greatly appreciate that as well.

"Do you enjoy being my personal assistant, Jordan Wong?" I asked him out of this long, awkward silence.
"Would you like me to answer 'yes'?" he asked.
"I would like for you to answer truthfully."
"Um, well, no, not yet. But it has been quite interesting. So far, I have gained two Facebook friends from those people on the plane. But I'm sure, working for you will become quite a pleasure for you and I," he gave a long response.
"Wonderful," I said, closing my eyes.
"Please don't fire me."
"Ha-ha. I won't. I highly appreciate your services, Jordan Wong."
"Thank you, Nathen. Um, no one has really thanked me before."
"Really? Quite intriguing."
"Indeed. They just pay me without a 'thank you,' and I leave."
"Depressing. It shows how 'well-mannered' rich pricks are these days."
"Yep."

Then it was silent after that. I figured he was exhausted and didn't want to talk any more. I stepped out onto the balcony a few times to look up at the stars and listen to the clear ocean's waves crash onto the sandy surface. I took a picture of the beautiful night scenery and went to bed. Katie . . . how I long for her . . . how I longed for her all my life. I promised myself that I would find her here in Hawaii. What a joke! I thought to myself. *Am I really doing this? Am I really living through this joke? My life is quite a joke, and I am a joke myself.*

Jessica~

Last night, I had to drag Tiffany back to my place with her car because she was too drunk to drive back home. She was riding in the back with another drunk, her new boyfriend. They'd been ruining the car's seats back there with their stinky vomit. I left her new boyfriend outside in the cold. That was what he got for falling asleep on her.

I was on my computer all night searching for high-school pictures which I had found when early morning came. I kept myself awake with some coffee and a few interesting Korean dramas. No Haagen-Dazs that time. I had found more photos than I needed. I had found photos of Andy and me which I thought I had deleted a long time ago. Aw! Not to be conceited or anything, but I thought we looked cute together. So happy . . . something that Freddy failed to keep alive . . . happiness. Tiffany got up and went to throw up in my toilet . . . how delightful! I'd remind myself later to clean up the toilet when she left. I logged onto my Facebook to catch up on updates which I hadn't done since . . . wow, almost a year. I had several friend requests and accepted all of them without knowing who they were, except two people. The two that kept popping into my life when Freddy was not around. It was Austin and Andy. I smiled and took a look at their profiles. Andy had posted his phone number on his profile information, and I decided to call the number. I picked up my phone and dialed his home phone. Then, I called, my heart pounding really fast, not knowing what to expect.

"Hello?" he yawned.
"Oh, hi, Andy," I whispered into the phone, not wanting to wake up Tiffany.
"Who is this?"
"This is Jessica."
"Jessica? Um, I think you got the wrong number."
"No, Jessica, from way back then," I said, stopping him from hanging up on me.
"Jessica . . . Oh! Jessica! Oh, hey there."

"Hi!" I waved at my computer screen as if Andy knew I was waving at him. I didn't know why I did such an act. I guessed staying up all night made me do hysterical things.

"You called me at three in the morning. Nice to hear from you at this time. Ha-ha," he chuckled lightly.

"HA-HA-HA! You are so funny!" I yelled and quickly covered my mouth.

"Um, sorry to end this chat so quickly, but I really need some shut-eye before I head to work in a few hours," he said.

"Oh, right. I have work too, okay. I'll talk to you some time later then." I quickly remembered.

"Yeah. All right. I'll call you back," he ended the conversation, hanging up the phone.

I stayed on the line for a few more minutes mesmerized by the sound of his manly voice. Ah . . . it was so nice to hear from him again. I really did miss him now. I finally hung up and went to bed. I needed to leave for work in three hours, might as well catch some Z's. After two hours had passed, Tiffany woke me up with the sound of her musical puking. I got up and made ourselves some cereal.

"Oh my god! I feel so sick. I think I threw up all three of my meals," Tiffany mumbled.

"There's some leftovers in the back of your car too," I added to her misery. "Oh and I think your 'boyfriend' is sleeping outside."

"'Boyfriend?'"

"Um, yeah, you picked him up last night and gave him a few 'nip tips.'"

"Ugh, damn it. Hey, can you drive me to work?" she asked me, placing her unfinished bowl of cereal in the sink.

"Sure. And next time, never invite me to night clubs during the week."

On the way to work, Tiffany told me about how Cindy, a coworker who was recently hired, gave herself an abortion. It was quite disturbing as she went into vulgar details. I thought I was going to leave some leftovers in the back seats of my car. But on the brighter note of dirty toilets and bloody self-abortions, I was happily waiting anxiously for that phone call from Andy.

Nathen~

I had sent Jordan Wong on a little quest for any information on the location of Katie with only one measly photograph of her. Hopefully, he would get something out of his search for the day. I had promised him a spa treatment at the end of the day and a two-hour break. I trusted that he wouldn't spend anymore leisure time than those two hours. Myself? I took myself to a Luau and spent a lovely afternoon/night interviewing random young Asian couples.

Out of the whole day, only one couple intrigued me the most. They were a Japanese couple from Yokohama, Japan, that were here for their honeymoon and had arrived just a few days before we arrived. I had taken Japanese back in high school and still remembered a few words, and I asked them if I could stalk them for the rest of the night. With a few minutes of hesitation and arguing, I introduced that the outcome of this stalking would be hundred dollars for them . . . each. They gladly accepted. The entire day, they acted as if I wasn't watching them. Well, I found out as it seemed that there was this PDA the female had bought for the male, and now this PDA was the man's life. He literally had everything on there. This piece of technology seemed to be of more importance to him than his lovely female. She was always insisting him to put the wife-stealing contraption away, but he continued to use it. Even during the Luau, his face was in front of the palm-held object. He did take some time away from the machine to take pictures of his beautiful wife with me in some of their pictures. They had even asked for my assistance in taking a photograph of them for them.

Why was I doing this? I had no idea. I never really focused on why I was really doing this. I believed that the other lives of human beings tended to be of more importance to me than my own. I believed their lives were far more interesting than mine. My life was quite boring and tiresome. Now that I thought about it . . . is that why we turn our attentive heads to the lives of celebrities and other important people? Are we so tired of our lives that we must pay to every attention and detail of these celebrities such attributes, including picking of the nose, relationship statuses, and other private matters? To believe that people make money off knowing these things that should not be revealed to the public. Idiotic paparazzi . . . "the rats of showbiz" as my father would call them . . . but I was being a paparazzi at the moment as well . . . but I paid them, so does it still count? I paid them to allow me to spy on them.

After the Luau, capturing a few photos of them as well, I waved to them good-bye and handed them their two hundred dollars. When I got back to the hotel, Jordan Wong was nowhere to be seen, and I found he was still on the job. I called him to come back to the hotel, and that he was off the search for the day. He came back, unfortunately, with no information on Katie.

"I'm sorry, Nathen," he apologized.
"It's fine. There is always a tomorrow. We'll just have to wait for the right tomorrow," I told him, staring out the window.

Mitch~

Today was Friday, so I had to take Monica and Austin to school today. I didn't bother to talk to them because of the fact I had a lot on my mind, and I was tired. I saw Austin give Monica something but couldn't quite catch what the object was. I might ask Monica about it later. Then I took Howard to his little school and drove back home. It was my day off today, and I had the whole house to myself. The only thing on my list for the entire day was sleep. I had nothing else planned today. I was about to pick up the phone and call Nathen to see how he was doing, but I forgot he went off to Hawaii. Hawaii did sound nice right now, and since I had nothing to do, I did the only thing that came to mind: work. I worked and prepared for my presentations for the weeks to come forgetting that my plan for the day was sleep, sleep, and sleep.

Later during the day, I found that Monica had an iPhone. I was lying on the couch and immediately got up and stopped her and asked, "Monica, where did you get that iPhone?"

"Um, Austin gave it to me," she answered, trying to escape around me.

I blocked her way.

"Why did Austin give it to you?" I fired back.

"He gave it to me as a gift for my birthday, Dad. He thought about the day I was born before you did," she vigorously retorted, pushing past me and marching up the stairs.

Damn, I forgot her birthday? All this time, I spent the day doing nothing. I didn't even spend a little bit of time to get her something nice. I ran to the calendar, and there it was; today's date circled in red ink was where I wrote "Monica's Birthday" with a little smiley face at the end. Damn it, how could I forget? It was the day she was pooped out of Leslie. Was it too late to run to the nearest convenient store and get her something? What would I buy her? Oh, I got it! She'd been asking for an iPhone a lot; I could get her that . . . shit . . . she already had one . . . I was yelling at myself internally in the kitchen. My wife crept into the kitchen with a cake in her hands and hid it in the fridge.

"Mitch, make sure to bring out the cake when I call her down for dinner, all right?" she whispered to me.

"Okay. Um, Leslie, did you get her somethin'?" I whispered back.

"Yeah, it's in the car, I'm gonna go get it right now," she said, heading out.

"Wait!" I stopped her. "What did you get her?" I quickly asked.

"Some clothes. You?"

Life's Manifesto

"I didn't get anything!"

"What? What do you mean you didn't get anything?"

"I blew it! I totally forgot about her birthday!" I whispered, my voice rose.

"How could you? You are one cruel dad. You had the whole day to think of something! Go get her something!"

"I don't know what to get her."

"Get her an iPhone like she's been asking for one."

"Austin got her one."

"Aw, how thoughtful of him! That boy of Andy's is really somethin'," she squealed quietly.

"Yeah, sweet of him. What else does Monica want?" I asked, grabbing my car keys, about to head out of the door.

"Um, a poster? I don't know," she shrugged, taking out things from the fridge, preparing food for dinner.

"Maybe a half-naked poster of Taylor Lautner or Joseph-Gordon-Levitt would work out just fine for me," Monica answered without looking at us as she came down the stairs, placing ear phones into her ears.

"Now, Monica, you know how I feel about half-naked boys in your room, even if they're printed on large pieces of paper," I told her, looking over at her.

She was sitting on the couch playing around with her new phone Austin gave to her. Half of me said that she didn't deserve anything because of her stupid attitude, and the other half of me said that she did deserve something because it was her birthday, and that I forgot about it, and because I'm a horrible father. Oh, well, I'd just get the posters, and we'd all be one, big happy family having a happy, happy birthday. I quickly jumped into my car and drove to the nearest Wal-Mart. I ran over to the posters and searched for the posters of people Monica asked for. I had no idea who the hell this Lautner or Jospeh people were. I quickly looked for a girl Monica's age and ran over to one girl next to the DVD racks. I quickly tapped on her shoulder.

"Hey, um, do you know who Taylor Lautner or Joseph-Gordon-Levitt is?" I asked.

She spun around and screamed in my face.

"Oh my gosh! I love them!" she screamed into my ear.
"Ha-ha. Um, so could you maybe show me a picture of them or show me what they look like so I can get a poster of them?"
"Sure thing!" she said, turning around so that I was facing her back. She lifted her shirt and there, she had a tattoo of two half-naked stars on her back. The colors of the tattoos were fading a little. "You like them too?"
"No, for my daughter. Okay, thanks," I said, running back to the posters.

I had a sort of a clear image of the two guys in my head as I searched for the posters, and when I found them, I ran to the cashier where I would pay thirty dollars for these two lousy posters of these guys staring intently at you like if they were interested in you. The kind of interest where they would want to make love to you . . . disgusting. What are these boys? Like seventeen? Eighteen? These boys were aiming for girls at Monica's age or even younger? Terrible, just terrible. I handed the posters to the cashier, and she unrolled them, taking a long look at the poster.

"Mmm-mmm-mmm! Damn! Look at these boys and their bodacious deliciousness!" she exclaimed. "You took a good pick," she said, scanning the poster's bar code.
"Oh, um, they're not for me, they're for my daughter," I quickly told her.
"Mm-hmm," she retorted, rolling her eyes. "I know your kind when I see them."
"No, I'm not . . . no. I'm married."
"Sir, that is considered illegal in this proud non-gay state of California," she yelled at me.
"No, I'm married to a woman!" I corrected her.
"Oh . . . that'll be thirty-two-ninety-five, please."

I gave her a thirty-five and got my change. What the fuck was her problem causing a scene? Everyone was practically staring at me. I was never buying posters ever again, even if it was for a birthday present or even for my own daughter. She placed the rolled up posters in a plastic bag and handed it to me.

"Have a nice day," she said in her sweet tone that I didn't want to appreciate, but might as well pretend to. But why pretend to this woman? She was an asshole.

"Don't tell me what to do!" I shouted at her and left immediately.

I didn't know why. I didn't know why at all, but I just ran out of that Wal-Mart as fast as I could, bumping into a few people who dropped their groceries because of me. I didn't know why I ran, but it felt good. It felt . . . exhilarating. Running away from trouble/embarrassment never made me felt alive before.

Nathen~

I gave Jordan Wong a day off today since he seemed quite overworked. He told me he was going to spend his day on a boat on the clear Waikiki waters with a sea woman. He said he was going to have some "fun" on this boat with the female, and I had asked him not to go into further detail. He informed me that his cellular phone would be on if I needed his assistance. For me, I decided to go on the search myself. I didn't think I went as far as I wanted to during my short exploration because of the tropical heat and small, short showers that tropical islands are well known for. I had stopped to take a rest after entering a few shops and eateries.

I sat down in an uncomfortable iron chair at a coffee shop with a small, dainty, decorative plastic bag of miniature marshmallows. I popped them in my mouth as I was on the lookout for Katie and Asian couples. I was more focused on Asian couples with my camera to my side. My pockets were half-full of money that I had stolen from the pockets of a few unwary people. I didn't think . . . um . . . I didn't think my father would have approved of this if he still existed above the surface of this planet. He wouldn't approve of anything I was doing right now at all. He had always told me that I needed a job—a good paying job that would help me throughout my life. But he added that as long as grades were kept up higher than anybody else's, life would guarantee me that I would get one. He lied. I didn't get a high-paying job. I had failed fifty-one times on getting one. His death, and the rest of my family's death, encouraged me to keep grades at the top. I stayed up all night studying and reading throughout my life, ready to expect the unexpected on tests and quizzes. But now, after so many years, I found that I wasted my life studying and reading. I studied and read for nothing; maybe for knowledge's sake, but not financially. As Jessica or Mitch or Andy or even Katie spent their lives happily with their heads outside of the hard back covers of textbooks and their minds roaming away from the thought of studying, I stayed in my room and did what my father had lied about. That lie, to be completely honest, was the only unforgivable thing that rested on his grave.

I didn't feel like finishing the bag of marshmallows. There were about four or five left in the crumpled bag, and as I was about to dispose of it, I spotted an Asian female sitting in a chair, crying to herself as her cell phone vibrated in front of her. I quickly turned my camera on and snapped a photograph of her.

"Young woman, are you all right?" I asked her, turning off my camera.
"Um, yes. I'm fine," she sniffled, wiping the tears from her eyes with a napkin.
"Care to explain why you are heavily sobbing?" I asked, taking a seat in front of her.

Talking to strangers/foreigners was a hobby of mine. I liked the idea of talking to strangers because they do not know you, and you do not know them giving you and your chosen stranger unlimited possibilities of many conversational topics which is quite different from having a chat with a person you do know because you know some things about them, and they know some things about you, and some subjects of conversation had already been covered giving you fewer topics to discuss. Not knowing anything about a person and having a conversation with them was a thrill to me.

"My aunt is in the hospital right now, and I'm here on a vacation with my boyfriend, and I don't know what to do and where to go. My boyfriend left me, and I can't find him anywhere. He won't answer his cell phone," she sobbed, dropping her head onto the table along with her arms.

"Well, if the man you spend a great amount of time has a heart, he'll come back," I told her, sliding the bag of marshmallows toward her. "Here you go."

"No thanks," she sniffled, pushing the bag away.

"Well, I'll just leave them here with you in case you decide to direction yourself to comfort food," I told her, getting up from the chair.

"Thank you," she said as I was about to head out of the door. "Wait. Can I ask why you came up to me and gave me tiny marshmallows?" she asked, looking up at me with wet eyes.

"One—I think it's best for you to try one because they are quite delicious, and two—I just didn't feel like finishing my bag of delectable sweets. Good day," I said, leaving the coffee shop.

I went back to my search for a few more hours and called it a day. Jordan Wong had come back to the hotel quite tired and a few hours after I was already in bed. I looked at the clock before I looked at him. It was 11:46 p.m.

"Did you enjoy yourself?" I asked him, rubbing my eyes.

"Yes, Nathen, I did. I think . . ." he stopped himself and laughed. "I think I knocked up a sea woman," he told me, cleaning himself up in the bathroom.

"Well, then, that doesn't make us 'single buddies' anymore, does it?" I said.

"I guess not," he chuckled.

He was to be back to the search tomorrow morning. When I closed my eyes, attempting to go back to a peaceful sleep as the sound of shower water hitting the tile of the bathtub annoyed me, I thought about the sobbing woman and the bag of marshmallows I had given her. Not only did I leave her a bag of marshmallows, but inside the bag included a small card with my name and my phone number and e-mail address. Hopefully, she would tell me if her boyfriend came back for her or if she got to see her aunt in the hospital. I was quite anxious to know, but wanted to wait after a week of my stay in Hawaii and see what I would receive from her.

Andy~

After two weeks of George's absence, he came back. Not once did he talk to me, look up at me, or even come near me. Everyone else on this floor was eyeballing us, expecting some random and explicit outburst from him and me staring at him defenselessly as he exploded. I was with the rest of the department too.

"Please enter your Jedi master's office, Andy," Janet called me.

I finished up a few and left to her office. I cleared my throat and kept my head down as I felt my coworkers' eyes on me. I could really feel George's eye stab my back as I walked into her office. I closed the door behind me and stood by the door. She asked me to close the blinds as she wrote something down, and usually when she asked you to close the blinds of her office, you knew it was going to be about a private matter. This private matter was probably about this triangle of craziness: me, Yoda woman, and a lunatic who had something for strange unmarried women with a fetish for Yodas. How did I get mixed into this? Oh, yeah, that stupid raise.

"Surprised, I am, that young George has words not said. Happening between us, this thing . . ." she said, getting up from her desk and slowly trotted toward me. I stepped back, placing my back to the door. "Something, is it really?" she asked me.

"No, um, Janet. There is nothing, absolutely nothing, going on between us," I told her, my hand firmly gripping the knob of the door as she literally placed her body against me.

Whoa, okay, this was getting out of hand. I quickly turned the knob and ran out of her office. What the hell! My boss was hitting on me on the day the lunatic came back from his absence. I needed to get myself out of here. I needed to quit, but I just couldn't quit. It was hard to get jobs right now; that was probably why Nathen didn't have one right now. I didn't want to work with these people anymore. I left work without granted permission and left the building, driving myself back home. On my way, I stopped by a Carl's Jr. to pick up lunch.

When I got home, to my surprise, I found Austin home with Monica who were arguing with each other about a problem on their homework.

"Hey, Austin. Hey, Monica," I greeted them, opening the greasy bag of Carl's Jr. and ate.

"Hey, Dad," Austin answered casually.

"Hello, Andy," Monica answered in her sweet voice. Sweet girl. I didn't know why Mitch always complained about her attitude.

It ended up Monica being right with a deserved slap across Austin's face. I quickly downed my lunch and didn't know what to do afterward. I turned on my computer and checked my Facebook. I'd forgotten that I added Jessica and decided to browse through her profile. What did I find? I found that she was in a relationship, she talked to this Tiffany person a lot, and her phone number. I picked up the phone and dialed her number.

"Hello?" she answered.

"Oh, hey, Jessica. It's me, Andy," I said.

"AH! OH MY WORLD! HI, ANDY!" she screamed, piercing my ears.

"Ha-ha, yeah. So how's life?"

"Life's okay for me. You?"

"It's good," I semi-lied. I had a group of coworkers who thought I was weird, one who hated me, and a boss who'd been hitting on me. "That's good. So you're not married yet?" I asked.

"Sadly, no, not yet. But I'm engaged!"

"That's good news."

"Yep. Hey, we need to meet up some time."

"Um, sure. Does right now sound good?" I bit my lip.

"Surprisingly yes! Where?"

"The gym?"

"The gym it is! Okay, see you there!"

"Okay," I said, getting my stuff and leaving the house with Austin and Monica home alone. They could take care of themselves. "Austin, I'm goin' to the gym. I'll be back."

Jessica~

Oh my world! Andy saved me from boredom! I used MapQuest to find out how to drive to the gym, printed out the directions, and hopped into the car with a cold bottle of water which I had finished by the time I got to the gym. Andy! I was meeting Andy at a gym after so many years. This was wild! Wasn't this wild? I thought it was wild. It was wild. I found a parking spot and met him in front of the gym after a ten-minute drive.

"Hi, Andy!" I greeted him as I ran up to him with my hands flailing in the air. I might have looked stupid, but I'd look stupid for Andy any day . . . okay, maybe not, but most of the time, I looked stupid for lots of people . . . especially, parties with coworkers and friends, not family 'cause family didn't like me very much.

"Hey, Jessica," he greeted back as I ran into him for a hug.

"Long time no see, eh?" I said.

"Yeah," he agreed, guiding me inside the gym.

"Wait, where's your car? I wanna see your car first," I said, coming back outside, searching for anything expensive because I knew he made good money unlike me.

"Oh, I jogged over here," he said, scratching his head with the cap of his water bottle.

"Oh, then why come to a gym?" I asked.

"To work out."

"But isn't running over here a good work out already?"

We entered the cool, air-conditioned gym where we found a small amount of people exercising. There were probably one or two fat people eating Twinkies while they slowly walked on the treadmill which I thought was a grand idea, but instead of Twinkies, I'd prefer Haagen-Dazs. Andy jumped on a treadmill, and I jumped on one beside him. We talked for a while, catching up with each other on the past and present. Then after we ran, we switched over to weights, but I was too tired for that, so I ran over to a vending machine to get a bottle of cold water. I watched him from a distance as I gulped down the refreshing taste of nothing. Oh my god! I knew it was wrong to hit on a married man when you're in a relationship, but this was so right. Andy looked so hot when he sweated in his little workout outfit. Okay, what the hell was I doing? This wasn't good. Not good at all. I needed to think about something or someone else to get my mind off sexy Andy. What about cauliflowers? Somebody from work said that cauliflowers got their mind off hot guys and imagining having mad sex with them. Was it Tiffany? No, I didn't think so.

When I came back to him, he was back on the treadmill, and I decided to rest beside him on a bench. As I was finishing up my bottle which cost me a freakin' two dollars, I saw little Sarah and her little fat teddy bear. Andy's little princess ran toward me cutely giggling on her way.

"Oh my gosh! Sarah!" I exclaimed, running to her and lifted her up. I swung her in the air as if she was some airplane as I made quite "realistic" airplane noises. I set her down on the ground as soon as I felt a naughty urge to throw her in the air so that she could fly all by herself. Little Sarah ran over to the treadmill her daddy was running on and threw her teddy bear at his legs. Andy slipped on the bear, fell on the treadmill when it was still active, and he did this impossible stunt of a flip and got thrown off the evil exercising equipment possibly enduring a lot of pain and a skinned back.

"Oh my god! Andy, are you okay?" I asked him, running to his side . . . maybe checking out his body a teensy bit.
"Ow . . . geez . . . my back," he said, lifting up his shirt, and right there, I froze as if time itself just stopped for me and him. I was in awe.
"How does it look?" he asked me.
"Ah . . . hmm . . . I . . . errr . . . quite magnificent," I stuttered.

It was more than magnificent; the curves of his body were like beautiful cracks of mighty mountains that the Greek Gods could have been worshiped upon. Even though he only had a four-pack, it was amazing. This was quite a magical moment that no David Copperfield or Lance Burton could ever stunt up.

"Magnificent?" he questioned, taking me away from body-daydreaming and back to husband-less reality.
"I mean . . . I . . . it looks bad, big boo-boo . . . yeah, looks painful," I told him, still staring at his body.
"Um, can you go over to the desk and ask for Lily, please," he instructed me.
"Oh, um, sure," I said, running up to the counter where Andy paid our fee. I had to be honest; I was a sucker for doing favors for Korean guys with hot bods. You can "LOL" at that if you'd like.

"Um, I'm lookin' for Lily," I told the woman at the desk.
"Oh, I'm Lily. How may I help you?" she asked me.
"See that guy over there," I pointed to the beautiful, injured Andy, "Yeah, he's in bad shape and needs medical attention right away."
"Oh, ha-ha! That's my husband," she told me.

So there, I turned to her and found the perfect match that Andy had married. They looked nice together . . . almost perfect. I slightly envied her—an envy that I didn't really want to show or admit at all. She took her plastic box of her medical instruments and ran toward her husband, treated him, and bandaged him up with a cold bottle of water in his hands as he rested on the bench. Sarah's little teddy bear was sadly ripped in half. I didn't know how that happened, but mommy bandaged it up with some white medical tape and handed it back to her. Lily walked back to me with a tired smile on her face. I could see she worked hard and got paid fairly well.

"It's a pleasure to meet you, Lily." I offered her a handshake, and she took it.

"It's a pleasure to meet you too."

"The name's Jessica! Don't wear it out sista!" I exclaimed fairly loud. I was making myself look crazy again.

"Ha-ha, so, um, are you a friend of Andy?"

"Yep. Our friendship goes way back to high school," I told her. I wanted to add that the relationship between us used to be more than a friendship, but I didn't think she'd take it the right way.

"That's nice. So does that mean you're friends with Mitch too?"

"Oh, yeah. Him too," I said loudly again. Sheesh! I needed to control my inner craziness and not let it out for people to witness.

"Say, the four of us, Me, Andy, Mitch, and Leslie, are going out to dinner tonight. You wanna come with?" she offered.

"Oh my world! That sounds fancy! Sure, I'd love to come!" I exclaimed.

"Ha-ha, okay. Here, I'll write down the address for you," she said, getting a pencil and paper out.

Nathen~

"Nathen, sir, could you please awaken so I can deliver fantastic news to you?" Jordan Wong nudged me with his index finger. I was still asleep. I was still asleep? I had slept in. Sleeping in was a big no-no for me and quite a feature that I was not fond of. I immediately heaped myself out of the bed and ran into the bathroom to wash myself up. I came out feeling quite refreshed and opened the door to the balcony to have a nice, healthy whiff of our polluted planet and that tropical aura that Hawaii holds. "So about the news? Would you like to be informed now or whatever time you'd like to be informed?" he said again.

"Um, tell me about it now as we race down to the lobby for some complimentary breakfast."

"Yes, Nathen," he agreed as we walked out of our room to the elevator.

"So I had given the store-keepers my contact number in case they had sighted your beloved Katie, and, we got a call from Philip who owns a local fish market and claims to be an uncle of hers."

"Quite interesting. Does that mean we can celebrate this victorious search?"

"If you'd like, Nathen."

"I think we will, preferably celebrating it at a Todai with Katie. Well done, Jordan Wong."

"Thank you, Nathen."

After breakfast, we located Philip and the fish market that he so proudly owned and sold fish by the half dozen for about fifteen dollars. Jordan Wong had informed me that Philip advertised his fish sales on YouTube. I found the act of advertising things on a popular World Wide Web was absurd. Why would anybody want to watch a commercial about buying fish on YouTube? I believed the only people who would watch it was if they were suffering from a severe case of boredom. His logo was "If you smell something fishy, it's me!" I liked it; it suited him and his fish sales.

"It is quite a pleasure to meet you, Philip," I said, shaking his odorous hand. It was a good thing I had brought along my travel-size hand sanitizer.

"And who might you be?" he asked me, spitting into the corner of a building.

"Um, you claim to be a relative of Katie?" I questioned, holding up a picture of a smiling Katie.

"Yep! I'm her uncle," he said, spitting into the corner of the building again.

"Would you happen to have her contact information?" I asked as Jordan Wong prepared to take out his writing utensils.

"Um, sure. I'll be back," he said, running to the back of his car.

Disgusting as he was, I couldn't believe he was a relative of Katie. Katie! How beautiful she was! She probably still contained her beauty after many years. She was more beautiful than the fish this man had ever caught. I was sure she would appreciate this compliment if she were drunk, but I rarely indulge myself in alcoholic beverages so I don't think that compliment would fly by anytime. I recalled a flashback when I examined the rear end of her body as she went to throw away a tissue she had blown her snot into. During this secretive and lusty examination, the teacher of the classroom caught me in this monstrous and inappropriate act and glared at me. I quickly threw down my head, turning back to my test and wondered when the teacher would turn his eyes away from me and focus on someone more disruptive than me. When I looked up at the teacher, I found him silently laughing as he took off his glasses and wiped the tears of laughter from his eyes. She was the most sincere person I had ever met. After I was coping myself with dreams that wouldn't come true in the dreary, cold mornings of school as the naked trees shivered without their beloved leaves, she gave me some flowers. A female sending flowers to a male like me? I believed it should be the other way around, but it was nice of her anyways. I thought she knew what I should've done with the flowers—rest them on the graves of my deceased family. There was another time when she caught me struggling to peel a banana or open a bag of low trans-fat chips. She kindly helped me out without saying a word. I would always reply with a soft, sometimes inaudible, "thank you" as she replied with a petite smile that made me feel oh-so-warm inside. A feeling of warmth that included party members of giddiness, butterflies that danced around in my stomach as if it were some kind of mad/angry competitive dance competition, and knots that slowly writhed as if they were going through a concentration camp. My heart was another party member beating as fast as a hummingbird in need to escape from a predator on an empty stomach during its lunch break. Feeling the need to spend time on the toilet to dispose of waste from the bottom was also a happy and quite proud member of this party as well. All these uncomfortable feelings all happening at once led to one word—love. This is love. This is how it feels to be in love or the way my body interprets it. I disliked the sensations of love, but it made me happy. Katie made me happy. I loved Katie. Although, loving Katie is a wee bit awkward, especially, when there comes a possibility I marry her. More weak than a strong possibility.

Philip came back with a piece of paper in his hand and handed it to me after he spat in the corner of the building again.

"Here ya go. That's Katie's cell phone number," he said.
"Why thank you. I appreciate this very much," I thanked him, taking out a twenty-dollar bill. I waved it in the air with a hint of a smirk on my face and tucked it in the pocket of his tacky, faded Hawaiian T-shirt with the price tag still attached to it. I lightly patted his chest pocket and left with a simple wave of good-bye. Jordan Wong looked back at the fish salesman who held the bill in the sun to check if it was as real as his claim to be Katie's uncle or as counterfeit as his worker's breast job.

Jordan Wong and I went back to the hotel room and dialed the number Philip had written on the piece of paper. The phone in my right hand was slowly slipping from my sweaty palms, and I quickly placed the phone on the table as it rang. My heart pounded faster than a child dancing after they had drugged themselves with sugary delights, and my throat was becoming dry and raspy. I couldn't take it and shoved the phone into Jordan Wong's hands.

"I . . . I can't call her," my voice cracked, and somehow changed.
"Why not, Nathen?" he asked again, the phone still ringing.
"I don't have a solid explanation, but I just can't. Um, I just have a sudden urge to take a poo, and I need to lubricate my throat with bottles of spring water. I'll be back, Jordan Wong," I told him, rushing to the small refrigerator to retrieve a cold bottle and into the restroom where I turned on the fan and sat on the toilet. Dear lord, what was I doing? Why

was I not the one to speak with Katie? Why did I hand the phone over to Jordan Wong? Was I . . . was I scared? Was that it? From this small bathroom that any claustrophobic would die in, I couldn't hear if he was already having a phone conversation with her or if the phone was still ringing or if the voice he heard from the phone was her voicemail.

"Hello?" Katie answered.
"Um, hello. Hello, Katie," Jordan Wong answered, tangling his fingers within the chord of the phone.
"Um, hi, who is this?"
"Oh, um, you don't know me, but you know the person who I'm working for. It's, um, Nathen? Do you remember that gentleman . . . fellow?" Jordan Wong introduced my name.
"Nathen? Um, I don't think I know a Nathen," she said.
"No? You don't remember a Nathen?"
"Nope, I think you have the wrong number, sir."
"Um, no, no, we don't. Your uncle Philip directed this number to us so that we can contact you, because we know you, well, I mean, Nathen knows you."

I stepped out of the bathroom and whispered into Jordan Wong's ear to inform Katie to check her high-school yearbooks.

"Um, Nathen wanted to inform you that you should take a skip-down memory lane and check your handy-dandy yearbooks," Jordan Wong awkwardly told her.
"Um, fine. If I remember this Nathen person, meet me by the fishing dock at either 8:00 a.m. or 8:00 p.m. where my uncle Philip fishes at. Okay, bye," she said, hanging up the phone with a click.

Jordan Wong hung up the phone and looked at me for further instructions. I looked out through the screen door to the balcony and said, "Now, we wait." Then we should wait until those given times and arrive there ten minutes early. I kept the phone number on that dirty piece of paper in Jordan Wong's manly man purse that he carried along all the time. Now that feeling of waiting anxiously for something or someone, in this case someone, felt like such a long time . . . longer than the ten or fifteen years that had passed since high school.

Mitch~

Andy and I had nothing to do so we planned a dinner for ourselves and the wives. Yeah, we took out our ladies for dinner when we're bored. But then, Andy gave me an unexpected call saying that someone else was joining us. I prayed to god it wouldn't have to be his kids because then I'd have to bring my kids, but then I realized that Austin and Sarah were staying over at my place with Monica and Howard. So then, who was it? Jessica. "Jessica," he told me. High-school Jessica? Yep, it was going to be high-school Jessica. Jessica didn't really like me back then; hopefully, she let go of the grudges she held on me way back then. I laughed at flashbacks of when I used to annoy her as I sat back in a chair.

I didn't really feel comfortable leaving all the kids stay in my house, not because I didn't like them getting all the floors dirty which were just cleaned the other day, but because of the police cars that stopped by a house a few doors down. A woman blended her newborn kitties and puppies in a washing machine. She had accidentally mistaken one of her small grandchildren for another puppy or kitten and added that in the washing machine too. Then when she opened it up after ten minutes, blood was spilled all over the place in her Laundromat. She found she had killed her own grandchild and carried it in her arms, soaking her clothes with the child's blood and walked a mile to enter a market and screamed, "I'VE SINNED!" I didn't know if the sidewalks would be cleaned up or not, but one long trail of an innocent child's blood did not set a good or clean image of this town we all called home. It was really disturbing and scary. I didn't want my kids hearing about this, especially Howard. When he was exposed to *The Exorcist*, he had to sleep in our bed for a few months. But Monica, I think she could handle it but wouldn't want to even know about it in the first place. The world could be a really sick thing sometimes.

But on a happier note, I was honestly psyched to see Jessica after such a long time. When the time came to meet Andy, Lily, and Jessica, I was stunned to see she was looking, um, a little attractive, but no. No way can she be more attractive than Leslie though. Ha, no way, never. When she entered the restaurant, she flailed her arms in the air, did this little dance, screamed, and came running across the room to our table to give Leslie a hug. I found it kinda funny.

"Oh my god! Leslie! I haven't seen you in such a long time!" she said, hugging her tightly.
"Ha-ha! Nice to see you too, Jessica!" she replied.

Then Jessica turned to me and gave me a weak smile. She rolled her eyes, laughed, and gave me a hug. "Hug, hug, kiss, kiss to you too, Mitch," she said.
"Ha-ha! It's nice to see you again," I said casually.

She continued her way around the table to give free hugs to Lily and Andy as well and made her way around again and took a seat beside me.

"So you still haven't told me how you and Freddy are coming along," Andy started the conversation as a waiter gave her a menu.
"Oh, um, it's going . . . fine . . . fine," she said, turning her eyes away from him and to the many pictures of seafood on the greasy menu. "Did you guys order yet?"
"Yeah. Yep," the rest of us said in unison.
"So, near marriage?" I asked her.
"Um, close. Engaged."
"Oh my gosh, Jessica. You still look pretty after all these years. You're skinny, you're in good shape, and I think you've grown a little taller as well. I'm envious right now!" Leslie joked.
"Yep. I've blossomed!" Jessica shouted, stretching her arms out in the air.

We were eating at the same Chinese restaurant Nathen and I had lunch at, and apparently, the same one Jessica's soon-to-be-husband worked at as a part-time employee. We had a long talk with a few laughs, and I kept quiet most of the time. I just really wanted to talk to Jessica alone about a few things. She was always closer to Nathen than me, and there were a few mysteries I wanted to know about him. I care for people because I'm a caring person . . . half of the time, but in Nathen's case, it was urgent. Besides that, I obviously wanted to know more about Jessica too. This was like some kind of high-school reunion, and the only person missing out on all of this was Nathen, the oddball.

Our food came after about fifteen minutes, and we dug in. Beside me, Jessica was having a fight with a packet of soy sauce, and it began to get serious when she started cursing at the small packet under her breath.

"Do you need some help with that?" I offered, placing my chopsticks down.
"Um, no, I can win this battle by myself. Thank you, though," she replied, not looking up at me.
"Okay," I said, picking up my chopsticks.

So then, she won, but after such a long battle, the soy sauce packet took quick revenge and splattered itself all over her dress and a little spittle on my coat.

"Darnsy, well, I think I'm gonna take myself on a little trip to the little girls' room," she said, getting up, dabbing lightly at her dress with a napkin.
"I'll go with you," I offered. This was a chance to speak with her in private.
"To the restroom with me?" she asked.
"Um, I'll walk you to it."
"Oh, okay."

We set off zigzagging through busy tables and waiters/waitresses.

"You know, I still kind of think you're an asshole," Jessica whispered into my ear.

"Yeah, I thought so," I smiled.

"So why are you showing me to the restrooms? I know where they are. I've been to one because there was this one time Freddy gave me this one dumpling, and it completely gave me this massive stomachache, and I really needed . . ."

"You know Nathen well, right?" I asked, cutting her off.

"Of course. I know him like I know all the Korean dramas ever produced. For the record, I watch tons of Korean dramas," she answered.

"How's he holding up?"

"He's okay, I guess. He wanted me to go on a trip to Hawaii, but I declined 'cause this woman has got to go to work! You too?"

"Yeah, me too. I also declined, and it was nice of him to send me a basket of bread."

"Yeah, the bread was good. The butter too."

"He told me he didn't have a job, but he makes good enough money. How the hell is that possible?" I asked, as we stood next to the doors to the restroom, out of view from Andy, Lily, and Leslie.

"I don't know. Prostitution?"

"What the hell? Really?"

"No, I'm kidding. Nathen would never stoop down that low, unless he was really desperate to lose his virginity. Gosh, why are you so worried about Nathen now? I thought your heart was a cold, dark, life-sucking black hole."

I was asking myself the same question. Why was I worried about Nathen? The guy lost his family, didn't have a job . . . could life be any worse for him? Hopefully not. But he should be okay spending some time in Hawaii.

"Well, I'm gonna go wash myself up now. I'm starting to smell salty," Jessica said, heading toward the door to the restroom, but as soon as she did, she ran into a waiter carrying numerous plates and they fell on top of each other. They were drenched in sauces and seafood.

"Great. Just great," Jessica said to herself, wiping off as much of the food and sauces off her. I helped her up, and she quickly ran into the restroom. I was going to go after her but had forgotten that what I would be walking into would be a women's restroom. I decided to go back to the table.

"Is she okay?" Leslie asked me.

"Um, she got into a bit of a mess, so we'll have to see," I told her.

Jessica finally came back after we finished our dinner. To be honest, she still looked the same with her dress patched with smudges.

"Aw, I'm sorry guys," she apologized. "Um, I think I've caused enough trouble, so I'll take care of the bill."

"No, no. Don't bother yourself." Andy stopped her from digging in her purse as he took out his wallet. "You've gone through enough trouble."

"I'll take care of it," I said, running up to the front desk.

Then it became a race. Andy and I tried to move each other out of our way as we literally jumped over chairs and tables, bumping into a few people. In the end of this epic battle that proved who was faster than who, and who understood Asian customs better than who, I won and coughed up a heaping amount of about one hundred and fifty dollars.

Nathen~

.Five days passed, and during those five days, I had not once seen Katie at the dock as I waited for both times of each day. It was the sixth day today, and the time was 7:53 p.m. I feared it was going to be another day . . . very similar to the past five. The search must have been a success, but finally seeing her was a failure. This whole trip to Hawaii was a failure. I was a failure, and adding Jordan Wong to aid me in my search to find her made me a complete failure. Failure . . . I always had such strong animosity toward that disgusting, degrading word of the English language. Not only was it disgusting or degrading, but it was the last word my father had screamed at me at the top of his slimy lungs. It began as a small conversation about what I would have as a career in the distant future between my father and me. In a few measly seconds, it morphed itself into a mutated, irate creature which is sometimes known as a fight. The fight ended with an abrupt "YOU ARE A FAILURE!" from his dry mouth and the slam of my bedroom door. No matter how much I wanted to forget it and erase it from my memory, it was the last thing to remember from him. I did regret having such a nasty talk with him, but what was done was done, and there was nothing you could do to change the past; you could only tamper with it.

"Do you think she'll show up, Jordan Wong?" I asked him, looking out at the ocean, watching the waves crashing against rocks and their fellow brothers.

"What would you like me to say?" he asked.

"Your honest opinion that I so wish would be 'yes'," I told him.

"With my full honesty, I don't think she'll show up at all, Nathen. To be even more honest, I think this entire search for her and waiting for her at the dock at this very moment is a waste of your time, Nathen. Um, please don't fire me," he quickly answered.

"Ah, the truth hurts, doesn't it?" I said.

"Do you want me to add something to that?" he asked.

"No, it's quite all right."

We stood out on the dock for a few more minutes until 8:10 p.m. struck. After that, we left back to the room. Maybe I should call her once again. Maybe the sound of my voice distorted over the phone would help her remember me. Whether my father was in hell or heaven didn't really matter to me; he was probably laughing his bottom off from the flaming bowels of the devil's palace or from the peaceful, cheery kingdom of heaven. I was wide awake in the hotel's bed. I doubt Jordan Wong was still awake.

"Jordan Wong?" I called out into the dark.

"Yes, Nathen?" a call answered mine.

"Oh, you're still awake, how convenient."

"Yes, Nathen. I am at your service."

"Oh, well, this statement you are about to hear is rather unnecessary, and it might cause some discomfort or awkwardness. Do you mind?"

"Not at all, Nathen. I'm being paid to listen to whatever you say."

"Well, if you were a female, which you are not, as obvious as it is, I'd ask you for comfort and a shoulder to cry on," I quietly sniffled.

"I'm flattered?" he chuckled.

It was quiet after that. It was an awkward silence that somehow mysteriously put me to sound sleep.

Andy~

I didn't want to go back to the office and encounter any problems with anybody. I sent Janet an e-mail saying I'd be working at home. I didn't want to give her a phone call because I was afraid she was going to say something provocative while I was on the line. I didn't want to include how long I'd be working from home because I wasn't sure myself. Probably, until I felt comfortable going back to the office. I told everyone about it at the restaurant that Saturday we went out to dinner, and everyone laughed at me. They just didn't understand how serious this could get. This crazy Yoda lady kept sending me invites to lunch with her, and I hadn't responded to any of them. I thought this was going to be a win-win situation for her because if I went to lunch with her, she obviously won, and if I didn't, I had a risk of getting more work piled up on me. I thought I should bring this up to the branch or the authorities or something because this was ridiculous. I couldn't blame myself for being so irresistible. I blamed Janet and George. You know, Janet was a freak and George was a lunatic, and with those characteristics, I pronounce Janet and George were made for each other.

Besides, I liked working from home because you could get up and get yourself food whenever you felt like it and take a crap as loud and long as you want where nobody could hear you. I had the place to myself on work days, and you didn't have to work in un-cozy chairs or on cold desks. I could sit back and relax with my laptop in bed, on the couch, on the patio swing, or even on, get this, the toilet, baby! The only downfall was that I didn't think I was working as hard as I did back at the office.

Jessica~

You know all of this Andy mumbo-jumbo processing through my head made me forget about Freddy for a while. Freddy had not once sent me a phone call, a text message, or an e-mail, nothing at all. Maybe this was all over: this relationship between Freddy and I. Should I send him some sort of personal message saying that this wasn't going to work anymore and just stay with each other as friends? Then it would be back to square one for me, loner status. I'd been frequently meeting Andy and Mitch because I had nothing better to do on the weekends. Before I left my apartment to Mitch's fancy home and Korean barbeque, I sent Freddy a text message saying, "Freddy, with full trust in my heart, I believe we shouldn't see each other anymore." He probably wouldn't read it for like a few weeks because he was so "busy."

When I was driving toward Mitch's lovely home, I heard on the radio about this music teacher that went on a rampage because his wife left him, taking all of his money from his bank account and his pockets, and he pushed a piano into a student, crushing the kid's legs and snapping them in two. Then he bashed a girl's head with a violin case and whipped another student with a violin bow and shoved it down their throat. Before the authorities arrived, the teacher choked himself with the use of his tie and one of his student's harp's strings. It was really disturbing to hear about while driving to a happy barbeque. The story just ruined my mood. Wow . . . the things people do because of pain, hatred, and madness.

Nathen~

    While Jordan Wong and I waited at the pier again, I asked him what he knew about me. At first, he had said that he knew nothing about me and apologized for not studying my background information. After 8:00 a.m. had passed, another no-show, he said he had heard of me through newspapers and the media. He had lied. It's a human thing, I believe. It's a human thing to lie about things to avoid the uncomfortable and sad things in life. He must have thought that he would "hurt" my feelings for bringing up my past. He apologized to me once again, and I sent him off to a little eight-hour break until 8:00 p.m., the time Katie was supposed to be here.

    After my days of living and observing humans on this wretched planet we call earth, I had found there were good people and good-looking people. It was rare to find people with both traits: good looks and goodness in them. Eighty-six percent of the time, you'd find at least one of those special people such as Katie. Katie, one of the rare few.

    For the rest of the day, I allowed Jordan Wong to enjoy himself while I sat down at a public bench, looking back at the past. It was nice once in a while to look back and to know what you've experienced and lived through before you grew near to your death and have Alzheimer's. There was this young Japanese male that walked down the street carrying bags of small necessities that he had bought for his wife that reminded me of a student I had helped out with his payments for college. Yes, I was once a geometry teacher, and if I remembered correctly, many of my students hated geometry more than I. I believed I was a somewhat good teacher who gave out homework and lessons on a rigorous scale and spared time to digress to humorous and unnecessary topics that had nothing to do with the class once in a while. There was one student whom I found extraordinary—an excellent extrovert with a very strong charisma who kept up with his grades quite diligently even when he took a time-consuming sport such as tennis. The boy did keep up with his grades and flattered me quite a bit. He flattered all of his teachers so I'd heard back in the lounge. It was his nature. So with this, his attitude toward things, I decided to pay for his future college payments: such as tuition, books, and a nice dormitory of his choice. I never liked eating lunch with other teachers who bored me with their conversations about... whatever they were talking about, so I ate lunch with my students. Their lives were far more interesting than the people in the lounge, and it was an attempt for me to know what the new trends were, what was going on around school, and what was "hip." It was also a chance for me to go back to what I had missed as a student myself. After a few more years, the student that I helped pay for college thanked me very much at the front of my door step at my apartment. He had looked through files of teachers, talked to neighbors, and his graduating class for information of the location of where I slept. He gave a long "thank you," we had a small conversation over a bottle of spring water, and he left. After that, I never heard from him again. During that time, I believed I had read an article about him saying he was creating hotels in Hawaii and Las Vegas. It was a shame that I had forgotten his name. It was a shame I had forgotten the name of his hotels, so I was unable to find it here. Sometimes, I wondered if he had forgotten who had paid for his college bills or if he still remembers me. Sometimes, we do forget who is or was important to us. That's another human thing, right?

I felt like I was wasting my time on this island of many islands. But if I went back home, I would have nothing to do, nothing at all. It was obvious Katie thought I was some random person who had called the wrong person with a coincidentally same name. Jordan Wong was right; I should give up.

Mitch~

I didn't know if I should believe what I just witnessed. I didn't know if I should say anything to Andy about it. I found the whole thing kinda awkward and weird. Jessica was in the passenger seat beside me because she asked for a ride. She told me her car was wrecked up by some troublesome teenagers, and she'd been complaining about how children weren't disciplined anymore to me, and blah blah blah . . . I wasn't really paying attention to anything she was saying; you know I never actually listened to anything she'd said. But back to the thing I just saw. When I drove into my old school's parking lot, I saw, with my very own Asian eyes, Monica and Austin holding hands. When they saw my car, they immediately unlocked their fingers and kept them to their sides. Andy was right; there was something going on between those two lovebirds.

"Holy! Jessica, did you see that?" I shouted out.
"And they're annoying! They're like stupid little Furbys! Oh, see what?" she asked, looking around.
"Them! Monica and Austin! They were just holding hands."
"Aw, how cute! They look so cute together. By the way, nice job producing such a pretty daughter."
"Ha-ha, thanks. This is weird. I think I'm gonna call Andy about this," I said, pulling out my Bluetooth and speed-dialed his number.
"Oh, you didn't know about the two?" Jessica brought up.
"No, was I supposed to?"
"It should've been pretty obvious to know about the two."
"Wait, you knew about this?"
"Hmm," she nodded her head yes.
"Why didn't you tell me?" I yelled at her, canceling my call when I spotted Monica and Austin walking toward my car.
"I thought you knew!"
"No! I didn't!"
"Why do you have to be so stupid," she muttered, turning away. In between her mutter was a disgusting scoff.

I didn't say anything, and I parked by the curb for Austin and Monica. They hopped into the car and greeted us with casual "hi's" and "hey's."

"AH! Austin! Let me pinch your cheeks!" Jessica screamed, reaching her hands out performing this grabbing motion as her seatbelt stopped her in motion, a few inches away from his face.

Austin blushed and moved up forward a little. Jessica grabbed his cheeks and wriggled them adding this weird sound effect. Monica hid her laugh with her hands cupped over her mouth. I tried not to laugh as well. I quickly drove out of the parking lot and headed toward Jessica's house. On the way, Jessica and I were trying to eavesdrop on their quiet conversation. We didn't pick up anything but giggles from them. Mission failed. Then it was a drive home, stopping by Andy's place to drop off Austin. I got on my computer and Facebook, chatted with Andy about the whole thing between his son and my daughter. Andy told me not to worry about it, and I went off to bed to tell Leslie about it. She gave me the same response: "Don't worry about it." Maybe I wouldn't let it bother me too much. It was not such a big deal, right? But what if they got too close and got married? Then Andy and I would become step brothers. Woah!

Nathen~

I'd been sending Jordan Wong off on long breaks for the past few days, and he told me if I continued doing this, he wouldn't like to be paid. After a few words, we both agreed. I sat myself down at a coffee shop and slowly drank my black coffee in very petite sips. I had never taken my coffee black and thought it would be somewhat nice to try it out. So here I was trying it out, and I didn't like it. I did not understand why I didn't just dump it after the first few sips. I was almost finished with it. It was 7:45 a.m., and I didn't feel like mobilizing myself to the pier and wait for another no-show from Katie. I gave up. When I finished my disgusting coffee, I got back in line to pay for a refill. The women in front of me dropped her wallet, and I quickly bent down to pick it up for her. Our hands reached and touched each other's, both hands resting on the leather wallet. I believed, if I glanced correctly, it was a Louis Vuitton.

"Oh, um, I'm sorry," she apologized.
"Yes, quite an awkward touch we had there," I said, looking up at her. At that exact moment, when our eyes came into contact, my heart

completely stopped for a few seconds. Mission accomplished. The female standing in front of me was Katie. I couldn't say anything or move anything, as if she had sucked me into a hypnotic stage with her medusa-like eyes, turning me into stone. I had always wondered what kind of stone Medusa turned men into. I mean it could be valuable stone for all we knew, and she probably would keep her stone figurines as a collection and would probably sell them off to people at high prices before her head would be ripped off and placed in a nifty nap-sack.

She picked up her order of a latte and a bagel and a side of cream cheese. I stared at her with my mouth open wide enough for small birds to nest inside as she walked out the door. I quickly snapped out of my trance and followed her out of the door, dropping my empty coffee cup on the floor of the small shop. I didn't realize I was littering until after I walked out the door. I tapped her shoulder and said, "I believe I know you." She turned around and gave a long, hard stare at me, but I felt her eyes looking past at me.

"Oh my god!" she said, still staring beyond me, "Nathen?"

She pushed me into a hug, and my body felt like it just melted. I was quickly perspiring for every second the hug lasted. This was a moment to cherish and remember. I hadn't received a hug like this since I watched the coffins of my family go down into the ground. I cried harder and harder every time the men with shovels dropped dirt down on them. Jessica had run into my arms and hugged me until I couldn't breathe anymore.

"I have missed you," I spurted from my mouth.
"Yeah, oh my gosh. So that wasn't a prank call after all," she chuckled lightly.

She moved away from me and gave me her oh-so-beautiful smile that made me crack a smile.

"Well, I would love to spend the rest of the day chatting with you and catching up on some stuff, Nathen, but I have to go to work. I'm sorry," she sighed.

"It's quite all right," I told her.

"Well, okay, how about you meet me at the Sunshine Apartments room 4220 at six tonight? Is that okay?"

"Why yes, it would."

"Okay then, see you later, Nathen!" she waved good-bye, running toward her workplace.

I immediately took out my cell phone and called Jordan Wong.

"How may I be of service, Nathen?" he asked me.

"Mission accomplished," I told him, hanging up the phone afterward.

I jogged back to the hotel room waiting for Jordan Wong's arrival and for this "date" with Katie.

Andy~

Was Jessica hitting on me? I thought she was because of what happened a few days ago at Mitch's barbeque. I went inside to get more dip for the chip . . . s . . . chips, and Jessica decided to come along. There was a bunch of awkward touching in the kitchen between the two of us. I used to date her until she dumped me. She had a reason, but I forgot what it was. She dumped me. I was always dumped, the dumpee, never the dumper. One time, I was about to dump this one chick, but she beat me to it. I was freakin' slow back then.

Well, I was still working from home, and I did make a phone call to the branch, and they said they would come over in a few weeks for an inspection and a talk with Janet. Boy, was I psyched to see everything cleared up in a few weeks? I kinda missed the office. It was like another home for me, except no wife or kids. I didn't mind working from home or work. I liked both. I saw a lot of interesting things happening around the neighborhood. Just a day ago, there was a house owned by a Mormon family just a few doors down who burned down their house on purpose and danced around naked shaking maracas and singing something in Latin. It all happened during the day, and I was the tenth person in the neighborhood to notify the cops. I found out they were Satanists *and* Mormons. I was just glad the flames of their house didn't catch onto my house.

Nathen~

I arrived at Katie's apartment while Jordan Wong spent his time at a night club attempting to "pick up females" with his "fabulous" charms he had once bragged about when he was overdosed with alcohol I had bought him. I was standing in front of her door not knowing whether it would be polite to just wait until the hand reached six or if I should just ring the doorbell now. It was currently five forty-seven. I feared my malodorous self would creep up on me even though I had applied several body-odor removal products such as a bottle of shampoo, which I finished through twenty showers, and canned and stick deodorants. I really didn't want to embarrass myself in front of her after so many years. In my sweaty palms, I held a boxed gift which was beginning to be blotched with salty water marks created by my sweat. It was a cool night, and the sky was speckled with stars and a full moon. I was hesitant to push that button next to her door, the one that goes *ding dong* or *ring ring* or whatever sound her doorbell would make. Then I decided to wait until six, so I stood in front of her door for the remaining time while she was busy doing whatever that was necessary to her. I was beginning to grow bored and began whistling the night away while drunken Filipino men in sombreros were drinking their night away with bottles of vodka, beers, and cartons of milk. The sight of them in Hispanic hats made me question: Did Filipino people wear sombreros? Then I thought to myself: *Well, why not? People had the freedom to wear whatever hat they wanted.* They were laughing and hacking, spitting out their globs of phlegm when needed in their native tongue. They wolf-whistled at women pushing strollers and shopping carts of babies as they slept soundly with a plastic pacifier in their mouths. About 78 percent of the women took the men's whistles offensively and responded with a verbal "FUCK YOU!" in both Filipino and English or a flash of their elegant and beautiful middle finger. The men replied with a loud laugh and nudged one another, whispering something to each other. What a lovely neighborhood my beloved Katie was living in! Oh, wouldn't she appreciate it if I had given her my home in Hawaii? I had no use for it, and I had never stepped in it at all. I had only looked at it on one breezy day and thought to myself: *What a bunch of money my father spent on this . . . when he complained about how money was spent around the house!* The only thing that existed inside the house was a grand piano a friend of my father had crafted himself with, of course, the helping hands of machinery.

After staring for too long, I took a quick look at my watch to find myself a minute late. I quickly rang the doorbell, and in seconds, Katie opened the door dressed in a beautiful pair of jeans and a simple blue and white striped T-shirt. I looked at myself, finding I was the only one who was dressed formally in suit and tie.

"Ha-ha, you didn't need to wear a suit just to see me," she laughed.
"He-he," I coughed an embarrassed laugh.
"Come on in," she said, leaving the door open for me, and for me to close.
"Quite a magnificent sight you have here," I complimented, looking at her detailed ceiling, walls, and lamps.
"Thanks, I had a friend do all of it for me. I just told her what colors to choose and what not," she replied from the kitchen.
"Do you mind if I take the time to examine your bathroom?" I asked, popping my head into the kitchen.
"Be my guest. Just don't forget to have the seat down when you exit," she joked.

Such an artist and a visionary for color she was! I had never seen this shade of color of her bright personality. Just standing and observing her bathroom with the door locked behind me made me perspire profusely. The crown molding was quite extraordinary which embedded small sculptures of simple flowers and bees. I flushed her toilet, and the sound was music to my ears as it was silent and had a light, sweet flush. Her marble sink sparkled underneath her dim-lighted Japanese lanterns. It was quite a sight for a bathroom so unique. I walked out and found that the table was set with refreshing bottles of water and delicious Hot Pockets that seated themselves on fine China.

"You might want to eat now, or else, the Hot Pockets are gonna get cold," she smiled.

"Oh yes, I should. I do admire Hot Pockets," I told her. I was completely stunned by this act performed by her. A dinner? With the main course being Hot Pockets? And the beverages? Bottled water? I was slightly outraged, but my anger was toned down a wee bit because of her sweet smile and her beautiful eyes.

But overall, the dinner was exquisite, and the chatting was nice. We caught up with each other. Later on, during the night, we went out for some Hawaiian ice cream at a dairy shop her aunt ran. The ice cream was exceptional—a nice spherical clump of rich, creamy vanilla ice cream with thin strands of coconut combed neatly inside. And there was surprisingly no tax, but I tipped because I felt bad not having to pay tax. Then we walked along the Waikiki strip watching street performers perform their bizarre talents, such as contact juggling, the art of music, and difficult modernized dancing. Some even had a simple yet tiring talent, such as standing still either covered in some sort of liquid or solid like squares of cardboard box, paint, and long bands of edible and non-edible plastic sausages. All of this amazement led me to remember Willy Wonka's quote: *We are the music makers, and we are the dreamer of dreams*, which was originally created by Arthur O'Shaughnessy, the author of *An Epic of Women,* so we should give the man some credibility.

It was a brilliant night which was ended with a walk along the beach without the use of our footwear, which we carried in our hands, and an "I missed you so much" from the lips of Katie. Then it was a farewell. This night was probably the longest night I had ever spent with Katie.

Later on in the evening, Jordan Wong informed me of something shocking.

Jessica~

There was like a blender in my head right now because images of Andy are seriously swirling through my head right now. I photocopied the note Andy had given to me back in high school and pasted it all over my bedroom wall. I thought I was in love with the guy again. This feeling, this love, was turning into an obsession. Obsession . . . ha-ha! I liked whispering "obsession." It sounded sexy. Ha-ha! Oh, what to do with my life? I was completely bored, and this is a HUGE shocker—I ran out of Korean dramas to watch. It was a Friday night, and the only thing I was looking forward to was something that would uplift and enhance my boredom. I took a coat and walked out the door and went for a night's walk. Where I was walking to wasn't the question, but where I would end up was. I was in high heels; I didn't know why I preferred them as a choice for my cool night walk, so I didn't think I'd go far. I'd probably stop by at a liquor store to buy cheap water and walk back home, but I really did want to go somewhere, see something.

I took off my high heels, clasping them in my hands, and zoomed down the sidewalk, running a red light. I almost got myself killed as the driver who almost ran me over ranted at me incoherently. I smiled and laughed, wiggling my high heels in the air. I passed by houses with lights out; the only light illuminating the rooms were TV sitcoms and reality shows—none of them any better than a Korean drama . . . not even a lousy Korean drama. Maybe I wasn't bored . . . maybe I was just . . . lonely. I needed someone . . . or maybe something . . . like a dog or a cat or a goldfish I could have a conversation with. It wouldn't matter what they would reply with because I would always reply for them. No, I needed a *someone*—a *someone* who would give me their honest reply, not a bark or a meow or whatever sound a goldfish would make.

"Oh, woe is me, woe is me," I said aloud to myself, buttoning up my coat.

My cell phone rang, and I answered, "Hello?"
". . ."
"WHAT?"
". . ."
"Nathen, I don't appreciate your sense of humor. That's not funny," I told him.
". . ."
"Nathen, you're so stupid!" I yelled into the phone, hanging up and throwing it back into my purse.

God, why did Nathen have to joke about things like that? Sometimes he doesn't know what kind of humor to use around people. One time, Nathen joked about the KKK at my friend Aretha's birthday party. You guessed correctly; Aretha was black, and 98 percent of the people in the room were black. The other 2 percent were . . . I didn't know what they were, but I knew that they were Europeans. Nathen's face didn't turn out too pretty after the party. Sometimes, he was just so stupid and lost his common sense. I stopped myself at a liquor store and purchased a chilled bottle of water. As I took out my wallet to pay the cashier with the eye patch and cigarette in his mouth, I glanced over at a pregnancy test.

"H . . . How much is that pregnancy test?" I asked the cashier.
"Five bucks, but, since you ain't lackin' no ugliness, I'll give it to ya for two bucks," he grumbled.
"Oh, I think I'll stop by at a pharmacy instead," I told him, taking my bottle and leaving the man with a two-dollar bill and two quarters. I didn't trust liquor store pregnancy tests.

So I did. I bought myself a pregnancy test even though I said I was going to go to the pharmacy instead. I decided it would be best to save money and buy it from the smoking eye-patched man. Yeah, I'd had safe sex—REALLY REALLY SAFE—with Freddy . . . a few times, but I'd never actually taken a pregnancy test. You know I just wanted to check, just to be safe.

Andy~

HA-HA! YEAH! Janet was suspended from her job for a few months, and now I could go back to the office again. Hopefully, George wouldn't be acting up again. The supervisor that was sent by the branch told me if he did, then he would have to leave, and if that happened, I would get to live normally and happily. Everyone welcomed me back with a small cake which I was highly surprised by. Who knew office buddies could be so nice to get you a cake because I worked from home for practically two months? This was awesome.

Over a phone call, Mitch told me he saw a glimpse of Monica and my boy Austin making out. Way to go, Austin! That's my boy! Ha-ha! No, the boy should really learn about abstinence and should keep his lips to himself or to his mirror or pillow or his arm if he practices kissing . . . kinda weird, but whatever. I did find this all kinda weird and awkward that Mitch's girl was dating my boy, and if their relationship turned out like Mitch and Leslie's, that would be a huge jaw-drop. Then, Mitch would be related to me . . . and . . . and . . . yeah, that was pretty cool I guessed.

Nathen~

"Jessica does not wish to believe me," I told Jordan Wong, walking around in circles in our room. "Are you positive that all of this is true?"

"Aren't pictures and a voice recording good enough, Nathen?" he asked.

"Okay, yes, I do believe you, Jordan Wong. Maybe in order to convince her that this was all true, we should send her a copy of the pictures and the voice recordings you took."

"On it, Nathen," he said, hopping onto his laptop and editing his secret findings.

I did find all of this mind-blowing and shocking enough that I didn't want to believe the pictures and the voice recording Jordan Wong had shown me so urgently. I could understand why Jessica would not believe the found news for it was absolutely absurd coming out of my mouth, but if it were coming out of Brad Pitt's or Angelina Jolie's mouth, Jessica would surely believe their words. Even though it wasn't much of a shock, I took it as a shock for it crushed me to believe that Katie was married. Whom did she wed? Whom she wed shocked me even more. Whom she wed was Freddy; the same Freddy that Jessica was engaged to. I had called Katie to confirm if her husband's name was Freddy and that he was Korean, and it was a yes she said to both questions. She had asked why, but I told her I was just curious. Why hadn't I asked her such a question when we were out walking on the beach or discussing it over our delicious mediocre "date" meal? Why hadn't such a question struck me? Did her charm or beautiful self blind me for thinking about such a question? Maybe such a question didn't occur to me because I assumed I would be the only one that would marry her after all these years, which was far-fetched to say in the first place.

"I just sent Jessica the photos and the voice recording through e-mail, Nathen," Jordan Wong had told me.

It seemed that I came all the way to Hawaii, in search for my long-lost love and find her married to my best friend's boyfriend. Oh, what a nasty situation this was! As I sat down on the side of the room's bed, I pondered about whether to leave now or stay for a little longer. I decided it would be nice to see Katie for at least one more day and then leave without letting her know that she was the only girl I ever liked and loved. I heard a loud bang on the door that made me jump out of my pondering stage. I got up, and as I was about to stick my eye inside the small peephole, the door violently banged again as if a rabid dog was ramming its skull into the door. I opened the door to find Freddy. He moved his fist back and hurled it directly into my face. I fell back to the compelling force he had mounted in one punch, and my body collapsed against the wall with a loud thud making me slide down to the floor where I blacked out.

Mitch~

Shit. Shit. Shit. I was passing red lights and cutting my way through small traffic, heading my way toward the hospital. Leslie was already over there with him, and Monica and Austin were in the car with me. She was wiping her tears away with her shirt as Austin comforted her. I almost started to cry too, to be honest, but I didn't want Monica to see me do so. "It's okay to cry if you want," Monica told me about fifteen minutes ago. "No, I . . . I'm all right," I told her. My Bluetooth was in my ear so that Leslie could keep me updated.

"It's gonna be okay, Monica," I heard Austin whisper. I hoped so.

We were only a few minutes away from the hospital. I had to leave work immediately and call the school saying Monica and Austin would have to leave early. I knew they were probably excited to miss their chemistry test that I'd studied with Monica for. I didn't think they really cared about the reason why they were leaving early until I told them, until Monica burst into tears. Neither Andy nor Lisa could pick them up because they had to work late tonight, and their daughter Sarah was still at preschool. Ugh, I might have to pick her up too. I tried calling Andy, but his cell phone was off, and so was Lisa's.

"Yes! No chem. test! Thank you, Dad!" she had exclaimed.
"Thanks, Mitch," Austin thanked as well. "So why are we leaving school so early?"

"Howard was hit by a car," I told them bluntly, my voice slightly cracked in the middle of the sentence.
"What?" Monica had shouted.
"We're heading toward the hospital right now."

That was when she cried her eyes out. That was when Austin put his arm around her, and she rested her head next to his. It reminded me about the time I found Leslie crying behind the PE buildings after school, after her dance practices, and I just sat down with her for like three hours which had only felt like one hour. We didn't say anything to each other. We didn't need to say anything to each other. I didn't even know what to say to her unless she said something. Our parents were freakin' worried about us, and we told them we were at Andy's house, and they believed us. I neither could nor couldn't remember if we kissed during that day or not. I'd ask Leslie later. I think it was our junior year of high school when it happened. Why was she upset and crying? Her grandpa died. The man was so close and meant so much to her because when she was about five years old, her parents lost their jobs and were going broke. They were so broke that they were going to lose the house until her grandpa saved them with a large sum of money that allowed them to survive for a quarter of the year until they got their jobs back. I loved her so much, and I still love her. I'll always love her.

As soon as the car was parked, the three of us ran into the hospital and asked for the room where Howard was resting in and took the elevator up. Floor 44, room 413. Was it just a coincidence or were these numbers for this room unlucky? The number four is an unlucky number in Japan, and of course, the number thirteen is unlucky as well. Ugh, I couldn't let superstition decide where this situation was going.

"Leslie, is he okay?" I ran into the room with Monica and Austin.
"Shhh, the doctors said he needs some rest, and they'll see what happens afterward," she explained.
"Um, Sarah still needs to be picked up. And . . ."
"What? Why?"

"Andy and Lisa aren't picking up their phones."

"Here, you can stay and watch Howard. I'll pick up Sarah," Leslie sniffled, picked up her purse and jacket with one hand, and in the other was a crumpled tissue. She gave me a kiss good-bye on the cheek and left.

I took a seat in the chair as Monica and Austin stood by Howard. Monica slowly moved her hand toward Howard's, and when her hand came in contact with his, his fingers twitched, and she held his hand. Her other hand was busy clasping Austin's. I thought they knew that I knew about their relationship. Eh, it didn't bother me as much as before, but if they're gonna end up like me and Leslie . . . no way, am I going to let them marry 'cause that is just . . . weird. Being related to my best friend is just . . . plain weird. Ugh, hopefully, he'll turn out all right. I hope he's okay. Every minute sitting in this chair with Monica and Austin felt like an hour as I bit my fingernails in worry.

Not too long, but it really did feel like a few hours. Leslie came back with Sarah who was asleep.

"You should take the kids home, Mitch," Leslie whispered to me in my ear.

"Okay, um, call me if anything happens," I whispered back.

The two followed me out the room and to the parking lot. It was a silent ride home, and when we got there, I tried to call Andy and Lisa again, but they still wouldn't pick up. Austin and Monica were in her bedroom doing whatever they were doing. I wanted to know what they were up to, you know, just in case, they didn't do anything inappropriate, but I respected privacy and the privacy for others. I didn't know what to do after I got home. Should I go back to the hospital? The only thing on my to-do-list was to worry about Howard. I climbed up the stairs after staring outside through the front window of the living room and entered Howard's room. In the corner, covered by a dresser, were his hand prints when he was in preschool. I remember I was painting his room, and he decided to dump his hands inside a different can of paint, different from the color of the walls, and he printed his hands on the wall in the corner. Below it, he wrote his name and the date with a little help from me. After sitting on Howard's bed and looking around at what I had bought for him and what he had made himself; pictures he drew, really short stories he wrote, stuff like that, I knocked on Monica's door and told her that I'd be going back to the hospital and would be coming back until Howard was home again.

Nathen~

After that hard blow I had taken from Freddy's manly fist, I woke up and found myself tied to a wooden chair with thick ropes, Jordan Wong seated beside me also in the same fashion I was in, except he had duct tape around his mouth. As I tried to pull away from the ropes, my entire body ached, and a massive headache was bothering me.

"Awake now, eh?" Freddy asked me as he took a sip from his glass bottle of Korean beer.

"So it seems . . . hello to you, Freddy," I said monotonously. since when did I never say anything in a monotonous tone?

"Yeah, hey," he burped. "Who's this? Your gay lover?" he pointed at Jordan Wong who seemed to be still knocked out.

"No, he is my personal assistant, and who are you? A husband of Katie? Or a boyfriend of Jessica?" I retorted rather quickly.

He beat me on the head with his heavy fist and took another swig from his beverage. Then as soon as I believed he was done physically abusing me for a few moments, he kicked me in the legs. I silently squealed like a newborn piglet to myself. He brought his sweaty, dirty face close to mine and whispered, "Don't you say one damn word to Jessica about this. You understand?"

"No, I do not comprehend," I whispered back.

He struck me across the face with his beer bottle, the liquid spraying everywhere, and glass pieces darting toward the bleached hotel room's walls. There was a deep cut on my right cheek which was being painted with my own blood, running down to my neck. The blood and the alcohol mixed together stung my face.

"Now do you 'comprehend?'" he mocked me.

I didn't want to say anything, but when people ask a question, they always expect an answer unless it is a rhetorical question.

"If it avoids me from further pain, then yes," I said quietly, glaring up at him.
"Good." He smiled, pulling another bottle of beer from his backpack where I believed he kept his duct tape and rope in.

"And if you ever leak one goddamn word to Jessi, I'll have you dead. Understand?"

I nodded my head in shock; my eyes were wide in fear. Who knew that a man I gave orange chicken to, would turn out to be so violent, drunk, and just pure evil? I was in awe by the sight of his atrocious actions, his words, and he himself. A two-faced monster of a human he was. Has dear Jessica ever witnessed this side of Freddy before? If so, I feel the anguish that she has endured. If not, I do hope she comes to believe the photos and the voice recording that she'll see and hear once she opens up her e-mail and will find that Freddy is a monster.

Jessica~

Nothing to do on weekends or weekday evenings . . . sigh . . . Yeah, I was sighing a lot. I'd been sighing a lot lately. I'd turned to Japanese dramas since good-bye Korean dramas. I sat on my bed with a warm cozy blanket, which I stole from Nathen a while back, covered over my back with my laptop with three people and a tub of my beloved Haagen-Dazs. Those three people in my bed? The only three people that are allowed in my bed . . . well, Freddy *was* allowed in my bed, but not anymore . . .

okay, so there were only three people allowed in my bed. For right now, unless another man appears in my life, but yeah, okay, three people: me, myself, and I. Yep, those three, and I love them.

When a priest came up in this cheesy Japanese drama, it reminded me of the time when I attended church for a boring mass on a lovely Sunday morning, and there was this priest. He was young and attractive. It was the first time I felt so naughty in church. It was also the first time I ever listened to a homily. I know, it's terrible. I told Nathen about it . . . I forgot what he commented with . . . hmm, oh! He rhetorically asked, "Since when was preaching hot?" Oh my, I laughed my ass off that day. This went way back into like high school. Poor him . . . such an attractive priest who will never get married . . . to me! . . . Ha-ha! I'm just joking . . . halfheartedly. Right now, he's probably happy with his life in his megachurches with his home-dog Jesus, and if he's ever lonely, he could always look at his Madonnas with dirty thoughts or flirt with the nuns.

I wish I was a kid again. Maybe I should go to Disneyland. I haven't been in that kingdom of dreams since . . . my senior year of high school? It was like a farewell party with all my friends. I wonder what it's like now after so many years. Is the person in the costume of Mickey Mouse still alive and doing his job? Or is he retired or dead, resting in his coffin with a gold Mickey Mouse pendant pinned over his right breast? What about Mickey's beloved companion, Minnie Mouse? Is she single now because of her dead or retired Mickey? Who will take Mickey's place? Donald Duck? Goofy? Her pet Pluto? Ew . . . the idea of Pluto being her lover is weird although they are all cartoon animals. How can a cartoon animal have a cartoon animal as a pet? Weird! What was going on through Walt's Disney's head? But you got to love that man who created so many memorable classics. I remember after I finished watching *The Little Mermaid*, he inspired me to wrap a green towel over my legs as if they were fins, and I wished to live in the ocean, so I could befriend so many other mermaids and mermen and possibly marry one and speak to a talking crab about my problems and situations, but my parents said I would die, and that *totally* crushed my dreams of becoming a mermaid.

I was so pissed after my parents told me I would die if I wanted to be a mermaid when I grew up, and now, I feel stupid for being so pissed.

I picked up my purse and dug for some coupons. I needed to go grocery shopping soon. I wish I had someone else do it for me . . . like a slave or servant almost, and I need somebody to talk to. I don't want my slave or servant to be foreign. Well, I do want them to be foreign, making them foreign makes them more interesting. Well, they just need to speak English too, and that would be good enough for me. Now, all I need is to find a foreign person who can speak English and go grocery shopping for me. I'll pay them . . . a little. Wait, but most foreign people might take advantage of me and just run away with my grocery shopping money and list, but I don't think they would care much about my list; they won't really care what I buy. I don't think anybody cares about what I buy unless it's like an expensive fashion accessory or something like that because people only notice the fancy things in life. When I found my shopping coupons, I also found that pregnancy test I bought a few days ago. I didn't even try it yet. I knew I was not pregnant. God! What a waste of my money . . . stupid self-conscience made me buy a pregnancy test. I'd just throw this away and let some homeless woman or man . . . ew . . . use this for themselves. As I walked over to my trash bin to dispose of it, I thought twice. I placed it on my counter and told myself not to think about it. So I didn't when I went through a series of some Japanese dramas. They're okay, the dramas, the Japanese ones, but nothing, I say NOTHING, beats the Korean dramas.

Nathen~

I was untied eventually when the maid opened up our room. She was yelling something in Spanish at me in the process of my release. And then I tipped her. I released Jordan Wong from his rope shackles, and he had told me he got Freddy's words all on a small digital tape recorder. I asked him if he could send it to Jessica, and he agreed saying it would be the right thing to let her know who she was dating. When he did so, we ran off to Katie's house for a visit. She greeted me with a tired hello and was immediately woken up when I handed her the tape recording of Freddy's violent words. She was in shock. I personally revealed to her, in the most unhurtful way a gentleman could put this, that she was being cheated on. At first, she didn't believe me, but she just trusted me after the first few minutes of this information she was taking in. She quietly excused herself to the bathroom as Jordan Wong and I stayed in her living room, sipping on green tea Katie had brewed herself, and I must say, she makes excellent tea. I asked myself if I should compliment her tea brewing or not when she came out of the bathroom. Well, she was in a depressing mood; maybe it would be best to mention her wonderful tea brewing at another time . . . another *pleasant* time.

"Nathen?" Jordan Wong whispered to me.

"Yes?" I answered him, aware of his existence and attention.

"Um, could it be possible if I brewed up some more tea?"

"I don't think Katie would appreciate that although she did say to make ourselves at home, and at home, you would certainly brew your own tea whenever you wanted; am I correct?"

"Yes?"

"Then, I believe you may, unless the permission of Katie is necessary or mandatory. The answer to your question; I do not know. I apologize."

"Well, I'll just ask when she comes out I guess," he said, twiddling with his fingers.

I turned my head away and to the façade of her bathroom door. She was awfully spending a lot of time in there. I wondered if she was crying to herself. Should I knock on her bathroom door and ask if everything was all right? Should I come in there and comfort her like a gentleman should do? Neither of the two actions did I perform, but I sat there, on one of her pieces of furniture that you could consider a chair or an oversized-martini glass. She owned very unique furniture. After about a half hour, she came out of her bathroom with a crumpled tissue in her hand and her nose a wee bit stuffy and red. She wiped small tears from her eyes and said, "I'm sorry. I just . . . needed some time alone . . . in the bathroom, my bathroom."

"I understand," I said, nodding my head.

"This proof . . . that you've given me . . . I don't want to believe it . . . but the truth is the truth. This is why he probably goes out on 'long business trips' and 'works really late.' I feel like a complete idiot. I'm so stupid. I mean, why didn't I think something was going on? I must be eligible to have the status of being legally blind, or even worse, legally blind."

"No, you're not. Don't say that to yourself. It shows that you have low self-esteem, and that's not something you really want to get into. Or it shows that you are looking for pity, but I doubt that is the case for you."

"Yeah." She looked away at the ground, spacing out as it seemed.

"If I may add another debacle to this debacle, Freddy's other companion, back in California, is Jessica," I told her, afraid she would run away to her sanctuary of a bathroom and cry to herself again.

"So why should I care?" she scoffed.

"Jessica . . . from high school," I added.

"Jessica . . . oh god . . . Jessica? Really? Jessica . . ."

"Yes, funny, how we're all connected . . . in a horrid way! It's a cruel, small world out there. But please, don't blame her or hold a nasty grudge against her. She didn't know either. Just last night did I deliver this terrible news to her, but she didn't believe me. I don't think she *wanted* to believe me."

"Well, when you get back to Cali, tell Jessica I said 'hi' and that I'm sorry and didn't know either," she said, leaving to the kitchen to retrieve more tea.

"This is my last day in Hawaii," I told her, standing up.

"Leaving so soon?" she asked, popping her head out of the kitchen.

"Actually, I've been here for a while now. It took me quite a long time to finally find you and meet you and see you." I smiled.

"Aw, you could've called Mitch or something to get my contact information or something."

Then the idea struck me. How could I be so stupid to not ask Mitch? Well, he did know I used to like her, and asking for her number would cause somewhat of a commotion of harassment and teasing . . . just like the good old days, but still.

"I hadn't thought of that when I came here," I blushed.

"Ha-ha! Well, the least I can do for making you search for me is drive you to the airport." she smiled.

"Oh, okay. Agreed."

Jordan Wong ran over to her with a small card which had the address of our hotel and gave it to her, and that was it. We left with a small farewell, and Katie agreed to pick us up at noon tomorrow. I hated so much to depart from this tropical island of islands and leave Katie live with terrible news on her. I thought she would be looking forward to a divorce when Freddy came home to her, and Freddy would run back to California and kill me like he proclaimed he would do, and to leave without saying that I had loved her since high school. Well, if I did such an act, the outcome would be quite awkward, and this awkwardness would remain between us till the day we died. Well, there was a sense of awkwardness between us back in high school because I had complimented on how good her hair smelled which was like a springtime garden of ripe and delicious watermelons that had a sense of warmth as it tickled the tiny hairs of your nostrils. But it seemed that awkwardness had died off after ten years.

Andy~

Whoo! Yes! Life is so sweet. Since the director from the branch couldn't stay for another few days to watch our office to see how things were turning out after Janet's absence, the director put me in charge, and I have to say, being boss is totally awesome. My first objective was to take over Janet's papers that she was supposed to finish a week ago, but the branch decided to give her a three-day extension. Her excuse was that Yoda grandma has passed away and had to tend to funeral business. Her grandma didn't really die; Janet was just lazy. My second objective was to dump all my other work on my coworkers. They didn't like me too much for doing so, and I felt bad for making them do *my* work, so I was nice enough to give everyone a longer lunch. How long? An hour longer which totaled up to a two-hour lunch break. After they had taken their breaks, they thanked me very much and called me "nice" and a "good guy with a kind soul and warm heart" and "sport" and "young man" and words like that.

"Andy, thanks man, thanks. Thanks to you. I had enough time to stop by the strip club and have a couple of bunnies hop all over me. Thanks, man, you're the best," George told me, shaking my hand.
"No problem," I answered awkwardly.

Did he lose his interest in Janet and aim his life-long dream girl to a couple of bunnies? Realizing where he had been and what he had done, I ran to the restrooms and washed my hands with soap. As I was scrubbing my hands with water and soap real good, someone was heaving out their lunch with a few grunts in one of the stalls. I didn't say anything. I didn't want to say anything, and I didn't think I should say anything. Maybe something along the lines like "Hey, what's going on in there?" or "You okay in there?" might be okay to say . . . no, it wasn't okay to say. It might be okay for Nathen to say something like that because he was just awkward and would say a lot of awkward stuff. I remember the time when Nathen and I met, excluding the time I officially befriended him. I was in the bathroom washing my hands and was in a hurry to turn in a slip to the office during break when Nathen came from behind me and told me I had very moisturized hands. He went on explaining he didn't have very moisturized hands because of his issues with dry skin and that it might run in the family and asked me what kind of lotion I used. I told him I didn't use any lotion. Then he went on asking if my skin was naturally moisturized, and I replied with "I guess so . . ." Then he told me his name, and I told him mine, and at that moment, I thought he was some kind of weirdie. Before I departed and left the bathroom to turn in my slip, he gave me a bottle of some kind of Korean lotion. Then he went on explaining how one culture should use their own culture's kind of lotion because their lotion was specifically designed to deal with that culture's kind of skin. When he was about to go on further about it, I told him I had to go, and I left without a good-bye when he gave me one which I sort of heard. He was one weird kid back then. I wonder if he still is . . . people do change . . . don't they? Yeah, people change. If people you know didn't change, wouldn't you find them a little boring?

Well, Nathen changed from weird to awkward . . . which I don't think is a very *good* or significant change but at least he says less weird stuff. Well, I wouldn't know that. I haven't talked to him in a while even after I met him again after so many years. Maybe I should call him right now. As I took out my cell phone, I realized I didn't have his number in my contacts, and it was written on a piece of paper somewhere at home. I put my cell phone away and turned to Janet's papers. No wonder why she procrastinated with her work; it was all so boring to read, and it was in small print. If I'm lucky, I can get half of it finished by the end of today if I don't go for coffee or bathroom breaks. Maybe life isn't so sweet anymore . . . a little bitter. Life is bittersweet.

Mitch~

I was still at the hospital. My wife was sleeping in a chair next to me, her head resting against my shoulders. I'd been briefly looking at my documents for work and just looking at Howard. The doctors said he was in a coma. He could wake up at anytime . . . in a few seconds, minutes, days . . . "soon" was the word I was looking forward to. From time to time, when my wife shifted her head to the pillow to her left, I stood up, stretched a little, and went up to Howard, scratching his head, kissing his forehead, and whispering for him to wake up. A few minutes ago, Mrs. Maybell called me telling me what exactly happened the day he got hit. She said he kicked a ball over the fence into the street, he jumped over the fence, and when he got to the ball, the car just . . . it stopped just inches away from him, but the car skidded and the bumper hit his head real hard. *Why the hell didn't you stop him?* I wanted to yell at her, but she said she didn't know about what had happened until she saw the kids gathered around the fence. Aren't teachers like her supposed to act as a babysitter for adults like me who have to work almost the entire day? I don't mean that in such an offensive sense, but back then, when I was in school, that was what it seemed like to me. Or were teachers like her there just to sit around and do whatever, say a few lines, feed them cheap food like stale animal crackers and wait until the parents came to pick them up? My cell phone rang.

"Hello?" I answered wearily, not having coffee for a while now. The time was about a little past one in the morning. Worrying kept me up through the night.

"Dad, is Howard okay?" I heard Monica sniffle.

"Um, I don't know . . . he's in a coma."

I heard her blow her nose and waited until she was done.

"Is Austin still there with you?" I asked.

"Yeah, he asked his mom if he could stay over for the night to, you know . . . cheer me up. She said yes. Is it okay if he stays over, Daddy?"

"Um, yeah. Sure. But why are you guys up so late?"

"I can't sleep, Dad. I just can't sleep when Howard is 'sleeping' like he is right now," she started to cry.

"I know; I . . . I can't either," I admitted.

"Is Mom okay?"

"Yeah, she's fine. She's resting."

"Dad, I hate to ask this but it's been stuck in my head for a while now and I can't get it out. Do you think Howard is going to be asleep forever?"

"Don't say that, Monica. Let's just hope for the best right now. Okay?"

"Fine."

The door opened as a doctor came in.

"Um, I'm gonna get off the phone now, sweetheart. The doctor just came in."

"Okay, bye, Dad."

"Bye."

I hung up the phone.

"Still in a coma, I see," the doctor pointed out the obvious as he looked over at his papers clipped to his clipboard. I didn't say anything.

I kept my hands in my pockets and waited for anymore words he had to say. "Well, I'll be taking an all-nighter too, like you," he told me. "Just ask the nurse for me if you need anything." Just as he was about to leave, he said, "You look like you could use a sponge bath. You want a sponge bath? It's free, no charge whatsoever."

"No, thank you, Doctor." I refused his strange offer.

"Yeah, I don't think I would want to take a sponge bath at the hospital either. To tell you the truth, we don't have very good soaps. It smells funny, and it makes you itchy, but it's good for you. Well, I'll be going now," he said, walking away.

"Bye," I said faintly.

Jessica~

Monday. Morning. Work. Dreadful. That was my rendition of my day in a wrap under five words or less. You can consider it a poem, or, better yet, a masterpiece. Everyone can relate to it, I know. Maybe you could add a "bleh" somewhere in there, so that it would make five words. Monday morning meetings today. I hate Monday morning meetings. I hate meetings in general. They're so boring; that's why I bring a pencil and notepad with me, sit in the far corner in the back, and write down my "cool" ideas for Korean dramas and cast people myself. I haven't really memorized the names of most Korean dramatists if you want to call 'em that . . . so, yeah, that's a big problem.

Big Idea!

boy meets girl

boy and girl get married

(insert few romantic scenes here)

boy cheats on girl for her sister

girl dies

boy devastated

girl's sister says 'don't worry about it baby; you have me to hold now'

that's all I have so far

Cast!

boy: can be that one cute guy with the short spiked-up hair with a nice four pack of abs

girl: can be that one skinny girl with her straight, brown hair that I want so badly and those pretty eyes

girl's sister: that one mean girl from that one Korean drama with the ass that that guy drools all over for and her amazing wardrobe

Okay, maybe the Korean drama writing/casting department isn't for me after all. I have to admit, solemnly, that was really bad and too short. I'm going swimming with Tiffany after work today. Maybe that'll make up for all the boredom today. After the meeting, I met up with Tiffany.

"Hey, Tiffany," I whispered to her.
"Yeah?" she answered.
"Um, I think I'm pregnant."
"HA-HA-HA-HA! WOW! REALLY!" Tiffany yelled out for the whole department to hear. Everyone popped their heads up from their cubicles like groundhogs do on *Groundhog Day*.
"I don't know for sure."
"Did you take a pregnancy test?"

"No, I have one, but I don't know. I don't really wanna find out, but then I do want to know. Ah! I'm confused whether there's a baby growing in my tummy or not." I stressed.

"Just take the test!"

"I'm scared," I whimpered, "I can't sleep at night. I lay on my couch every night and that thing, the box, the test, it just stares at me with its cardboard façade. It bothers me!"

"Do you want me to be there for you? To watch you pee on a plastic or digital stick?" she asked me. I didn't really know if she was being sarcastic enough because I was so confused.

Mark, a guy who works in numbers, walked up to me with a manila folder labeled "I like Mai Numbers." Mark was a bit of a crazy fellow who liked to bring goat milk from home in a brown homemade jug and kept it under his desk. Whenever he was thirsty, he'd take it from underneath his desk and drink away. One time, Tiffany dared me to ask him if the milk ever spoiled, and so I did. He said, "No, not unless you add some Indian spices to it, so it preserves its yummy taste." Now I couldn't tell if he was joking, nobody did, all because he was a bit whacky.

"Psst. Jessica." He spat on my face. I wiped my face clear of his spittle and continued to listen to his words. "Are you pregnant?" he asked out loud for the office to hear.

"Uh-Um, I don't know . . . yet . . ." I stuttered.

"Do you know how I know?"

"Um, no."

"Your boobs. It's your boobs that's giving it away. At first, I thought you were stuffing yourself with some soft tissues or something, but no. You're pregnant."

"You look at her boobs, Mark?" Tiffany yelled out.

"Who knocked you up?" Mark asked, ignoring Tiffany's question.

"This is all very personal, Mark. Could you please just go away?" I told him, tightening my fists.

"Do you look at my boobs too?" Tiffany yelled at him.

"Yeah, sure. I'll be going now. I need to give 'mai' numbers to Sherry."

"Yeah, you do that, Mark! Yeah, you better walk away, and you better not stare at our breasts or anybody's breasts in this office or I'm filing a complaint of sexual harassment, you sick pervert!" she completely screamed at him.

Maybe Mark is right. Maybe I am pregnant. My boobs . . . they are a bit . . . perkier, I guess. Maybe there is a baby boy/girl in my tummy, waiting to be born.

Nathen~

Katie drove Jordan Wong and me to the airport while her stereo blasted music from its speakers, and Jordan Wong was asleep. I couldn't understand how he could sleep with such loud music playing. Is it a gift he was born with? Or is it a skill he obtained through practice? Katie and I were discussing a few things of the past, and I frequently had to repeat my sentences for the music slightly gobbled up my words. When we reached to the entrance of the airport, I nudged Jordan Wong awake with my index finger and took our items from the back of Katie's car. She insisted that she would help, but I told her not to bother herself. As we rolled away with our suitcases, we waved good-bye to the beautiful Katie and started walking off. When the automatic doors opened, something or someone bumped into me and wrapped its or his or her arms around me. I didn't suspect such an act from Katie, but when I turned my head to find her hugging me, my heart just melted. After I found out from Jordan Wong that the hug between Katie and I was about ten seconds long, it felt like ten minutes. She then took out a small piece of paper out of her jeans pockets and slipped it in my slacks pockets.

"Promise you'll call, 'kay?" she said to me.
"Indeed, I promise." I smiled.

She said good-bye once again and ran off to her car and drove away as I watched her go. After we went through the long process of getting through security and getting our bags checked, we rested our legs on seats next to our plane. I wondered if I should have told one of the security guards that I had a bomb in one of my suitcases as a form of pastime amusement, but I knew I would be jumped if I had said so. Jordan Wong was on his PDA looking through his schedule.

"Your time's almost up, Jordan Wong," I told him.

"Yes, I . . . I'm going to be honest here and say this: I am going to miss you very much, Nathen. My experience with you has been very extraordinary and very different from my other clients. I got hurt . . . um, physically. I've never been physically assaulted during my work ever before," he said, starting to sniffle.

"Oh, don't cry, Jordan Wong. I hope we will keep in touch," I told him as I handed him my personal number in exchange for his. I wanted to pat his back as a friendly gesture, but resulted in shaking his right hand.

"I . . . I'm trying my hardest not to cry, Nathen," he started to sob. I gently placed my hand upon his back.

An elderly woman stopped herself in front of us, her cane in her hand, and insulted us with, "You communistic homosexuals" and walked away. She had somewhat of a manly voice. I was always intimidated by women with the voice of men. I also had phobias of not aggressive women, but masculine women. Something about a woman being buff makes me wonder if she can kill me with her bare hands.

"Would you like to celebrate our parting, Jordan Wong?" I asked him, removing my hand from his back.

"I'll pay," he said.

He took this very emotionally. I did not understand why he should, but I would accept it. When we got on the plane, a question popped into my head. It was one where I wanted Jordan Wong's answer.

LIFE'S MANIFESTO

"Jordan Wong, what were my chances of coming to Hawaii and ending up marrying Katie?" I asked him, looking sternly at him.

"Um, do you want an answer you'd like to hear or my personal opinion?" he asked.

"Your very own personal opinion." I smiled.

"A ratio or a percent of the chances?"

"I prefer percents."

"My personal opinion says 0.01 percent."

"That's almost zero percent. Why didn't you just say zero?"

"Because you love her."

So there I sat in my seat, thinking about what he said. He chuckled almost inaudibly and turned away from me, facing the window beside him, and we were up in the sky in minutes. Jordan Wong took out the professional camera I had given him, the one with all the pictures of Asian couples on them. I had asked Jordan Wong to mail me the pictures of various Asian couples when he got home, and he agreed saying that he wanted to save some of the pictures of Asian people he had taken himself. That was fine with me. A friendship of utility was this? Well, I wasn't expecting this relationship between us to become a friendship which he took it as. I had always thought of this as a business acquaintanceship. Should I take it as a friendship? I guess I should. I don't have many friends, but you don't need a lot of friends; you only need good ones. Afterward, when we got back to sweet California, home, a taxi took Jordan Wong home to drop off his baggage and drove him to the restaurant. A woman was waiting for him at a table instead of me. I was attending a different restaurant. Yes, she is a prostitute, but a *legal* prostitute, the same one he met on the boat back in Hawaii. It took a couple of hundreds of dollars to bring her over to California. I believe he would find it most appreciative. He would probably take the liberty in taking her home and having some fun with her. Dear lord, images of them performing passionate love are racing through my head. I need to digress from this. I picked up my glass of wine and took a sip and looked around the tables. So many people talking amongst the people at their tables. Me? I sat all by myself with a glass of wine, a basket of cold biscuits, and several napkins. I looked around the restaurant for people who were sitting by themselves. No one. No one in sight. I was the only one sitting by myself. From knowing that, I left the restaurant and took a stroll along the pier. I slipped my hands into my pocket and there, in the left pocket, I felt a piece of paper, and I pulled it out. I soon realized it was Katie's phone number. Would it be a good time to call right now? No, it was the same day. No need to call on the same day. Maybe in a few days, I'll pick up the phone and give a call. There was also another piece of paper in my pocket, my back pocket to be precise. I unfolded it and it read, "Katie, I love you." Stupid of me! Why on earth did I write such a thing? Even though I hate being honest to myself when it comes to love, I know I don't have a chance with her. I crumpled the piece of paper and attempted to throw it out into the salty, ocean water, but I failed, and it landed somewhere in the rocks where many seagulls had pooped upon, and numerous crabs had crawled upon. Maybe a seagull or crab will take a stab at it and drift away, somewhere far from here and land somewhere where a different Katie will think someone out there truly loves her, placing the crumpled, wet piece of paper to her heart, when I don't admire her in any way, me being the one who wrote the daft message. This is all "crazy" talk. I am crazy. I took a taxi home and spent the night in bed staring at the ceiling and at my wall of many Asian couples. I was anxious about receiving new photos to post up upon this great wall. It was a great way to spend your time when you're laying in bed—to have a ceiling above you where it squeaks for every time those adolescent hooligans dance their night away like right now and the millions of Asian eyes, which all appear to be in a squinting form, staring back at you as you stare at them with the only two that you own unless you wear glasses when you go to bed and count your glasses as another pair of eyes.

Mitch~

I hugged him so hard. I kissed his forehead and just cried. I cried so hard, just as hard at my dad's funeral. Leslie went about screaming in joy and relief.

"Daddy, you hurting me!" Howard cried out, yawning.

"Ha-ha-ha, I'm so sorry," I said, pulling away from him, scratching his head.

Leslie picked him up and hugged him tightly, allowing him to take a look at the view through the hospital window. We were on the highest floor, so he was pretty excited. Ah, I'm so relieved! God, I'm so glad he's okay. I called for the doctor, and he congratulated me and walked us out of the hospital. We thanked him and drove back home where we found Austin and Monica still sleeping. Austin was sleeping on the floor and Monica in her bed. When I called Monica up, she screamed when she saw Howard and hugged him to death like me and Leslie did. Through the loud screams projected from Monica, Austin was still asleep. Monica quickly ran over to him and started kicking him in the sides and finally in the groin, and he woke up immediately.

"Ow! What the freak was that for, Monica?" he yelled tiredly at her.

She just kept screaming and pointed at Howard, jumping up and down.

"Oh, hey, there buddy," Austin welcomed him back, giving him those "cool" handshake kids do these days.

It was nice, relieving to see Howard at home. Leslie called the school saying Howard would be absent for a few days as she stuffed him with a bunch of junk food, my kind of diet. Hey, I could survive off junk food. Potato chips, soda, ice cream . . . you got yourself a complete diet of vegetables and calcium . . . soda? I'm not exactly sure how that'll benefit me in a healthy way, but still, it tastes GOOD. I mean, come on, who hasn't drank soda before? Everyone has, right? Soda is a universal beverage. A person has *at least* once gulped a soda before.

Jessica~

Okay, all I have to do is confront the box, open it up, take out the stick, and pee on it. Simple as that. I need to show the damn thing who's boss. I'm boss. The box isn't boss. I am. Yeah . . . okay. I walked over to the counter where the box was sitting, waiting for me. I downed a bottle of water before I tore the box apart with my wonderful Wonder Woman masculinity. I took the stick and ran to the bathroom. Okay, all I need to do is pee on it. I'm almost done with this process! No, I can't! I'm still scared. Okay . . . okay . . . going to pee on it . . . relieving myself at the moment here . . . and done. Okay, now I wait for the results . . . plus or minus . . . addition or subtraction . . . I waited for a few minutes, staring out my bathroom window to pass the time. There was an old woman pushing a cart of aluminum cans and plastic bottles. Poor her, if that was her occupation, her way of making a living, I should give her my cans and bottles, yet I recycle bottles and cans to make little money too, a side occupation, so I don't think I can sacrifice my cans or bottles . . . okay maybe one or two . . . no, one or two bottles make a difference; it's like ten or twenty cents of a difference right there, and that's a BIG difference right there, but only when you're referring to the subject of recycling bottles or cans. You can't apply the BIG difference rule to anything else like going to the movies or eating out at a restaurant. "Oh, it's only ten cents more, no big deal," you could say when buying popcorn or a movie ticket or "No problem, just twenty cents more," when it comes to the price of the bill, but when recycling pops up, "Whoa, twenty cents? Now that's a HUGE difference." You could apply the rule to gas money as well. Yeah, well, that's what I put my faith into. I snapped out of my beliefs and looked at the plastic stick. No, this is wrong. It doesn't even look like a plus sign. It looks like a freakin' division sign! What's a division sign supposed to mean? No, this can't be; I'm not pregnant. This thing is messed up, broken. I'll go out and buy another one . . . now, yes, now. I ran out of the bathroom and to my car, driving all the way down to a Wal-Mart. When I was about ready to pay when I was at the cashier, the person behind their little counter tried not to laugh.

"Hey, dude, what's so funny?" I fired at the guy.

"Nothin'," he smirked.

"I should just shove this plastic stick up your . . . how much . . ." I grumbled.

"You could have it for free if you stick it up my ass real nice," he retorted.

"I won't even want to use it after I stick it up there, jerk," I said to him, as I pulled out a five dollar bill, glancing at the price label of the item. "Keep the change, you filthy animal!" I yelled at him and ran to my car. Oh, I made a *Home Alone* reference! Ha-ha! Oh my gosh, I used to love that movie! I need to watch it again sometime soon. Okay, no time to laugh or think about good movies; this is serious business here. As soon as I entered my apartment, I just realized, I'm just being ridiculous. I know it's not a division sign, it's a plus sign . . . even if it looks like a division sign. Face it, I am pregnant. There was no use in buying another pregnancy test and no point for wasting five dollars—a waste of breath for messing with the stupid college prick behind the counter. I closed the door behind me and took a seat on the couch, tossing the test beside me. I yelled at my television screen because it wasn't working, and it was a lousy piece of broken junk. I didn't know why I did so until I realized I didn't even turn it on. Great, now I'm pregnant *and* crazy.

Mitch~

As I was working on a few documents on the computer, Monica knocked on my door, and after a few minutes of typing, I finally acknowledged her presence.

"Am I invisible to you or something?" she rhetorically asked me with a sense of sarcasm in her tone, her hands on her hips.

"Sorry. What's up?" I asked her, leaning back and spinning in my revolving chair with my hands behind my head.

"Can I go to homecoming?"

"With whom?"

"Ugh, you already know who!"

"Uh . . . no I don't," I told her.

"Austin!"

"Okay, yeah, sure."

"And you're paying right?"

"How much?"

"It's like sixty buck," she said casually.

"What? Sixty bucks? You think I'm going to pay for a sixty-dollar dance for you?"

"Okay, fine . . . it's not sixty."

"Okay, good . . ."

"It's ninety."

"What?"

"Plus gas money if you wanna include that."

"No, I am not going to pay ninety dollars, sweetie. No."

"Dad, it'll make up for my lousy birthday present."

"You're right. Okay, fine."

"Thank you, Daddy!" she exclaimed, literally pouncing on top of me to give me a hug.

"Yeah, yeah, yeah, you're welcome."

After a few minutes of finishing up a few more documents, I ran into the kitchen to get a drink of water, and there, standing by the counter tapping her fingers against the granite counter, my wife looked at me.

"Yeah?" I asked.

"I think it's time you told her," Leslie said.

"Told her what?"

"You know, the 'talk.'"

"What 'talk?'" I mocked her with her little air quotes.

"You know what I'm talking about! You know, the birds and the bees talk."

"Um, I think that's your job, Leslie," I told her, my arms folded across my chest, leaning against a wall.

"Go up there and talk to her!" my wife demanded.

"No! You!"

"Mitch, go!"

"Leslie, go!" I mocked her again.

"Mitch, you better go on the count of three or else I'm going to give you the slapping of a lifetime."

"Why can't you go?" I asked her, taking a sip of water from the water bottle on the counter.

"One . . . two . . ."

"Okay! Okay! All right, I'll go. Sheesh, since when did you become my mother?" I said, climbing up the stairs. While I was heading toward her door, I was wondering how I would word this "talk." God, so uncomfortable . . . I was hesitant to knock at her door when finally, I sort of knew how to say this.

"Come in," she called from her desk.

"Hey there, Monica," I said.

She finished typing something up and twirled around in her chair and said, "What's up?"

"Take a seat," I told her as I sat down on her bed. Her sheets were so soft. They were softer than mine. Did I buy these sheets for her? Huh, weird, why didn't I buy some more for myself?

"Dad . . . I am sitting," she told me.

"Oh, right. That's good." I clasped my hands together and rubbed them. "So whatchya doin'?"

"Um, chatting online with some friends, reading stuff. Why?"

"Are they friends from school?"

"Yeah."

"Whatchya readin'?"

"Just stuff."

"Good stuff?"

"Good as in worth reading or good as in beneficiary for me educationally or religiously?"

"Never mind."

"Dad, don't you have better things to do than small talk with me?" she asked me, crossing her arms over her chest.

"Oh, I just needed to talk to you about something," I told her, adjusting myself on her bed.

"Sure, hit me," she said leaning back in her chair.

"Well, okay, when a woman loves a man very, very much, they . . ."

"Dad, I will not have this talk with you," she said, turning away from me and went back to her business.

"Okay. Good. And if your mom asks if you had the 'talk,' please say you did. 'Kay?"

"Sure thing, Dad."

"Okay," I said walking out of her room.

When I came back down to finish up my documents, Leslie was sitting in my chair, looking up at me. "Did you have the talk?" she asked me.

"Yeah, done and done," I said, kissing her cheek as she got up and left. "Sucker," I murmured under my breath as she walked away.

Andy~

Well, if I heard correctly, Janet took an absence forever. Yep, she quit, and all her Yoda merchandise was being boxed up and sent to her door. She didn't want to pick up the boxes herself, so she sent some Hispanic movers to do it for her. She said she was too embarrassed and ashamed to come back to the workplace. I couldn't blame her. I would feel the same way too. The branch and I had a quick meeting in the conference room, and you know what? A drum roll performed by a huge group of drum lines should be playing right now because . . . I WAS PROMOTED TO HEAD OF THE OFFICE! Yep, I'm the boss now, and it's good to be the "king." I moved myself into Janet's room which means good-bye cubicle and dull walls and hello comfy chairs and bigger space. To be the nice guy that I am, I gave George my cubicle which was slightly bigger than his, and he accepted, and from there, everyone moved cubicles throughout the week. I was happy, and so was everyone else. Life is no longer bittersweet, but totally sweet right now.

So now that I'm here enjoying myself with a mug of warm coffee that I made myself with a coffee maker I put in my office, spinning around in this amazing swiveling chair, I kind of miss Janet. I miss her voice, her leaping from desk to desk swaying her green lightsaber around, knocking off mugs of pencils, papers, and sometimes even computers off our desks as if they were the evil, annoying droids. I missed her absurdity. I knew I should have recorded her in some way, shape, or form as a memory, so that I could prove to my wife that my boss was a complete nut job. I wonder where she works now. She's probably working at another office not far from here sharing with everyone her amazing impersonations of Yoda and having lightsaber fights with a *Star Wars* geek somewhere down in the supply room. There's always a *Star Wars* geek in the office. Always. You just have to find them. There's probably one lurking around here somewhere on this floor or another.

When I got home, Austin ran up to me and asked, "Dad, can I go to homecoming?"
"Ah! Who's the lucky lady?" I asked him.
"It's Monica, duh . . ." he grumbled.
"Oh yeah, right . . . sure thing," I agreed, patting him on the back.
"Yesh! Thanks Dad!" he exclaimed, running up to his room.

In the living room, I found little Sarah drawing a picture and a ton of other drawings all around the floor.

"Don sep!" she pouted, raising her hand in front of her face. "Stop!"

I looked down at the pictures, all of them almost exactly the same. All of them were a picture of us standing in front of our house. It was funny the way Sarah drew Austin and I. Austin was a little bigger and a little taller than me. I secretly took one, the one that looked the best as far as I could point out, while she was quietly concentrating on her like fiftieth picture of the same drawing. Lisa wouldn't be home until a few hours, so I spent my time working out. Yeah, need to get in shape before the next soccer game between Mitch and I, so I could whoop his ass again. The last time I went for an exercise was when I went with Jessica. I told

Austin to watch the house while I was gone and left the house, running around the neighborhood and the park a couple of times.

When I got home, really exhausted, I found a cold bottle of water waiting for me in the kitchen—good, I didn't really feel like getting one myself—with a small post-it note on it. I tore it off and it read, "Turn around." When I did, Lisa went for my lips and kissed me.

"Guess what?" she asked me.
"What?" I said, opening the water bottle and chugging it, waiting for her to tell me.
"I got a bonus!" she yelled jumping up and down and hugged me. "Ewww, you're all sweaty!" she said, backing away from me, attempting to brush away my sweat off her clothes.
"Oh, sorry, ha-ha. I went for a run. But that's awesome, Lisa!"
"Let's go out, just the two of us. Sound good?"
"The kids?" I brought up.
"I'll have Monica baby-sit. I'm sure she would accept because of you know who."
"Ah, smart. Okay, sounds good."
"All right!"

So we went off to a movie, then a restaurant, and then to my office where you could see the entire city alive at night with all of its lights. Yeah, I know, a little lame. The only person there was George, like always, madly typing away as if he was angry or something.

"Hey, Andy? That your honeybunch?" he asked me, stepping out of his new cubicle.
"Yeah, this is my wife, Lisa." I introduced to him.
"Nice to meet you, George," my wife greeted with a handshake.
"Ha-ha, we're all Asian here, you could bow," he said.
"Well, um, okay," Lisa said and did so. It was a bit awkward.
"Well, I'll give you two some privacy and leave for home. Okay?"
"Okay, thanks, George," I said.

"And I have some blankets and some pillows under my desk if you're interested in using them. Just don't forget to wash 'em when you're done with 'em."

"Oh no. No! We're not here to do that, George," I told him.

"Ah, okay. Well, you two have a good night," he said, walking away.

When we waited for him to go inside the elevator, go all the way down to the parking lot, and drive away, Lisa said, "Oh my gosh, you were right; he is weird."

"Ha-ha, I know, but he usually keeps quiet."

We looked out at the view, my arm around her. Then I led her out to the top of the building where the chilly air allowed me to place my jacket around her, and there, we embraced the city's lights, the full moon, and the cool, crisp air. I doubt there was a sign of pollution in the air I was breathing in, and for every breath I took made it more exhilarating to be on top of the building, the highest corporate buildings in the city. Lisa said the thing that always made me smile, "Andy, I love you." I kissed her forehead and replied with an "I love you too." After a few more minutes of embracement, we went back down to my office floor and said, "Oh, I almost forgot to tell you."

"What?" she asked.

"I wanna show you my office."

"Well, okay."

We walked into Janet's old room and she asked, "Aha, Andy, did you get promoted?"

"Yep." I smiled, my hands in my pocket.

She let out a scream and hugged me so tightly that I was about to fall to the floor, dragging her down with me. There we lay, on the floor of my office, almost asleep. I let her sleep for a couple of minutes as soon as I finished Janet's old documents and woke her up, telling her we needed to go home. She wouldn't budge, so I had to pick her up and haul her to the car. I accidentally let a wall hit her head, and she responded with a weak and tired "Ow"; her w's trailing off for a minute or two. I called

Mitch to pick up her daughter, and Monica was a bit depressed that she had to leave so early.

"Monica, you stayed here for about five hours. I don't think you can consider your stay short," I told her.
"Oh, why does your son have to be so adorable?" she asked me, giggling afterward as Austin stayed behind in the corner, blushing. I laughed and didn't say a word. I waited in the living room with Monica who was listening to her iPhone, the one Austin had given her. Mitch came after about a solid ten minutes and told Monica to wait in the car.
"But can't I wait with Austin upstairs while you two flirt? I mean, flirting is a healthy way of developing and enhancing your little '*bro*-mance' you two have kept for a while," Monica asked.
"No, in the car, Monica," Mitch told her.
"I know, I know, I was just joking . . ." she said irately.
"You know she's going to homecoming with Austin, right?" Mitch asked me as we both watched her walk out to his car.
"And you know he's going to homecoming with Monica, right?" I fired back.
"Do you find it weird that our kids are dating each other?"
"Just a little. You think it's weird?"
"Of course, I do! I mean, what if they get married, Andy? We would be related."
"What are the odds that they'll get married? Come on, totally unrealistic . . . well, I can't say it's unrealistic because of you and Leslie . . ."
"I don't know . . . but it's still weird."
"Yeah, well, okay. I need to hit the bed. I'm beat."
"Yeah, okay, I'll catch you later."
"All right, night," I told him, walking him out the door.
"Night," he replied walking out to his car.

I hopped into bed with Lisa who was fast asleep. I was about ready to close my eyes. Ah, could life be any better for me?

Jessica~

I can't sleep and can't handle the fact that I'm pregnant when I'm about ready to go to bed. The fact that the baby would be born without a father just breaks my darn little heart. I don't want him/her to live without a father, and if I told him/her what his/her father was like, I don't think he/she would take it too well; he/she would be scarred. Yeah, I checked my e-mail and found proof, solid proof that Freddy was cheating on me. It explained why he didn't pick up his phone, why he didn't call, and why he went off for "long business trips." God, I'm so stupid. I don't really think I have the money or the time to actually take care of a little baby. Wait . . . what? What am I saying? What kind of a parent says that? Well, um, I guess I'm trying to say that I'm not really ready to be a parent, a mother yet. I need help.

So now, I've been eating, well, stuffing myself with a whole bunch of eggs, yogurt, cottage cheese, and anything else that's considered healthy for this baby jiggling in my tummy, and it feels good not watching my weight and eating like a pig, a healthy pig.

Nathen~

Well, I had no other objectives in life other than keep myself busy till the day I die. So I drove out to the Chinese man and his hot dog stand. It was sometime between 12:00 p.m. and 1:00 p.m., and I was a bit hungry.

"I'd like to order four boxes of your orange chicken, please," I told him, flipping out my wallet.
"You? You. You! I almost go out of business because you!" he scolded me.
"Sorry, I was enjoying a little vacation," I told him, apologizing.
"Well, good thing you come back. I almost lose apartment, hot dog stand, and twin-headed goats!" he shouted at me.

"Well, I am quite sorry to hear that."

I went off carrying four boxes of hot orange chicken in my arms. I hopped in my car and traveled my way to UCLA, found a parking spot, and took a stroll on the beautiful campus with my four boxes. On my way, I picked up three random students whose expressions that told me I was some crazy person. I told them I was a professor, and it is true, I *was* a professor on these school grounds. I took them to one particular bench where I had used to have lunch. Three students, one was a white female, another was a black male, and the last was an Asian male. All looked like geeks but our future successful doctors/engineers. I handed them a box of orange chicken and three pairs of chopsticks. I opened my box and dug right in.

"Go on, eat," I told them with my mouth full.

They opened their boxes and ate right away except for the Asian male.

"Young man, why aren't you eating your orange chicken? I would say it is the best of Los Angeles has to offer," I told him.
"Um, I'm a vegetarian," he told me, handing me his box.
"Well, your loss," I said, offering it to the other two students who happily accepted with their empty stomachs. "Do you have something in your little bag you could munch on right now?"
"Um, yes, yes, I do."
"Then why don't you whip that out and fulfill your stomach."
"I'm not that hungry, sir, but thank you."
"Well, your loss, again."
"Why are we here, sir?" the white female asked me.
"You are here, with me, to talk, to have an interrogation of getting to know you all better. Don't worry. Your professors won't mind your absence. I have good ties with all of them. Well, okay, shall we begin?"

They nodded their heads and continued with their Asian cuisine.

"Well, we'll start with you," I said, pointing at the white female. "You will be person A." I went further explaining that the black student was person B and the Asian male was person C which was all funny because they all had ties with their chosen letter. Like the Caucasian female, the first letter of her name began with an 'A' and the African American student, well, um, he was black and was person B. Black . . . B . . . do you see the connection? The Asian male was Chinese . . . and person C . . . I think you can find it obvious from there . . . Chinese . . . person C . . . No? Don't get it? Well, it certainly appealed to me in an amusing form.

"What are your religious views?" I asked person A.

"Well, I like Jesus . . . a lot. I mean, I have a whole bunch of pastel paintings of him up in my dorm room. I have about fifty? Yeah, fifty pastels of Jesus in there, and I have some back at home with my parents. Most of them I buy from random places like Michigan, Utah, and Mexico, places like that, and some of them, I paint myself. I'm a Christian, by the way," she explained.

"And what is it that you like about Jesus Christ?" I asked her.

"I don't know. I just like Jesus! I like him a lot! Like, he's a good role model for kids . . . of all ages! For adults too! I think it's his beard that appeals to me the most . . . I like his beard. You can like take Jesus' beard and use it as a sweater, and Jesus will make you feel warm internally and externally. It sure looks like you could keep yourself warm with it. His beard reminds me of my uncle's beard . . . and my uncle does look a lot like Jesus, so I like him too, but he's a biker and smells funny all the time when he comes to Thanksgiving dinners. I guess you can say he's a Jesus on wheels, am I right?" she laughed to herself. The rest of us didn't care to laugh with her. "And yeah. That's all I have to say."

"Person B, your religious views?" I turned to him.

"Well, I am a Jew, and, of course, the rest of my family are Jews. And the past, I've had a terrible past, my ancestors as well because they were Jews, and it seems nobody likes the Jews, and they were black and nobody seemed to like the blacks. And . . ."

"If you are at all offended by the way you say 'black,' you have the freedom to be politically correct and call yourself an African American." I interrupted.

"No, I'm fine callin' myself black, sir," he explained.

"Then you may continue."

"And yeah, nobody liked the Jews or the blacks. 'Who stole the plate of butter?' Blame it on the blacks. 'Who caused the death of one-third of Europe's population?' Blame it on the Jews. 'Who took this baby's candy?' Blame it on the blacks. 'Who was it that killed Francis II of France?' It was the Jew's evil juju. Yeah, bad past, and my family celebrate both Hanukah and Kwanza."

"How did you become a Jew, may I ask?"

"Well, there are some things the history books don't teach you. There was this group of Jews that either persecuted or converted non-Jews. And my family became vulnerable and became Jews that way."

"Um . . . quite interesting. Person C, would you like to share your religious views?"

"Well," he began with a whisper, looking around to see if anybody was watching him or eavesdropping on this conversation, "I was originally a Buddhist, but now I'm a Scientologist. First, they got my grandparents, then my mom and dad, and finally me. I'm telling you, they completely brainwash you and make you pay so much money just for these 'sessions.' And they have the power to blackmail me, so I can't really escape. Please, I need help. I need out," he whispered to us as we remained silent.

"Well, now, may we digress to another question? I think that would be most comfortable," I started.

"I need out, man! Out!" he shouted into my face, grabbing my collar, wrinkling it. Absolutely wonderful, wrinkled. You know, I just had this ironed last night. Oh, well. "Oh no, you see, you see that man over there with the suit and the dark sunglasses? He's obviously a Scientologist," he pointed to a man with a briefcase, casually walking over to a room. "He's a watcher; he's watching me. He's been following me since last Monday."

"Um, what is one of the happiest moments of your life?" I asked Person A.

"Well, the happiest moment of my life was when I painted my first picture of Jesus after taking four months of art classes. I . . . I, to be honest, I *almost* cried, no, okay, I cried. I have it framed and hanged in my bedroom back home, and I have a copy of it also framed and hanged in my dorm room. I just love it because it means so much to me, and

Jesus means so much to me. He's like . . . I consider him my second dad." Person A said, letting out a long sigh afterward.

"Please! Help me!" Person C shouted out from behind Person A and Person B.

"Um, Person B? Care to share?" I asked.

"Well, I have to say, the happiest moment of my life was when I got my first actual toy. As a young boy, I never actually had anything to play with, absolutely nothing. And um . . ."

"It's okay to cry and let yourself out, Person B," I told him.

"Um, thank you. And um, it was a dreidel, and I absolutely loved it. I just loved it," he started to cry. "We . . . we're basically dirt poor, and um, I just, I was very thankful."

"Um, Person C, would you like to share your happiest moment in life?"

"Hasn't happened yet. Not yet. Nope. It happens when I die, break free from the Church of Scientology."

"Okay, Person C, I think we have had enough of your . . . how about you take a deep breath and calm yourself down with some nice, orange protein. Sound good?"

"I . . . I . . . I'm sorry. Well, okay. Fine, then I think I'll leave then. I'll just take this orange chicken with me and go. Well, I will say good-bye now. Good-bye." He bowed walking away.

"Well, that was quite eccentric," I stated as they nodded their heads in agreement.

Then we heard screaming and found it to be coming from Person C who was running around, stripping himself and went his way until he was the size of a piece of pocket lint from our point of view.

"The world sure is one crazy place," Person B said.
"You could say that again," Person A laughed.
"The world sure is one crazy place."

It was quiet after he repeated his belief in the world as we looked a yonder at his clothes on the ground.

"I like his boxers." Person A laughed.

"I have the same pair." Person B revealed.

"Oh, really? That's cool. Where'd you buy it?"

"Abercrombie and Fitch. I bought it in Vegas. It's about eighteen dollars. A little expensive if you ask me, but they're good. The quality of the undergarment is nice and comfortable, and I like it."

"Moving on, what was one of your depressing moments in life?"

"My most depressing moment in life," Person B began, "was when my father died. He got shot by some white folks. My father was the engine of my family; he kept it movin' and protected us real good. He always wanted me to go to a good school like this one, and I did. I'm sort of surprised of how I got here; good grades. It took me all my life, all my hard work to get up to this point," he cried. I handed him a tissue to blow his nose in and told him he could keep it, and if he wanted anymore, I would be happy enough to give him more. They were finished with their boxes of orange chicken, and I threw them away as they told their stories.

"My saddest moment in life was when my family and I spent a whole lot of money on my new baby sister who was still in my momma's belly, you know for a new crib and clothes and stuff like that. But then . . . then . . . you see, it was a miscarriage. We didn't know why or how it happened, even the doctors didn't know why, and I just cried and cried that day, the day we buried the baby in the back of our house, not really the backyard of the house, but there's a cemetery behind the house, and we buried her there. I know it ain't such a pleasant idea to have a house next to a land full of dead people, but we bought that particular house because it was really cheap," she said with a heavy southern accent that I have never heard from her before. Maybe she only had that accent when she cried. I also handed her a tissue.

"Well, I hope I have tried to make you feel emotional, well, it is quite obvious I have since I reduced you to tears in an inoffensive and nonharassing way unless you consider me randomly interrogating you as some sort of personal threat, and if so, I apologize. That was my objective. Now would you like to hear my story?" I asked them. They nodded their heads yes as they sniffled, and I told them. I told them what had happened to my family and how I made money and my recent experience at the lovely islands of Hawaii. At first, they thought I was lying like I was retelling some sort of big screen mellow-drama, but then they believed me after studying my face. Then I left, with a little good-bye. Why did I do this? Mainly because I was drowning in boredom, and I had nothing better to do. But I also learned a few things about random college students and appreciated their cooperation with me . . . except for maybe Person C. I had always feared what happens to people like Person C. I had always been afraid of being brutally interrogated by a Scientologist, tied to a chair with duct tape under dim lighting making the interrogator seem more mysterious and eerie. "What are you afraid of?" they would shout into my face, and I would be sitting there, unable to wipe the little bit of their saliva on my face. "Well," I would start, "I am afraid of you, obviously, because you are such a demanding and authoritative figure I am guessing by the sound of your tone. I don't really do well with blunt authority; it makes me nervous. You're making me nervous right now, and I believe it would help if you just tweak down the bluntness and just keep the authority, and I'll be in a much more relaxing state of nervousness. I also fear being stuck in a cramped room full of drag queens because I am a wee bit claustrophobic, and I do fear men in heavy makeup and fraud bosoms. I really do! I am really being honest here because honesty *is* the best policy, am I correct?" I would chortle nervously. He would spend a few seconds circling around me, his head down, his eyes covered by black sunglasses for a reason I do not understand. There was dim lighting; why would he need sunglasses? Maybe I should be a little more objective; maybe his eyes are highly sensitive to light. His hands would be clamped behind his back as he walked with small strides and quiet footsteps that made tension grow. This whole thing this Scientologist was doing to me would be unbearable, absolutely unbearable. I found all of this horrifying. "What are your crimes?" he would then shout into my face. "Y . . . You se . . . sound mad. Please don't get mad at me. Well, I . . . I, well okay, I'll admit," I would start, "I once stole a Klondike bar from my teacher's mini refrigerator because I was hungry and didn't have the opportunity to have a decent breakfast or lunch, and it was the last class of the day, and it was hot, brutally hot, the day almost near summer. Pigeons roasted in the sky and fell to the frying ground, and . . . and ice cubes skipped a stage in matter and just evaporated into the air. My biggest crime of all time:

I steal money from people in order to live, to survive! I have tried about fifty times to get a job and each and every one of them failed . . . failed . . . failed. I can't get a job; it's very difficult. But you have to understand that I come from an Asian background, and it makes it unacceptable for me to go out and get a job at a McDonald's or be the person that sits out in the sun all day twirling signs for what? Fifteen bucks an hour? No, highly unacceptable. Members of the Asian community would frown upon me from their cars and shake their heads in shame saying to themselves, 'You make us look bad.' and give me this dirty look. I . . . I couldn't. I could never do that. I'm sorry." Hopefully they would let me leave eventually and not let me die in this room of dim lighting. They would open the door for me, ripping the duct tape off me. "You are free to go," they would say to me, and I would reply with, "I have nothing against your religion or the Church of Scientology, really, I accept all religions; I don't really like to hate because I'm afraid of people opinionating me of what I hate. I hope you do understand that. Okay, well, have a nice day," I would say and go my merry way back to stealing money from people's pockets.

Jessica~

Ugh . . . I feel absolutely sick eating all this crap. My tummy's been getting a lot bigger as I sit around most of the time watching lame Japanese soap operas. I've been going to the restroom a lot which is a hassle. I have to get up, wobble all the way over to the stinkin' bathroom and dispose of my waste. Might as well just eat and watch my soap operas in the bathroom. I could sit on the toilet seat, but sitting on that isn't too comfortable if you spend a lot of time on it. Your butt aches after like half an hour if you do so. Yes, I have spent thirty minutes in the bathroom before. It was because I was reading a book, you know, to pass the time, and the thing just got me hooked and I ended up getting engrossed and read and read. I finally stopped when I reached to the end of a few chapters when the story was going bland. So now I'm considering whether or not to get a seat cushion for my toilet seat, but I'm afraid it might get dirty. And I want a seat warmer for my seat especially in the mornings when you have to poop or pee in the mornings, and when you sit down on it, it sends chills all across my body. Anyways, I have a human being growing inside of my stomach right now! Okay, that was unnecessary and uncalled for . . . sorry, I've been a bit moody . . . must be a side effect from being pregnant. If my mom was here with me, in my apartment, she would say something along the lines of "Now you know how I feel." But I love my mom. Just a few months ago, when I only looked fat and *not* pregnant, I went to my cousin's party. It was a pretty interesting visit, and I didn't want to add anymore interest to it by saying I was pregnant. That day, I found out that three of my uncles went for a beer at a bar without knowing it was *gay* bar, two of my aunts drink egg yolks for breakfast, lunch, and dinner during private settings such as at home, and that Mark, the freak, from work is half-Hispanic. Tiffany text-messaged me that. I sort of had fun. I caught up with news with relatives about other relatives and got to play tag with the cousins and nephews . . . even if I may be a grown woman. But I stopped halfway through the game because I didn't think it would be too good for the baby. Hmm . . . I wonder what I would name him/her . . .

The doorbell snapped me out of my state of flashbacks, and I walked over to the door. It was probably just Mrs. Pritz asking about her lost cat again. She's been bugging me about it. "Have you seen my cat? Have you seen my cat?" I would mock her after I told her no in a high-pitched tone. Sometimes, my voice cracks when I say it. Sometimes, I don't even know which cat she's missing because you see she also refers to her husband as a cat. Sometimes, I see her husband on top of the roof licking the back of his hand or walking in the middle of the street on his hands and knees in the middle of the night when there aren't a lot of cars . . . when he would be more likely not to get hit by a car. But most of the time she asks for her real cat, the one with four legs and a tail . . . not the one with two legs, two hands, and a huge ass. The two of them have like some kind of disorder. I opened the door to find him.

"Hey Jessica! I'm back from my business trip!" Freddy exclaimed.
"Oh . . . Freddy . . . you didn't get my message?" I asked him.
"What message?"

"The one where I said this whole thing going on between us isn't going to work out?"

"What? Why? Of course, it's going to work out. What are you talking about?" he raised his voice.

I quickly slammed the door in his face and locked it before he could come inside and start yelling at me. I didn't need this. I went back to my place on the couch and just laid my fancy little head on a pillow, Nathen's pillow to be exact. Just when I was about to close my eyes and probably sleep through the rest of the day, Freddy was pounding on the door. I quickly rose up and stared at the door. God . . . if he continues this, the door is going to break down. My weak door isn't meant to be pounded on; it's meant to be knocked on *gently*.

"Open up! Open up!" he started yelling.

"Leave me alone Freddy!" I yelled at the door, stuffing my head into the pillow, but he kept pounding the door. Should I call the cops or something? No, I can't. I don't want to cause a scene; the neighbors would think differently of me. From sweet, happy Jessica to some trouble-maker. Ugh, why can't he stop? "Go away, Freddy!"

"Did Nathen tell you? Did that bastard tell you? I told him not to tell!" he started punching the door, and if I heard correctly, I think he was crying as well.

"Don't forget that that *bastard* paid for the wedding ring you gave me, Freddy! He has a better heart than you! He doesn't go around telling his fiancé that he's on a business trip when he's actually going to see another woman, a *woman* that you're married to! You're the freakin' bastard, Freddy! You are!" I yelled at the door, a little closer than before. I was going to add more about how he got me pregnant and how the child would hate him, but I couldn't say more, I just couldn't. I looked at him through my teary eyes in the little peephole. He was on the ledge, both of his hands gripping the iron bars with his head down. I watched him walk away. He didn't look up, he didn't say anything, and he just walked back to his car and drove out of the parking lot. I began to cry, slamming my back against the door and sliding down to the floor. For the rest of the day, instead of sleeping as I had planned, I just cried my eyes out right by that door.

Mitch~

Tonight's the night Monica heads off to homecoming with Austin. I had to drive Monica over to Andy's house where the limo was waiting for them. One of Andy's cousins was a limo driver and did this for them for free . . . they should consider themselves lucky because when I went to homecoming with Leslie, my mom took me, and before I left the car, my mom kissed me good-bye. Yeah, Leslie did laugh at me afterward . . . and told other people about it . . . completely embarrassing.

"Here we are," I told her as I parked in Andy's driveway and as she was texting away on her phone.
"Okay, thanks, Dad. Um, how do I look?" she asked me.
"You look amazing." I smiled.
"Thanks, Dad," she said, giving me a quick hug and running off to Austin in her high heels.

For me, I get to stay over at Andy's and watch the soccer game. After Andy's cousin was done driving them over to the school, he was going to join us. I don't know what it is about beer and popcorn, but it gave me one hell of a stomach ache. I felt sick and couldn't really focus on the game. It was a good game too, it was . . .

"Hey, Mitch, you don't look too good." Andy brought up, taking a sip from his beer.
"No, I'm all right," I lied, rubbing my eyes.

He went back to the game, cheering as Korea . . . oh god . . . I thrust myself to the right on the couch and hurled on Andy's floor. Damn it . . . how freakin' embarrassing. When I was about to get up and clean it up,

Andy got up from the couch and said, "Don't worry about it Mitch, I got it."

"No, I'll get it," I coughed into my sleeve. Honestly, I didn't want him cleaning up my puke. I don't think you should let other people clean up your own puke. So I grabbed some paper towels and cleaned the place up with the aid of some carpet removal materials and such.

"You sure you're okay?" he asked me.

"Lesson learned; my stomach just can't handle beer and popcorn at the same time," I told him.

We continued watching the game, Andy to the right of me, keeping a close eye on me. God, this was so embarrassing. Because I ate popcorn and drank beer, and for the record, I am an occasional drinker and throw it all up, I'm being babysat by his eyes. I should just go, but I can't; I have to wait until midnight, the time Monica gets back. So when the game was over, which was not disappointing at all—an awesome game with Korea winning and Greece losing. We we're going to rent a movie but we had a pretty heavy debate on what kind of movie to rent. I was in the mood for an action because I was pretty pumped up and feeling alive after hurling, Andy was in the mood for a horror, and his cousin was in the mood for a romantic comedy. His cousin said watching those kinds of movies gets him the ladies . . . I couldn't agree more if I was single. So we just ended up playing with Austin's Wii. Yep, the Wii does solve debates when it doesn't come down to a solution. We just played Wii Sports for the rest of the night until Austin called the limo driver who enjoys watching romantic comedies just to get a girl. He left in a hurry and came back with two sleepy kids. From there, I drove Monica home.

"The best day of my life so far," she mumbled, her eyes closed.

"I remember I used to say that; that homecoming was the best day of my life," I whispered to her.

"That's sweet, Dad." she smiled.

"Yeah, just wait until prom comes up. Then compare your 'best day of your life' to that." She fell asleep on me.

When we got home, I had to carry Monica upstairs to her bedroom where she fell asleep in her warm bed in her homecoming dress. I gave her a goodnight kiss and went to bed myself. I didn't mind the smell of beer and popcorn in my mouth and was too tired to mind, so I just went straight to bed. I could brush my teeth later.

Andy~

The scariest thing happened today when I was waiting to have a blood test. I dragged little Sarah along as well because she needed to have a few shots, and she's been crying like crazy all day. So when I was waiting in a chair with Sarah in my lap, the woman beside me told me my daughter was cute, and we grew on that. Now in the corner of the room was this one woman who couldn't shut her baby's mouth, and it was crying really loudly. There were no tears on the baby's red face, and she couldn't figure out what was wrong and how to calm her child down. Then, this shaggy man who's been trying to yank out all the hair from his roots jumped up from his seat and just exploded. He yelled until he caught everybody's attention in the entire hospital waiting room and ran over to the woman's baby. He pulled her baby from her hands and chucked it against the door head first. When the baby hit the wall, I jumped a little from my chair, and I'm pretty sure a few other people did as well. Just that loud *thud* when the baby hit the wall just completely horrified me and stopped the beating of my heart for a few seconds. Now, there wasn't any blood, and the room grew real quiet, and the only sound you could hear was the shaggy man's heavy breathing. Everyone was staring at the guy, and I held Sarah real close to me who hid her face in my shirt making it wet with her tears. He sure did shut that baby up . . . forever because now it's dead. The woman rose from her chair screaming and crying and assaulted the man, punching and slapping and kicking him when he was on the floor, but the strange part is he didn't even care to defend himself; he just stared at God knows what with his wide, blank eyes and didn't say anything as the woman cursed at him after every kick in the stomach, slap in the face, and mucus she spat at him. His blank face showed terror and innocence. She was in angry tears, and her face was as red as her dead child's. Sooner or later, the security guard came to break up the fight and sent the man down to jail. The woman who sat beside me, the one who thought Sarah was cute, said, "The damned things sick people do these days." Why didn't anybody stop him? Why didn't I stop him? Well, my excuse is that because I didn't know what to expect . . . I didn't know what would happen.

My birthday's next week, so life does just keep getting better and better. Birthdays mean free gifts for me, lots of food, and cake. I love cake. Jessica makes a mean chocolate cake . . . maybe I'll invite her. Yeah, I think I will.

Mitch~

Monica yelled at me for not waking her up when we got home because she's complaining about how her dress is wrinkled. "Calm down, girl, it's just a dress. You can always drop it off at the dry cleaners," I told her, but she was still pretty upset. Not to be insulting or anything, but Monica is a bit of a spoiled brat. Yeah, I got the guts to call my kid a spoiled brat any day. But why am I complaining? Yeah, I know it's a little annoying, but, hey, I was a spoiled brat too. I got whatever I wanted whenever I wanted with a little courtesy and politeness which Monica lacks in her attitude. Speaking of getting stuff for spoiled brats, what should I get Andy? Hmm . . . I'll ask him later.

Austin and Monica have been . . . spending a lot of time with each other lately, and I'm sort of surprised that her grades have been . . . up ever since they got together. I like this—this thing goin' on between them. I like it, I approve of this . . . greatly. This relationship seems to be a huge benefit for her emotionally and academically. Now I have to drive her and her boyfriend over to the tennis courts, so they could practice for tournaments in a few weeks.

"You know," I started, taking a turn, heading toward the park, "you could always join soccer. It's . . ."

"No, Dad! We talked about this already . . . No soccer!" Monica yelled, quickly becoming irritant.

"Okay! Okay. I'm just saying if you're ever interested just sign up and tell me 'cause I can hel . . ."

"No, Dad! I'm not interested or ever going to be interested in your *pussy* sport!" she shouted. Okay, now what the hell happened to "respect your elders?" Huh? It just like completely died! Kids need to be more disciplined. I think I'm gonna ground her . . . for the second time of her life. The first time was when she got an 'F' on her report card back in middle school, but it was only for like a day or two, but she took it poorly. She threw a freakin' tantrum and wouldn't stop yelling or crying and made such a huge deal out of it, something insignificant.

"Hey! Soccer is not a 'pussy' sport, Monica. You know NOTHING about soccer. Now, tennis; tennis is a pussy sport," I shot back.

"Ugh! Why do you have to be so UGH!" she pouted.

"I like soccer, Mitch," Austin said.

"Yeah, see, see, Monica! Austin here likes soccer. Attaboy, Austin," I said. I would give him a pat on the back if I wasn't driving. Austin smiled and put his hand on Monica's shoulder. What a suck up!

When the car was parked, they jumped out of the vehicle, and I heard Monica say to Austin, "Oh my god, my dad is so ugh! You know how I feel, right? Okay, so when I was like in fifth grade, my dad made me play on a lousy soccer team at some youth place, and I was the only girl . . . me, the only girl! It was so stupid because the team wasn't even into it! All they did was just stand around and talk to each other scratching their stupid heads and picking their disgusting noses! I was like, 'Why are you signed up to play soccer if you're not going to do anything?' It was so irritating! I swear! One time, we played this team, and half of the players thought I was a guy. So stupid. Worst experience of my life," she huffed, Austin just nodding his head after every sentence she said.

I sat in the car, watching them, and I'm surprised that Monica is better than Austin. I should rub it in Andy's face later. "My girl's better than your

169

boy" sort of remark. But I didn't want to discourage Austin . . . but I'll tell Andy anyways. I'm sure Andy wouldn't discourage his own son . . . or would he? Eh, I doubt it. "You could've hit that!" I heard Monica yelling and smacking Austin across the head with her racket. Poor Austin. After like ten minutes, I grew bored. Man, I should've asked Andy to tag along and then we could beat each other's asses. I'd totally beat his bum . . . and today's a nice day too . . . today's a nice day to beat Andy's bum . . . it's perfect outside. Well, I guess I'll take a jog, something to do to pass the time. I got out of the car, locked it, and started jogging on the sidewalk. I passed by the bench Nathen sat at where he would eat his orange chicken. My stomach grumbled. God, now I'm hungry. I knew I shouldn't have passed breakfast. It is the most important meal of the day. I might drive down to a Chinese place to get some orange chicken.

Jessica~

Andy just called me. He wants me to go to his birthday party. Ugh, I don't feel so good. I've been stuck in my prison of an apartment, afraid to go outside and find Freddy waiting for me. It's like this eerie presence just overcastted my home making me believe there's a monster out on the loose waiting to yell at me and possibly beat me like he beat my door which I did NOT appreciate. I loved him, and now I fear him . . . Fantastic. I think I'm going to bake a cake for Andy. A chocolate cake. Ahhh . . . chocolate cake sounds about good right now. I should make one for myself as well. I hope they won't notice that I'm pregnant. I don't really want them to know yet . . . or at all . . . ugh! I feel so stupid! I got pregnant before I got married, and I know I won't be getting married anytime soon. I should have listened to the stupid sex education guy during my middle school years. It was all about abstinence. Abstinence. Abstinence. Abstinence. Why didn't I listen to the teacher? "Remember, kids, wait until you get married to have sex. None of that premarital sex, ya hear, folks?" I remember I used to mock him for saying that in this deep, retarded voice . . . all the time. But now, he should be the one mocking me of mocking him of what he said—if that does . . . make any sense at all—in an even deeper and retarded voice. I deserve it. I hate myself now! I need a hot chocolate . . . I got up from the couch and poured some hot water in a teapot and pulled out the packet of hot chocolate mix. I think I'll have some marshmallows with my warm drink as well. I grabbed a bag of king-size marshmallows and decided to eat some while my water was boiling. Oh, what should I get Andy for his birthday? I should get him something really amazing like a William Shakespeare action figure. "It might not have karate chop action, but it can destroy you with the power of poetry!" Maybe I'll just get him a card. Yeah, just run over to Hallmark and pick up a decent card for him. Eh, it makes me look cheap. Well, I am baking a cake for him, and isn't that the best present you can give to a person? Because you put your heart and soul—not to mention your tired blood and sweat into it too, but it doesn't make the cake sound as appetizing anymore—into it. The cake will come from the heart of my bottom. I mean, the bottom of my heart and the bottom of my bottom. Oh, wow, heart of my bottom? I'm going crazy. Maybe I should get him a new phone. I don't like his phone. I remember the night when we had that Korean barbecue: Andy's hands were all sticky and his cell phone was ringing in his back pocket and he couldn't pick it up.

"Hey, Jessica, can you get my phone for me?" he asked me as his ring tone was slightly annoying me.

"Um, where is it?" I asked him, pulling a strand of hair away from my face.

"It's in my back pocket."

"Ew! Your butt pocket? I'm not putting my hand down *there*."

"Aw, come on, Jessica! Pick up the phone!"

"Okay, fine." I let out a long scoff. "Promise not to fart on my hand."

"I promise," he said as I dropped my hand down in his pocket, my hand in contact with his butt as I pulled out his cell phone. I held it up to his ear for him to talk into it. When he was done, he asked me, "Can you put it back in my pocket now?"

"No!" I yelled, placing it on the kitchen counter.

Even though it seemed like I didn't like it, I liked it . . . Yes, naughty me . . . shame, shame, shame, bad Jessica, but I can't help it. I think he caught my smile when I was reaching down there and knew that I liked it, but I don't know. But oh, it was magical. He has such a nice butt . . . nice and firm, like a ripe grapefruit. But no, his butt cheeks aren't as big as grapefruits. No, they're about the right size . . . to my liking. Aha-ha . . . okay, the water's done boiling. I got up and carefully poured the hot water into a ceramic mug I made back in high school. It was ugly, but I wanted to keep it because I didn't want to go out and buy one. Mugs are expensive these days. It was slightly crooked, and it was white with black stripes . . . or black with white stripes. The whole mug was supposed to look like a bar code you see on the back of cereal boxes and other items you can purchase from the grocery store, but . . . yeah, I failed, and it looked more like a zebra, so I added eyes, a nose, and ears to the mug. It doesn't look that cool anymore. Maybe I should just toss it and go buy professionally made mugs. I dumped two or three marshmallows into my hot chocolate drink and waited for it to cool down a bit, as I stirred it with a spoon.

Andy~

Ah! My birthday! I woke up to find breakfast in bed from Sarah and Lisa. It was like a little Denny's in my room. When I came downstairs, I found Austin on his laptop. He quickly got up and pulled out a CD. He lazily handed it to me and smiled. "Happy birthday, Dad." I took the CD. "It's a playlist of all your favorites."

"Aha-ha, okay, thanks, Austin," I said, scratching his head.

"Happy birtday, da! Happy birtday, da!" Sarah kept on screaming, as she clumsily came down the stairs. She ran over to me with a hug and a homemade card. I opened it to find that picture—the one with the family in front of the house, and this time, I was taller and slimmer than Austin. It was the best one she made so far.

"Thank you, sweetie," I said to Sarah, kissing her head.

Lisa came down and threw her hands over my neck and kissed me. She pulled out a card from her pocket. I read it and thanked her. "Is this all I'm getting from you?" I laughed.

"No, there's more, Andy." She winked. "You'll get it later."

She walked away, and Austin went outside to mow the lawn for me. Me? I sat at my desk to do a little bit of work. It's always nice to do a little bit of work on your birthday, right? "Dad!" I heard Austin yell.

"What?" I shouted back from the room I was in.

"Come out here, quick!" he shouted again.

I ran out to see if anything was wrong, and there I stood in the doorway, my mouth dropped to find a brand-new red Porsche sitting in my driveway. Austin went over to it and checked the thing out. "Is someone here?" I asked Austin, who pulled out a card from the backseat. Austin came running to me with the card. It read:

I apologize for not making it to your celebration or anniversary—or whatever you wish to call it—of nativity because of the fact that I am busy. I really do wish to be there celebrating your descending to bereavement with various "party" finger foods and singing cheerful songs from the public domain such as "Happy Birthday" or "For He's a Jolly Good Fellow" in an attempting sweet tone that would not puncture your eardrums because who would want to puncture their eardrums on the day of their birth unless they were going to a live loud concert which you are not, I believe. Well, I leave you with this, a present from thee, a brand-new car. I wish you a happy birthday.

Sincerely,
Nathen

"Who's it from, Dad?" Austin asked me.

"It's from Nathen," I told him, running over to the car. I ran my hand down the hood of the car. The touch of the new sports car sent chills down my spine; its slick and cold hood. I hopped into the car, landing in the driver's seat and running my hands down the passenger's leather seat.

This was absolutely amazing. My heart was beating really fast right then. I found the keys in the glove compartment and decided to take the car for a spin. Austin hopped into the back. "Hey, watch the leather," I told him. I roared the engine, and it made my heart beat a little faster, and I took a test-drive around the neighborhood, stopping in front of people standing out in front of their yards to show off my sweet ride. Yeah . . . they all had the same expression on their faces—jealousy. Yep. This has got to be the best birthday present I ever got. When I brought the car back into the driveway, I turned on my cell phone and wanted to call Nathen and thank him. I tried calling a few times, but he didn't pick up, always leading to his voicemail.

"Dad, can I have this car . . . since you already have one?" Austin asked me.

"Um, obviously, the answer is 'no.' You can have my old car when you hit sixteen," I told him, laughing at his question. Me? Give him *this* car? Pshhh, yeah, right! This car can be officially declared as my second wife. Yep.

"But your old car is a piece of poo," he grumbled.

"Well, if I could handle riding a piece of poo for ten years, so can you. Then maybe in the future you'll get a new car like mine," I told him.

"Hey, how's Nathen doing?" Austin asked me, propping his legs on the headrest of the car.

"Um, I don't know. I just tried to call him a few seconds ago, but he wouldn't pick up, so I don't know. Why'd you ask?"

"Oh, just curious."

"You like Nathen?"

"Yeah, he's cool, a little awkward, but cool."

"Yeah, hasn't changed a lot since back then."

"But your relationship with Jessica has, hasn't it?" He laughed at me.

"Ha-ha, very funny . . ." I said sarcastically, pushing his legs off the headrest.

"Ow, what was that for?" he yelled at me.

"I told you to watch the leather, didn't I?"

When noon struck, Jessica came over with a big ol' cake in her hands and exclaimed, "HAPPY BIRTHDAY, ANDY!!!" when I opened the door for her. Then Mitch and Leslie and their kids came by. Like always, Austin and Monica met up, and Sarah and Howard drew pictures together. I heard that Howard was in a coma and thought that was really scary. I told them about the story of the baby that was thrown against the wall in the hospital and Jessica just excused herself to my bathroom and stayed in there for a while. What did I get from these people, these friends? I got a pretty nice Rolex from Mitch and a somewhat-expensive soccer ball from Leslie. Jessica got me a gift certificate to Todai and said she was going to give it to her parents for their anniversary but said I seemed to be more important to her than them which, of course, made me feel bad for her parents. When night fell, we all went out to Todai to use that gift certificate, and all ordered beers except for Jessica.

"Come on, just one glass and that's it," I told her.
"No, I couldn't. I'm, I-I just can't. Not today," she said awkwardly, looking down at her lap, her hands over her stomach. We ate the night away with so much sushi and other seafood . . . yeah. I haven't been to this place in a while. The last time was when I took Lisa out for dinner, and that was a long time ago. When everybody left—when I was completely exhausted, full, and happy about this lovely day—I found a soccer ball lying on the bed.

"Lisa, I thought I asked for you to put the soccer ball in the garage," I called to her who was in the bathroom taking a shower. I don't think she heard me. I picked up the ball to find it autographed . . . oh . . . my . . . freakin' . . . GOD! T-This ball! T-This ball in the palm of my hands was signed by Lee Jung Soo! Oh my freakin' god! I was literally jumping on top of the bed with the ball grasped tightly in my hands, and I jumped so high that I hit my head on the ceiling a couple of times, not minding the pain because of this amazing gift. Lisa appeared from the bathroom, wrapped in a towel, and laughed at me.

"I had to pull a lot of strings to get that thing signed," she told me.
"Thank you so much!" I yelled in her face, giving her a kiss on the lips.

To end the night, we had some fun—"Dirty, Sexy, Money" type of fun.

~

A figure sat in a chair in the dark room. To the human eye, his silhouette could only be seen in the darkness. The time was nearing to 9:00 p.m. The person in the chair slowly tapped the baseball bat in his hands against the wooden floor. Thud . . . thud . . . thud . . . the simple rhythm echoing throughout the home. After a few minutes, the figure got up and played a song on the old record. As soon as the figure went to his post at the chair, returning to his facile tempo, Stravinsky's *Petrouchka Danse Russe* played, the sound a little scratchy. He eventually matched the beating of his bat to the tempo of the beautiful song. There was a knock on the door, and it unlocked. The door closed behind the person that entered, and when he was about to turn on the lights, he froze at the sight of the silhouette in the chair.

"Honey, I'm home." The silhouette stopped his rhythmic beatings, got up from the seat, and slowly walked over to the man that entered. "Well, well, well. Lookie what we have here, Nathen. What did I say about telling Jessica about me and Katie? I said if you told Jessica anything, I would get you . . . and lookie, lookie! Here I am, in your apartment with a lovely bat," Freddy said, as he raised the bat above his head. The person that entered fell to the floor and pushed himself inch by inch closer to the door, his hand shaking as he grabbed the knob, his fingers slowly slipping away from it because of the sweat between his fingers. Not a sound came from the person that entered. "Don't worry, Nathen. I won't *kill* you. I'm just gonna fuckin' bash your brains in! If you're a horror-lover, you would realize that was a Stephen King reference from his personal masterpiece, *The Shining*! You should know, 'cause you gave it to me for a fuckin' birthday present. And seriously, only a dumb shit would give books to people for their birthdays . . . shows how fuckin' cheap they are."

Freddy smashed the bat against the man's head once and then several times in the rib cage and legs, as Stravinsky's song continued to play. The man grunted and screamed as Freddy was going berserk. "Aw, don't cry like a little girl, Nathen! Don't cry! Don't cry like that pretty little Jessica! Don't!" Freddy yelled. "AHHHHHHHHHHHH!!! BECAUSE OF YOU, JESSICA DOESN'T LOVE ME ANYMORE! BECAUSE OF YOU, KATIE SETTLED A DIVORCE AND KICKED ME OUTA HER APARTMENT! BECAUSE OF YOU, I DON'T HAVE A PLACE TO STAY AT AND HAVE NO MONEY IN MY FUCKIN' POCKETS! I'M HERE, WASTING MY TIME BASHING UP YOUR BODY! BUT IT'S ALL WORTH IT! IT'S *ALL* WORTH IT! IT'S *ALL FUCKIN'* WORTH IT! AHA-HA-HA!" Freddy screamed at the top of his lungs as he repetitively swung the bat at his body. "I HATE YOU! YOU CAN ROT IN HELL AFTER I KILL YOU!"

"I'm not Nathen!" the man suddenly said. His voice cracked, in tears and in pain. "I'm not Nathen!"

Freddy took a few steps back, lowering his weapon. He took a long time to try and find his face, to try and find out who he was beating to death. "Then who the fuck are you?" Freddy asked.

"I . . . I . . . I'm Nathen's o . . . o . . . old person . . . nal ass . . . sistant," Jordan Wong trembled.

Freddy walked up to him and flicked on the lights.

"Please don't kill me!" Jordan Wong sobbed as he shielded his eyes with his wet and bruised and possibly broken hands as a sign of weakness and from the bright lights.

"Why are you here?" Freddy asked.

"I came to give him a few photos," he cried.

"Get the hell out of here. I'll be sure to hand these to Nathen," Freddy said as he snatched the orange-yellow portfolio from Jordan Wong's hands. Jordan Wong left very quickly, his steps soft. During his escape, he fell over, landing into a wall, but continued. Freddy closed the door behind him, turned off the lights, and threw the portfolio of pictures on the kitchen counter. He walked over to the center of the living room and stood there in the darkness. He stood there until the song ended. He huffed and quickly smashed the wide, flat-screen TV's screen. The screen cracked, and the TV fell off the wall landing on the floor with a big crash.

He then jumped on the couch and stomped over to the piano where he heaved and pushed it through the balcony and out into the air where it landed with a mighty *bam!* He smashed Nathen's windows and knocked everything off the kitchen counters, until pots and pans chattered as loud as the annoying traffic. He pushed bookcases down to the floor and jumped on the couch again, laughing maniacally. He took the portfolio, ripped it open, and found photos of many Asian couples. He ripped all of them into tiny bits and threw them in the air. He laid his body on the ground moving his arms and legs in order to make "snow angels" as the small bits of snowflakes of paper gently and gracefully fell down on him.

Mitch~

Lucky, Andy . . . he got a freakin' car for his birthday. A car from Nathen! Not any old, regular car, but a Porsche. Damn . . . where could Nathen get all that money if he doesn't even have a job? It is practically impossible to get a car like that if you don't own a job, and I highly doubt all that money spent on that car came from his bank account. Geez . . . I wonder if Nathen will get me a car for my birthday. I want a Porsche. I want a black one. Yeah, I'm jealous of Andy right now, him and his car . . . He's been rubbing it in everybody's faces, and I hate it. What do I have? I have a Honda, a lousy Honda . . . Oh, well, you gotta work with what you got, I guess.

Jessica~

Five months have passed, and my tummy is huge! I feel like using my stomach as a large drum and slap my hands away on it, making music for the baby and hoping that the baby will come up with an accompaniment with my beats inside. He/she could maybe use my umbilical cord as a string or something and pluck that. Or maybe music making isn't healthy for the baby. Now, I'm terribly afraid of what I bump into and eat, and so

I have become careful. Now, I don't think I can see Mitch or Andy or any other people of that crowd. I am ashamed, disgraced. They can't see me like this. They'll think differently of me . . . and I don't like to be thought differently of . . . I'll just hide myself in my apartment, this refuge, this sanctuary until I pop the baby out. Hmm . . . now would be a good time to name the baby, my baby. If it's a boy, maybe I'll name him after the great Nathen . . . I wonder if he'll appreciate that . . . "Hey, Nathen, I named my son after you." I would say. "Please change the name of your child . . ." he would probably say along those lines. Well, I can't think of a name . . . maybe some time later.

Nathen~

Well, I would like to say that I have been busy for the past few months with some financial business. I had kept my cell phone off for a while because I wanted to exclude myself from the world I lived in and just went away. I left my normal living habits for something different, a new environment, but only for a few months and that was it. When I returned to my regular lifestyle, I turned on my cell phone to find several missed calls which I was surprised about. Mostly no one ever leaves me messages. A few were from Andy, and the rest of them were from Jordan Wong. All these messages from Jordan Wong had told me to call him back as soon as possible, and I did so because it sounded really urgent. He had told me he had a broken arm and leg, and I asked him why. He had told me Freddy had done it and had wrecked my home. I was stunned, shocked, and appalled. I quickly came back home to find everything I owned destroyed except for my old record player. Bits of photograph papers danced along the surface of my wooden flooring, when the wind blew its cool tune. My piano was smashed into bits. I found it out in the alley where a hobo was using it as shelter. My books were trashed, and my furniture was thrashed. Some of my walls had holes in them, and my TV was marked with large scratches and multiple cracks. My kitchen wasn't as nearly wrecked as my room, where I found my wall of Asian couples, the wall of degradation, gone. All the photos were ripped and scattered everywhere—on the floors on the bed, in the bathroom, and caught in between broken glass of my shattered window. And that's when I said, "All my life's work ruined . . ." rather depressingly.

I wasn't so much angry at the sight of this disaster, but more shocked. I didn't think Freddy would go beyond the limits I had thought he would never reach. Not only damaging the house, but a human being who was covered in casts. Jordan Wong was merely giving me the pictures I had taken and those that he had taken, but instead, he meets his demise. I dearly apologized to Jordan Wong and told him I would repay him very soon. I was disappointed in Freddy, very disappointed. Freddy is a grown man and should be more mature; he should be mature about this whole thing. But no, he decided to take his life on a rampage. I guess love makes you blind *and* crazy.

With my hands in my pocket, I walked around my house, not minding what I stepped on, not minding the little pieces of everything getting stuck to my shoe. Instead of repairing and repaying for all this damage, I decided it would be easier to simply move to another apartment, and so I did. I would move into a vacant room a few doors from my bashed room in a few days maybe. I didn't care to clean up, so I paid a few maids. I would buy new furniture sometime later; necessities such as furniture didn't appeal to me at the moment. I went down into the streets, the active ones where tourists and people who enjoyed night walks, roaming the streets to make myself some money. All I have focused on the past weeks was picking pockets for financial purposes as I had explained—and have become in a state of greediness. This state will probably leave my system in a few days when things go back to normal.

On my trip, I mainly spent my time in Europe picking pockets of, obviously, Europeans . . . and tourists of different ethnicities that I tried to guess myself when I spotted one or two that looked interesting. Surprisingly, these Europeans carry a whole lot more money than our proud Americans do in their pockets and purses. Coming back home, back in Los Angeles, I miss pockets that are rich in bills. Because of today's economy, there haven't been many pockets with a lot of money;

America's pockets lack money! Woe is us . . . woe is us . . . On my way to and back from Europe on a lovely plane flying first class, I read the Bible to pass precious time. I had never actually read or touched the Bible before and found this holy item to be quite a read. I had always wanted to write a book myself. I wouldn't know what it would be about . . . probably about people. Yes, people and their lives. Yes, people and their lives and the themes of life. But who would even care to touch a book like that; a book about people, their lives, and themes? Even I wouldn't really hanker for that type of reading, but that's what I want to write, something to share with the public. Books are meant to be enjoyed and be learned from for the public, and the public should appreciate that. Then I would walk down the street and pass by a local bookstore's window and say to the elderly woman beside me who spent her time window-shopping, "Do you know who that book is by?" "No," she would reply. "It's by me!" I would tell her. I don't think she would even care and carry on with her window-shopping and probably reply to my exclamation with a "that's nice." If I'm wanted or lucky or they don't have anybody to put on the air, I can speak with David Letterman and talk about my book which I do highly doubt will happen. If it does become a bestseller, it would be nothing compared to the Bible, for it is *the* national bestseller and will always be for years to come.

I stood outside on my balcony, inhaling the polluted air of the city and exhaling carbon dioxide. Then a question popped into my head: What is the meaning of life? What is the point of life? That was a question I had once asked myself before but never had a solid/definite answer. There are various philosophies to this question that various people believe in. Only philosophies, not answers. I never wanted to ask this question to a person before because I know somehow in some way, shape or form, their religious beliefs would be tied into their answer. Really, I don't have anything against their religion. It's just that it'll bring up a bit of a controversy, a debate especially when you are discussing it with more people with their different religious backgrounds. Well, I have found some philosophies:

"To grow through your experience."

"To enjoy yourself."

"Don't worry, be happy . . . that's a song, right?"

"To contribute to society."

"'Dream as you'll live forever, live as you'll die today.' James Dean, my boy."

"If you ask me, I would say, it's just like asking what the point of a book is. We would hunt down the author and find out what the author was trying to tell us through the plot of the book. It is the hidden message. We don't have points unless there's a message conveyed. If there is a message hidden in your life to be conveyed, then who could the author possibly be? It has to be your God or else there isn't a point. If you want to find the point of your life, find your creator. So there you have it, the secret message; find your God, have a chat with him, a nice cup of tea. Yeah, that'll work."

"Does it matter?"

"I guess the whole point in life is to hopefully find out the answer to your question."

"To live forever in a paradise."

"Sex, sex, and more sex. Scientifically speaking, to reproduce."

"Learn to earn."

"Learn to be a lover of or for God."

"Bein' kinder to others."

"Laugh, cry, and love."

"To correct the past's mistakes."

Life's Manifesto

"'There are just some kind of men who are so busy worrying about the next world that they never learn to live in this one.' Learned that little sweetie pie from *To Kill a Mockingbird*."

"Change every five years, and if you see no change, you can guarantee a new president in eight . . ."

"To carry on."

"To ask philosophical questions in the category of cars and transportation of course."

"The meaning of life is to live. Nothing else makes 'sense,' it's all rhetoric."

"Life is just one long movie full of actors and props and social issues. Just wait til' it ends."

"The point is to die. But life ain't the absolutes of birth and death. It's about what's in between. There ain't no absolutes in life, only 'in-betweens.'"

I have kept that last philosophy to my beliefs for a period of time. Now then, the in-betweens. I would say, a lot of things have happened to me in this period of "in-betweens," but none of it is highly significant. I do not consider myself as significant, and I don't think anyone else thinks I'm significant. Well, I'm not exactly sure . . . I haven't worked with a lot of people. Well, there was this one guy named Phil who was a mechanic and worked on my car for a few hours. He only had one arm, and I was surprised he was still working in such a difficult condition in an environment like a car repair shop. He made me feel significant by demeaning himself very brutally. Therefore, he looked at me as a significant person . . . is that right? Yes, well, he did give me this look though from time to time. It was this look that said he was thirsty for my arm. He did indeed lick his lips during this look, so . . . never mind, I'm digressing. Well, allow me to digress again as I enter into my nostalgic mode. I remember when I argued with my father, the matter being what is the point in going to school, going to a better school, paying taxes, and bills when we'll just end up six feet under in an expensive box? And then I asked him, "What is the meaning of life?" He told me, "You can waste the rest of your life with philosophical ideas and thoughts or you could find it through this book," he said as he pulled out a dictionary. "The meaning lies in this 'Bible' of words and definitions." All right, I'm done digressing. The point of life is *to die* as pessimistic as it sounds. Well, then, might as well check in early. I-I did have thoughts of suicide, I do admit. I never thought of actually *doing it* though.

I decided to pay Freddy a visit. Jordan Wong had told me that he was in jail. Jordan Wong did call the authorities reporting a "crazy being" had beaten him and the intrusion of private property. When I saw Freddy in his orange jumpsuit, I noticed that the outfit had given him the appearance of being quite corpulent. I had a box of chocolates in my hand. They were indeed for Freddy. I handed him the box, and he just tossed it under the table not saying a "thank-you" or a simple "hello." He lacked enthusiasm. Well, maybe because he was in jail, and jail is not a cheery Broadway production full of gay and happy actors and actresses.

"Well, hello, Freddy." I gave him a small wave through this glass in between us, communicating through black, greasy phones.
"Why the hell are you here?" he asked me abruptly.
"Well, um, I thought I might just pay you a visit."
"Why? So you could laugh and harass me in my fuckin' face? Huh?" his voice rose, getting up from his chair. A security guard placed a hand on his shoulder and guided him back to the seat by the telephone.
"Um, no. It's because I think this is going to be my last day," I told him, scratching my head.
"Your last day of what? Puberty?"
"No, my living, my life."
"You're going to kill yourself?"
"Um, yes, a suicide."

"Ha-ha-ha! You're a joke. You don't have the guts to kill yourself."

"I know! I really don't know if I *can* do it! Just the fear of not existing anymore frightens me!" I broke out.

"I know you can't," he said, his hands folded across his chest, the phone caught in between his cheek and shoulder, leaning back in his chair. "'cause you're weak. You're a pussy," he whispered to me.

"Yes, I-I'm well aware of that. I have been aware of that for a while now."

"Oh, fuck it up the ass." He laughed making me feel like a piece of poop. I was not enjoying this talk with Freddy nor was I feeling comfortable about it. My stomach was churning my breakfast, lunch, and last night's dinner which was a bowl of noodles, orange chicken, and crab bisque.

"Well, I just came here to say that I am not at all angry at you, a little aggravated, but not mad. But I am disappointed in you, Freddy, that you took the liberty in destroying my home instead of turning the other cheek. It was immature of you to do so and beat the-the . . . poo out of poor Jordan Wong who has, now, a broken arm and leg. Now you're here, where I personally believe you belong, Freddy."

"I told you not to tell, Nathen. I specifically told you not to tell! But you told! You told! Then I just wanted to bash your brains in because of that. Bash your brains in!" he began to scream into the phone; his spit flew and landed on the glass between us. He slammed the palm of his hands onto the glass and screamed, his breath leaving a temporary imprint on the glass. "BASH YOUR BRAINS IN! BASH YOUR BRAINS IN! BASH YOUR BRAINS IN! BASH 'EM RIGHT THE *FUCK* IN!" he screamed repeatedly with his mad eyes that showed he really did want me dead, as he was being dragged away by the authorities.

I quickly left and had found out that he was using a Stephen King quote specifically from *The Shining*. It was a Monday morning, a rather dull day of the week for some people. I tried to contact Andy, Mitch, and Jessica through my cellular phone but could not get a hold of them. I assumed they were busy. What a lonely day for my death! I ran over to a drugstore a few suicidal acquaintances—the ones with the long, black hair and thick black makeup that sit underneath the eyes and tight pants—had asked me to visit if I ever felt like joining them in coffins, but I had always insisted that my answer to their repetitive questions would be "no" until now, today. I entered the store that held a strong stench of cigarettes and liquor. The man behind the counter was grizzly, his arms flocculent with long, black hairs that seemed to weave together in this combed pattern and his face was full of facial hair that supplied him warmth for his face, possibly during the winters when necessary.

"Hello, there," I greeted him.

"Hey, what can I do you for?" he asked me nicely with a thick New York accent. He smelt of cigarettes, cheap perfume, and lipstick. I didn't bother to ask if he had a one-night stand or if he was a part-time drag queen.

"I heard from a few people I knew that you sold poisons. Is that correct?"

"Were your friends suicidal and are presently dead?" he asked me, shuffling through a couple of bottles which I believed to be poisons.

"Yes."

"Then you came to the right place. What are you looking for?"

"Something that will kill me instantly when I finish the last drop of whatever you got."

"That'll be fifty dollars," he said, pulling out a small bottle of this clear liquid.

"Do people normally tell you why they're going to kill themselves?" I asked as I pulled my wallet out and handed him the bill.

"Yeah."

"Do you want to hear from me?"

"You gave me a fifty-dollar bill. Why not?"

"My high school dream girl . . . finally found her after what? Fifteen years? In Hawaii. Then I found out that she was taken, disabling me from saying the three words that I've always wanted to say to her. But fun fact here is the man she was with, cheated on her for a friend I have back in my community, and she finds out, and they both leave him. The guy goes crazy, beats the poo out of a friend of mine, wrecks my apartment, and is now whistling a sad tune to himself in his happy little jail cell. End of story."

"Aw, man, I know how you feel. Listen, I'll give you the poison for half price," he offered me as he opened up the cash register to pay me back twenty-five dollars.

"I'm going to die today, it won't matter," I said, waving away the twenty-five dollars.

"Oh . . . right. Have a nice day."

"What a nice thing to say when I'm going to die today! Thank you."

So I went back home with my purchased bottle. I held it in my hands for a few minutes as I sat on the couch. I couldn't die like this. I need something from somebody and so I decided to call Jordan Wong.

"Hello?" he answered his cell phone.

"Um, the man you are speaking with is Nathen," I told him.

"Oh, hello, Nathen! How are you?"

"Fine, thank you. Listen, I just needed to call for a quick question."

"Shoot me."

"Well, what would you say to me right now if I told you I was going to kill myself?"

"Well, I would say, just live till death meets you, Nathen. Why?"

"Thank you for your answer, Jordan Wong."

I quickly hung up the phone and opened the bottle of poison. I confronted my record player, placed a disk on the platform, dropped the needle on the disk, and listened to *Midnight, the Stars and You* performed by the lovely Henry Hall and his Gleneagles Hotel Band.

"Well, this is it," I told myself. I sweated between my fingers and the glass of poison. "Oh yes, my last words."

I quickly ran to the counter to retrieve a notepad and a pen so that I can write down my last words in case anybody wanted to know what they were. I did so and placed it on the floor beside my feet. Then it was time to recite my last words from William Shakespeare's *Macbeth*. "'Life is a tale told by an idiot, full of sound and fury, signifying nothing.'" I quickly downed the little glass bottle and waited for my death. Well, so far so bad. I feel absolutely fine . . . I am not dying instantly. Then I began to think that maybe that grizzly of a man was a cheat, a con, until my head felt heavy. I became dizzy, my vision becoming blurry and soon black. My steps became unbalanced, as I fell into a wall and down onto the floor.

The glass bottle gently rolled across the floor and into the notepad. The song continued to play as Nathen lay lifelessly and still, his face to the ground.

Midnight, with the stars and you;
Midnight, and a rendezvous.
Your eyes held a message tender,
Saying, "I surrender all my love to you."

Midnight brought us sweet romance,
I know all my whole life through
I'll be remembering you,
Whatever else I do,
Midnight with the stars and you.

Jessica~

A Saturday morning. I have no work to do over the weekend, and I have no plans. Well, then, what is it shall I do? A Japanese drama perhaps? Or should I just stay in bed all day and complain about how tired and overworked I am? Ugh, somebody got laid off the other day, and all their work got piled onto my desk, and so I finished all of it last night, and then I went home to celebrate with a glass of wine taking out the aged bottle and a glass. And as I was pouring the delicious wine into the glass, I forgot I was pregnant. So I tried dumping the wine back into the bottle, but I was spilling it everywhere, so I just dumped it in the sink and decided to have yoghurt instead. The yoghurt was lousy with lumps of god knows what. I think they were strawberries . . . Yeah, strawberry lumps.

Well, I needed to forgive Nathen about how I acted over the phone when he told me about Freddy. I picked up the phone and called him, but he didn't pick up after several rings and his voicemail. Ugh, why won't Nathen pick up? That guy always picks up. Maybe I'll apologize to him in person, and, as a matter of fact, it would be more formal and more appropriate. I haven't been formal or appropriate since my mom's birthday. Okay, but Nathen can't see me like this with my big belly. Ugh, well, I guess I'll tell him. It'll just be him and nobody else; Mitch won't know, Andy won't know, their wives won't know, their kids won't know, and my family members won't know. I can trust Nathen. I baked some cookies before I left as an apology gift. You know, some people say sorry without a gift, and I don't really appreciate and accept their apologies because of that, and then I have to pretend that I accept their sorry in front of them. Gosh, is it really that hard to run over to the store to buy something or make something before you apologize?

When I rang his doorbell, nothing had happened. I stood outside, in front of his door for like two minutes. So then, when I knocked on the door, the door opened. It was weird because he would always tell me to lock my doors before I go to bed. He would call me like at night everyday, especially on Halloween. Even back in high school when I was still a true trick-or-treater, knowing which houses to ignore and which houses to hit. Free tip: Don't hit the houses that are located in the Korean or Japanese areas because most of them are Christians, and Christians rarely give out candy because they go to their churches for parties. Yeah, so aim for Catholic or any other religion homes. He stopped doing that like a few months ago when he went on his trip to Hawaii. "Lock your doors, Jessica," he would whisper. In a way, it was kind of creepy with the way he said it and that sentence alone. It sounds like he's out to get me . . . like Freddy. What? I can make Freddy jokes about myself, can't I? Well, when I walked into his apartment, I found him lying on the ground. I gently tried to nudge him awake with my foot, but he wouldn't wake up. So when I stooped down to his level, I tried shaking his head, but that didn't seem to work either. Was Nathen hungover? Oh my god . . . I think he was. I placed my plastic container of warm cookies off to the side and turned him around so that his face was facing me. His eyes were still open.

"Nathen, oh my god, don't do that! You freakin' scared me." I chuckled.

He didn't move his eyes. He didn't blink or twitch. When I keep my eyes open, my eyes just water. Therefore, I suck at staring contests. I quickly kneeled down and placed two fingers on his throat, trying to check his pulse. When I couldn't feel it, I reached down to his heart . . . oh my god . . . I think he's dead. No pulse. There was a notepad on the ground that said, "Life is a tale told by an idiot, full of sound and fury, signifying nothing." There was a small empty bottle on the floor as well. I picked it up and smelled the lip of the bottle. It did smell weird. I placed it on the kitchen counter and called 911.

"Please, Nathen, wake up." I tried nudging him awake again. Nothing. If this was a practical joke, I am going to kick his ass.

When the ambulance arrived with all their little medical people running out of their small vehicle, they ran upstairs and quickly checked Nathen's pulse. They declared that he was dead. Nathen was dead, and by the looks of the small bottle, they declared the death to be a suicide.

"No, Nathen would never kill himself. He wouldn't . . . ever . . ." Even though I said this, I really didn't know if it was accurate. Would Nathen kill himself? Well, he did live a rather depressing life, but . . . oh, Nathen.

Mitch~

I went to pick up Monica and Austin from school on a Saturday in my *Honda*, not a *Porsche*, but a *Honda*. Yeah, I'm still not over that.

The kids had to take a PSAT on a Saturday which I thought was kind of stupid. What kind of school makes a person take a test on a Saturday? It would be best sometime during a school day or maybe after school or before school. Well, it is a four-hour test . . . and people may have before and after school activities. Okay, fine, never mind. Maybe it would be better if it was on a Saturday. I waited in the car, the windows rolled down, the weather a little warm, for the two. The test wouldn't be over for another fifteen minutes. I've only been in the parking lot but never actually walked on the school grounds in a long time. I jumped out of the car and took a walk around the school. It didn't change as much. It looked the same as it had been when I was the kids' age. I think it looks older, and there are a few new coats of paint, but through the cracks, you could still see the old school colors. I quickly ran over to the language arts building's wall where Andy, Jessica, Nathen, and I hung out and where I placed all of the gum I've chewed. I made all the dried pieces of gum into a smiley face and my initials. When I got there, I found Jessica sitting a few inches away from the wall in a fetal position. She was looking out at the leaves falling off from the large tree where the albino-freak girl back in high school used to climb up with her Puerto Rican boyfriend and make love in the mornings. To the far right of her, there stood my mosaic art of gum; my smiley face and my initials. I was surprised that it was still there.

"Hey, Jessica, what are you doing here?" I asked her, surprised of her presence.
"Oh, hi, Mitch." She sighed.
"Something wrong?" I asked her, taking a seat beside her.
"Mitch," she started, not wanting to look up at me, "I'm pregnant."
"Wow, congrats! I was wondering why your stomach was so . . . expanded."
"Aha-ha. I have been for about six months now."
"Congrats!"
"The baby's gonna be born a bastard, Mitch." She looked down at the ground, invisibly writing something on the concrete ground with her index finger. I couldn't make out what she wrote.
"How come? What happened to that Freddy guy?"

"He cheated on me, and I broke up with him before I knew that I was pregnant."

"Um, I'm sorry to hear that."

"You better be." She lightly chuckled as I saw that her eyes were getting a little teary. "No, I'm just joking. You know who he was cheating on when we were together?"

"No, who?"

"Your cousin, Katie. They were married."

"Oh my god . . ."

"Yeah. Oh, and the next time you see her or something, could you please tell her that I was just about as clueless as she was when she found out the news? I think she hates me for all of this and tell her that I'm so sorry."

"Here, I'll give you her number," I told her, taking out my cell phone, a pen, and a piece of scratch paper from my pocket. I quickly jotted down the number and handed it to her. I felt sorry for Jessica. Poor her to not have anyone help her out with the baby. Poor baby to not having a father to love . . . Sad.

"Thank you." She gently smiled, placing it in her pocket. "You want to hear some more 'depressing' news if you consider all of this depressing news?" she asked me. I did think all of what she said was depressing. I feel really bad right now. I came here to remember the past and then to find out about Jessica's troubles . . . and my cousin's troubles.

"Sure, I guess." I shrugged my shoulders.

"Nathen's dead," she said flatly.

"What?" I asked, in shock. At the exact millisecond she said that; my heart completely stopped.

"He's dead, Mitch. I found him on the floor, this morning. So lifeless . . ."

"How did he die?" I asked. My throat became dry and tightened as if I was being choked by some invisible Hulk. My breaths became short, and I couldn't breathe as well.

"Suicide."

I always saw Nathen as a suicidal after seeing him cope through that family massacre, but I never thought he'd actually kill himself. But what kept him so long from killing himself? I mean, if that was the case, the massacre being the reason why he committed suicide, then I'm sure he would've done it a few years back. Was it us? Was it us that kept him alive? Did we keep him from killing himself? God . . . he left us without a good-bye.

"Um, Mitch, could you maybe give me a ride? I kinda took a cab here," she asked me.
"Sure," I told her.

We walked to my car, passing by all the classes we've been in—some classes with Jessica, Andy, and Nathen. It brought back good memories.

"Nathen's blood is spilt everywhere, his memories, his nostalgia," Jessica said.
"*Our* blood is spilt everywhere, *our* memories, *our* nostalgia," I corrected her. What a weird thing to hear from her! Maybe this is why I ignored her most of the time . . . because she said weird stuff.
"Hold my hand?" she asked me.
"Uh, sure," I said, grabbing her hand and gripping it loosely. Her hand was cold, and mine warm. I took my hand away from hers and took off my jacket, placing it around her.
"Thanks," I heard her mumble.
"No problem," I told her as she grabbed my hand. Then she pinched my biceps.
"Wow, Mitch . . . been working out? It's a little squishy, like in between frozen and refrigerated meat loaf, but I think, a few more weight lifting, the meat loaf will blossom into a solid object like bricks or . . . bamboo . . . whichever you prefer. Oh! I remember one time when you were talking to Leslie, at the time when she didn't know you liked her, you were like sort of flexing your arms. Yeah, Mitch, I remember that real well. Oh my goodness . . . ah . . . so lame of you to do that. You were like Hulk status at the time . . . thinkin' you were all strong which, by the way, you weren't . . . aha-ha . . . FEE FIE FOE THUMB! That's a

Hulk thing, right? That's what he says? No? Well, anyways, good job," she told me.

"Aha-ha . . . thanks." I blushed, embarrassed.

"Mitch, I gotta say, I like the new you. The new you that lacks asshole aspects. Do you still reminisce those days where you stole my Rice Krispies and harassed me with cruel jokes?" she asked.

"Sometimes." I chuckled, pulling my hand away from hers and placing them in my pockets.

When we finally reached the parking lot, we spotted Monica and Austin waiting impatiently at the car. I knew Monica was about to yell something at me, but she saw Jessica next to me and decided to keep her mouth shut.

"Hey, Jessica." Austin waved to her.

"Oh, hi, Austin. How are you and—" she asked him, pointing to Monica.

"Oh, uh, we're good. You?"

"Pregnant."

"Ah, congratulations. Did you name him or her yet?"

"No, not yet."

When I was about to drop Jessica off, she said, "Oh, before I forget, here you go," she said, giving me a twenty-dollar bill.

"Wait, what's this for?" I asked her, the twenty-dollar bill in my hands.

"For the ride."

"No, take it back. Here," I said, shoving it into her hands.

"No, it's okay. Keep it."

"No, you don't have to pay people for a ride home."

"Yes, you do."

"No, you don't. You didn't pay me the last time I gave you a ride."

"Yes, I did. I just left it on your seat without saying anything that time."

"What? I thought that was lucky loose change. Okay, no," I said, pulling out a twenty-dollar bill. "Here."

"Wait, since when was a twenty-dollar bill ever considered 'loose change?' No! Just keep the money, okay, just keep it."

"Jessica, I am not a taxi driver."

"I know you're not. Oh, so you think I'm insulting you? Insulting you by calling you a taxi driver? Since when was being called a taxi driver an insult?!? You know, my uncle happens to be a taxi driver and—"

"Just take the money, please, Jessica," I cut her off.

Jessica didn't say another word and took the money from my hands and placed it into her wallet. "Thank you," she said and went out the door and to her apartment. She waved, we waved, and we left with me winning the battle, this battle of Asian customs. Ha. I win.

"Hey, Mitch, what was Jessica doing at our school?" Austin asked me as we drove home. He was going to be staying with us until Andy or Lisa came by. They were working late again.

"Oh, um, she was there to tell me some stuff and just, you know, revisiting the school because, you know, we went to school there, and it's just nice to see how the school is after so many years," I explained to him, still awestruck that Nathen was gone.

"What kind of stuff did she tell you?" he asked.

"Okay, Austin, do you know Nathen? He babysat you and your sister before, right?"

"Um, yeah. What about him?"

"He's gone."

"What do you mean he's gone? Gone as in . . . dead?" he asked. Monica looked up at us, not knowing who this Nathen was.

"Yeah . . . Austin," I assured him.

"How?"

"Suicide."

" . . . Why did he do it?"

"You should ask your dad, Austin. I think that would be best," I told him, ending this conversation.

"Dad, who's Nathen?" Monica asked.

"A friend." Austin and I answered in unison.

"Oh, well, I'm sorry to hear that . . . for the both of you . . ." she said awkwardly, looking down at her iPhone. The ride home was quiet. Nobody dared say a word, including me.

Andy~

When I came by Mitch's to pick up Austin, he told me that Nathen was dead. I was completely speechless. Why did he do it was the ultimate question, and we do have ideas for ourselves, but we wanted Nathen's answer which is obviously impossible to know. For the rest of the day, I just felt like doing nothing. I felt like sitting down and just doing absolutely nothing. All of us were supposed to go see a movie tonight, but I just let them go without me—Lisa, Sarah, and Austin. They tried to convince me to go, but peer pressure couldn't get me this time. I didn't cry. I just couldn't cry. I didn't know why I couldn't . . . I just couldn't. I found out that none of us did; Mitch, Jessica, and I. Austin didn't cry either. It was weird.

Jessica~

At exactly 10:00 a.m. of my Sunday morning, a man knocked on the door who identified himself as Jordan Wong. He had asked me to follow him to his limo, and I just shut the door in front of his face. Who listens to a guy who asks you to hop into his car? Okay, maybe small, stupid yet innocent children who don't know anything and have blind, irresponsible parents, but I am not a small child, and I don't have blind or irresponsible parents. Okay, maybe irresponsible. There was this one time when I was bleeding really badly, like the blood was gushing out. It was like a small Niagara Falls. I was about to be rushed to the bathroom for some cleaning up and a Band-Aid, the phone rang, and my mom ran to answer it, leaving me in the middle of the hall way. It was a friend of hers from work who called, and they talked for like half an hour or so as I, proud Old Faithful geyser, entertained imaginary tourists with my blood. All happened at the age of five. Who does he think he is asking me to hop into his car? He knocked on the door again, and as I was about to tell him that if he knocked on my door one more time, I would call the cops, and I don't care if my neighbors think differently of me when they see cops at my door, but then he mentioned Nathen and I decided that I could trust the guy. When he was driving me god knows where, he told me that he was the one who sent me information, the truth, about Freddy. Okay, this guy was either a true stalker or a good friend of Nathen's. Honestly, I was leaning toward the stalker side of my profiling because I like to choose the most ridiculous answers. He stopped at Mitch's house, and he came along with Monica and his wife and kids. Then finally to Andy's house, picking him and his family up.

"Would you like to listen to soft rock?" Jordan Wong asked us as he was driving us, yet again, god knows where.

"Um, no, thank you," we all said something along those lines, shaking our heads.

"May I offer you muffins or toast and butter?"

"No, thank you," we all replied again.

After a long, awkward silence, he spoke again, "Nathen insisted that I offer you a small breakfast for what you are about to hear."

"Where exactly are we going?" Andy asked Jordan Wong.

"Nathen said he wanted to keep it a surprise until you, his only friends, would get there."

Finally, he took us to this medium-sized building where the parking lot only had a few cars. The parking lot was fairly clean, and the building looked fairly clean itself. The building looked pretty old with appropriate stout bushes and puny flowers that leaned to their sides in the front. I gave the building my respect, and I'm sure that the building would respect me in return, hopefully not leading me to a crack in the sidewalk for me to trip over. Jordan Wong instructed us to step outside the car and follow him. He led us to a door which he unlocked. The room was small and dark. I didn't think we would all fit, but surprisingly we did . . . enough room to have my large stomach have some space.

The walls had a bland butterscotch color that just made my taste buds act up, and the room was mainly occupied with a large wooden desk probably the size of my refrigerator when laying it on its side and a large electronic safe that looked like it cost a fortune. Ha-ha . . . whoever bought it spent a *fortune* to keep his *fortune* safe. Ha-ha . . . I crack myself up sometimes . . .

"You are all probably wondering why you are present in this room," Jordan Wong brought up, kneeling down to the safe and pulling out a piece of paper out of his brown folder.

"Obviously," I replied which sounded really rude. Everyone's eyes were on me, except mine. "I didn't mean to be rude. I was just stating the obvious for all of us. If I offended you, I apologize," I tried to explain.

Jordan Wong ignored my comment and entered the code into the safe by pressing a long sentence of a bunch of numbers. The first time around, he messed up in the middle of the sequence, and so he started entering the combination in again. There was an awkward feeling to the room as the sounds of punching keys sang in the room. None of us knew what to do, so we just looked around the room, seeing what could be improved, how to make the room seem more lively. When he was done, the safe beeped and unlocked itself with its door slowly swinging away from whatever was inside. Inside was a single sheet of thin paper. All those numbers punched in for a piece of paper. It must have been really important.

"Well, I will start off by saying that this document in my hands is Nathen's will. I am sure most of you are interested in knowing what it has to say to you all," Jordan Wong started. "Okay, I will now begin to read this paper." He cleared his throat. "We will start with Jessica. 'I thank you for taking me under your wing when I felt like dirt after that unfortunate event and appreciate it very much. I know that your relationship with Freddy was a complete and utter failure that landed in a crash so unpleasant, but I hope that one day you will marry someone who is not a monster. I leave with you a condo which you can either live in or sell. The house is filled with new furniture which you can either decide to keep or sell.' Now, moving onto Mitch. 'Mitch, at first, I wondered if you befriended me because you pitied me or you wanted to take it as a joke understanding that you came from a high social class of the Asian population at school. But I do appreciate your kindness and thank you for that.' Finally, Andy. 'Andy, I admire you the same amount of kindness that Mitch had to offer and . . . that is basically all I have to say to you. I'm sorry, I couldn't find more words to say to you, so I'm apologizing to you now . . . even if I'm dead. Maybe I could add that you have wonderful children, but that wouldn't really be about *you*.' And for all of you, he says, 'You're all probably wondering why I wished to commit suicide which I will not reveal. I am sure enough you can figure out why.' So now Nathen wanted me to leave you with these." Jordan Wong finished, pulling out a small wooden box with plastic cards that were keys from the Zurich Bank International. Why did Nathen give us this? "He has also supplied you with tickets to Zurich, Switzerland, for whenever you wish to leave. He suggested that you go during spring break. Well, I will leave you with that and be in the limo waiting to take you all back home free of charge. Small tips are acceptable." Jordan Wong smiled, walking out the door with the safe locked and his folder in his hands. "And maybe you would like to have a muffin or toast this time because if you don't, I might have to throw them out which is a waste of food, and then it makes me think about the poor African children in . . . Africa, and then I stay up all night tossing and turning in bed with pillows and blankets tossed onto the ground wondering about those children because it makes me feel so guilty and ruins my whole evening. I-It just agitates me." Jordan Wong left the room to let us mingle about anything that was needed to be mingled about or that was worth mingling about.

"Should we go during spring break?" Mitch asked, placing the key inside his pocket.

"If that's what Nathen wants us to do, then let's do it," Andy said, placing his key in his pocket.

I couldn't place my key inside my pocket because I didn't have any pockets. I felt kind of left out. I was the last one to leave the room and turned off the lights, closing the door behind me. It was a little chilly, and

I was still in my pajamas, and if I remember, I need to remind myself to buy new pajamas with pockets.

The next day, Jordan Wong told us that Nathen was already buried. Nathen had wished not to have a funeral service, and I asked Jordan Wong for the directions to the cemetery Nathen was staying at. Whoa, I think it's best if I reword that: ' . . . to the cemetery Nathen was staying at.' It sounds like he's staying at a motel/hotel or something. I wrote them down and quickly drove myself to the cemetery. I wondered if I should call Mitch and Andy to come see where Nathen was buried and have like a small funeral service among ourselves, but . . . I wasn't really sure if that would be appropriate. My hands were in my pockets. My jacket was keeping me warm. The morning was cold, and the sun wasn't out yet. I looked down at his tombstone.

"Granite tombstone. Nice," I started, talking to Nathen. "Well, I want to be the first to, um, give you my eulogy, so here it goes. Nathen, you were a really good friend, and, um, I'll miss you . . . Why did you have to check in so early? Why couldn't you just stay for a little bit longer to see my baby? Oh, and by the way, I named my son after you. Yep, it's a boy. I hope you'll appreciate that. Ha-ha . . . You kept me not-lonely most of the time, you know that, right? Remind me to find the antonym of 'lonely' when I get home. Sometimes, late at night, you would stay on the phone with me no matter how many awkward silences there were, and I liked how you didn't mind if your next phone bill would be huge. Mine certainly were, and I certainly minded. I visited the school, met Mitch there. We talked a bit, and you know that gum thing he made on the wall? It's still there. I was surprised, and you would be too because it looks exactly the same as it had been like fifteen years ago. You know that song that was playing? On your record player? I think it's called *Midnight, the Stars and You*. Yeah, I downloaded that song onto my iPod. Oh, I forgot to bring you flowers. Well, the next time I visit and come for a chat, I'll promise to pick up some roses. Do you want red roses? Or white? Oh, well, I'll surprise you. Aha . . . I remember the time when you wanted some cake, and I cut the cake with a spatula, and you were simply fascinated with it. 'Oh my world, this spatula has a very unique design. Is it supposed to have an indent like that? That's strange . . . I never seen spatulas that were bent in the middle like that. I don't own any with an indent like that. Where did you get this? I want to buy something like this . . . oh and there's a small indent where you can place your thumb in. Quite fascinating.' Oh, Nathen . . . you're amazing. God, I miss you so much, Nathen." I fell to my knees and just cried. "Damn it, Nathen. There will never be another one like you, never another person who cares about others so much that they don't even think about themselves first, never another person who's-who's always there for another . . ." I grabbed a tissue from my pocket and blew my snot into it. I looked at my snot to find that it wasn't the most beautiful sight. "Well, I think I'm gonna go now. I'll come back soon, I promise you that. Bye, Nathen," I said, walking away.

Mitch~

We were packed and were ready to leave for the trip to Switzerland. I wonder what he was leading us to. What was in Zurich that Nathen wanted us to have? What was so important in Zurich? I kept the keys safe in my suitcase, everyone's trust in my hands. It was nice of Nathen to give us seats in first class and pay for our flight. How could Nathen do all of this for us? I mean, this takes a whole lot of money. It would probably take me a little over half a year to pay for this flight for this many people. Where and how does he get all this money? Was he an heir? Did he inherit the money from a relative or something? If he did, it must've been a fortune.

Andy~

"Honey, Sarah needs to go the restroom?" Lisa nudged me.
"Oh, uh, why can't you take her?" I asked her. Lisa was sitting behind him, the window seat, and beside her was sleeping Jessica. Her baby was due just a few weeks ago. Jessica's baby was in Lisa's hands, and it took forever to put the kid to sleep. My eyes were red and burning. I quickly

rubbed them knowing that I would eventually give in and escort little Sarah to the little girls' room.

"Hello?!? I'm holding the baby," Lisa whispered loudly.

"Fine. Fine. Fine. I'll do it," I said, getting up and picking up Sarah. We walked to a vacant stall, and I got in with her. I helped her get on the cold toilet. I turned away to wash my hands with the warm water and splashed some in my face. The restroom had a stench, but it was fairly clean.

"Daddy? Ausin say Nayten dead. What that mean?" Sarah asked me.

"Sarah, it means that . . . um, Nathen isn't here anymore." I sighed, afraid that she might not understand.

"Den where's he?"

"A better place."

"What betta place?"

"I'll tell you later, okay?"

I heard the toilet flush and helped her off the toilet. When we got out, I was afraid to make a sound because the plane was so quiet. Everyone was either asleep or watching something on the screen in front of them. Was this how rich people lived? I wish I could sleep and watch movies all day. Well, it depends on what I'm watching. It has to be a real good comedy or action or a really interesting nonfiction topic or else I'll fall right asleep.

Mitch~

When we finally got to Switzerland, we immediately called a cab to take us to the hotel we reserved our stay at. Now this money was coming from our pockets. We would head up to the bank the next morning, but right now, all of us were exhausted and just went to bed. The rooms were nice, clean, and it was really nice outside even though it was a little cold. The blankets and the pillows were so soft, and I just slept like a baby. I like European pillows and bedsheets. I think I might buy some online when I get back home.

The next morning, we passed by the burning of the Böögg. I found out later that it was an effigy that marked the start of spring. It's like this poor snowman that stands above a bunch of wood and . . . people light it and watch it burn. It does kind of make sense. Poor Frosty the Snowman represents winter, and when you burn him comes spring, a new season. Strange Swiss customs . . . I thought it was a bit satanic at first, but I enjoyed it and accepted their ways of the coming of spring. It was interesting.

When we got to the bank, we found, surprisingly, Jordan Wong. The guy got here before us. When he found us, he walked up to us.

"Hello, again, folks. I see that you have made it to the bank. How was your sleep?" he asked us.
"Good. Nice," all of us answered in unison along those lines.
"Well, okay then. Will you follow me, please?" We followed him to an elevator where we surprisingly all fit in. I was starting to feel a little claustrophobic being pressed against the wall. "You brought your keys with you I hope. Am I correct?" he asked.
"Yeah. We did," I said, the air tightening my throat.
"That's good."

He took us to a single room and was stopped by a man in a suit.

"Qui sont ces gens?" the man asked what sounded to me like French.
"Amis de Nathen. Ils sont là pour récupérer leurs biens. Vous vous souvenez il ya quelques mois, que l'homme a déposé un tas d'argent? Right?" Jordan Wong spoke. Wow, the guy can speak French. It sounds fluent too. That's pretty legit. I wish I could speak French. I took Japanese in high school as a foreign language . . . even though I am Japanese.
"Oh, oui, je me souviens. Proceed," the man in the suit said, stepping back for us to enter yet another room. So many rooms, so many doors leading to what? What was hidden behind all of these doors that Nathen kept for us? "Well, here we are." He guided us into this room with a single

keypad and some kind of revolving mechanism behind it. Wow! I say, Swiss technology comes in second behind Japanese technology. "Well, all you need to do here is slide your cards in the slot and enter your date of birth, and you'll be set." He moved out of our way. We couldn't decide who should go first, so we did rock, paper scissors, and I won best two out of three. I slid my card in the slot and punched in my birth date. My heart was beating somewhat fast in this cold, metal room. The revolving thing made a lot of incoherent noises, and out came a large wooden suitcase. I took it from the revolver and placed it on the floor. Jessica got up next, as I examined this beautiful case. On the front of the suitcase had my named engraved in gold, cursive letters. I gently touched the letters which were as cold as this room. Then I just realized that cursive was dead. I don't think anybody uses cursive anymore. People in the office don't use cursive. I don't even write in cursive. Well, signatures in cursive don't count . . . unless I don't think they should count. I think I should try it out sometime, to see if I remember how to. I unlatched the suitcase, and inside was a whole shitload of money. All of it . . . in bills. Some of the bills were wrinkled and old, and some were crisp and new. "There's one hundred thousand dollars in that suitcase, Mitch." Jordan Wong told me. "There's one hundred thousand dollars in your suitcases as well, Jessica and Andy. The kids have a suitcase of their own but with a smaller amount of money—*ten* thousand dollars each." Monica and Austin jumped in the air and screamed with excitement.

"Oh my god . . . how could he give this to us? All of this money? I mean, how the hell did he get all of this money?" Jessica shouted.

"Oh, there's a letter that'll appear later on when you finish collecting your suitcases. Hopefully, that document will reveal some answers," Jordan Wong explained.

"I can't take this money . . . it's just too much . . . I'm taking money from a dead guy . . ." I said. I felt bad for doing this. I just can't take the money. It feels wrong, absolutely wrong.

"He insists that you take it, Mitch," Jordan Wong said.

"How would you know, Jordan? He's dead."

"H-He arranged all of this . . . and I was to help him with this, all of this. He told me that he was going to commit suicide and do all of this, do all of this good, before he was gone. He wanted to leave and leave behind all of this for his friends, you people."

"Why didn't you stop him? Stop him from killing himself?" I fired.

"I-I-I don't know . . . I mean, I wanted to . . . but . . . I don't know." Jordan Wong looked down.

"I can't take this," I said, latching up the suitcase.

"Please, keep it . . . not entirely for your sake, but Nathen's," he said. I guess I should. If Nathen wanted me to have this, then I guess I'll keep it. I stood up with the suitcase in my right hand and nodded my head to him.

After everyone got their suitcases, Sarah and Howard had a hard time lifting it up. A small envelope rolled out of the revolver, and I picked it up, ripped open the letter and it explained how Nathen made money. He was a pickpocket. He got all of this money for us from picking pockets. I didn't believe him. This was completely outrageous. But if it is true, then I am completely stunned. This is how he made money. This is how he made money when he didn't have a job. This is how he supported himself. Amazing . . .

"Do you guys believe it?" I asked the others, specifically Andy and Jessica.

"Not really," they answered in unison.

"A little far-fetched for me to grasp, but if he really did make money this way, for us and little for himself, then it must've taken him day and night, 24-7 with his hands in other people's pockets. Geez . . ."

We left it at that and went our way back to the hotel.

"Um, may I borrow Austin for a second, Andy?" Jordan Wong asked.

"Um, sure," Andy said.

Austin followed Jordan Wong into a corner. He whispered to him, which was inaudible for us to hear, "In your briefcase, Austin, you will find a small notebook. That, my dear boy, is a handbook to all of Nathen's techniques, hints, and tips on how to pick pockets. Enjoy it and tell dear Monica that there is a special 'ticket' if you will, in her case. When she reaches to the age of sixteen, she can exchange that ticket for a Porsche specially made for her. There's one in your case too. I would pat you on the head right now, but that would make me feel uncomfortable, so I think I'll shake your hand." Jordan Wong shook Austin's hand.

"Yeah . . . thank you," we heard Austin say. It was the only thing we heard from their small talk.

He let us leave, and that was the end of that.

"What did he tell you, Austin?" Andy asked him.
"Oh, it's nothing. Oh, um, Monica? There's like a ticket in your case that you can exchange for a Porsche when you turn sixteen," Austin said.
"Oh my gosh! Really?" she exclaimed, quickly opening her case. "Oh my god, I'm gonna be sixteen in a few months!"

Jessica~

It's been about twelve years now, after our visit at Zurich, and life's been easy. Thanks to Nathen's money. He really helped me out even if he's dead . . . I've been trying to get rid of all my fat I put on for the baby, and I must say, it is NOT easy . . . at all . . . even after eight years. Wow, I'm like really pathetic . . . Well, it's because I've been lazy. I've been watching Korean dramas. Yep, new ones. I just picked Nathen up from school, and we were driving to an ice cream shop to get—no duh—an ice cream because he got an "A" on his math test for the first time. Yeah . . . I am proud of my little Nathen.

"Mommy?" He caught my attention.
"Yeah?" I acknowledged him.
"Where's my daddy?" he asked. My heart stopped.

I was afraid he would eventually ask this. I never had an answer prepared because I didn't want to or haven't thought about it in a while . . .

a while meaning twelve freakin' years. I was choking on words, searching for a legitimate answer, incoherently spewing out words that don't exist in the English language or, with a high possibility, any other language.

"Mom, do I *have* a daddy?" he asked.

"Um, he died, Nathen. He died when you were very little," I spewed a lie from my lie-filled mouth.

"How did he die?"

"Um, he died in a car crash. A drunk driver. The person that was drunk crashed into him . . . your father wasn't drunk. No. Never. He never drank . . . enough to get drunk. Which reminds me, don't drink, Nathen," I told him.

"What was his name?"

"He has the same name as you. I named you after your daddy."

"Okay," he said, turning away and staring out the window watching as we quickly drove past trees and houses. We were living in a house now. I sold the condo with the furniture inside and got a whole bunch of bucks from that. We were living right next to Andy's, just about five minutes away. I take Nathen up there once in a while, you know, to visit. Mitch, Andy, and I have been visiting each other a lot, like at least twice a week since after Nathen's death. Hopefully, Nathen won't ask about his "father" when we come to visit again. I need to like talk all of them into this lie, that Nathen was his real father. It doesn't sound right, and I know they will oppose, but . . . I can't tell Nathen that his father was a psychopath . . . no, I couldn't. I-I don't know if I did the right thing—to lie to Nathen about his "father." I don't know what to do. Should I tell him in the future? When he matures? Should I tell him the truth then? What if Freddy gets out of jail and finds me. Then what? Then he'll start a commotion and let the whole thing leak. Then Nathen would know. Oh my god . . . well, I wished the past changed. I wish I didn't choose Freddy. I think . . . I think I should have chosen . . . Nathen. With him, I would've been happier than I was with Freddy, so much happier. Well, you can't change the past, lesson learned, but you can tamper with it.

ABOUT THE AUTHOR

I was born and raised in Anaheim, California, and currently reside in California. I live with my mother and my two younger brothers. My father had recently passed away of lung cancer. I wrote this book through depression of the fact that my father was beginning to be hospitalized because of his condition. As some parts of my novel were humorous, I needed something to lift me out of being down in the dumps all the time. I began to write short stories at the age of thirteen in middle school and later on shared it with my classroom peers. And when I'm not reading or writing or studying for school, I like to perform magic.